Maybe Charlotte

Other Bella Books by Louise McBain

Claiming Camille

About the Author

Louise McBain lives in Washington, DC with her family and pets.

Maybe Charlotte

Louise McBain

BELLA BOOKS

2020

Bella Books, Inc.
P.O. Box 10543
Tallahassee, FL 32302

Printed in the United States of America on acid-free paper.

First Bella Books Edition 2020

Editor: Cath Walker
Cover Designer: Judith Fellows

ISBN: 978-1-64247-163-2

Acknowledgments

I had a wonderful time writing this book. From the outset, the characters knew exactly who they were and had no problem letting me know. Added to this bit of good fortune were the unconditional support of friends and family. Plot walks, proofreading, beta reading, endless cups of tea — thank you to John Menditto, Linda ReVeal, Eliza McGraw, Maggie Menditto, T. Elizabeth Bell, and Florence Williams. You helped me shape the narrative and called me on the bullshit.

Thanks also to Bella authors Cade Haddock-Strong and Stacy Lynn Miller for helping me navigate the world of lesfic publishing. I appreciate your handholding and value your friendship.

Maybe Charlotte would be a different book without editor Cath Walker who deserves more than a Birdies T-shirt for the cleanup job she did on the manuscript. Thanks for the spit-shine, Cath. It was fun having you in my head.

I started writing lesbian romance novels because I enjoy reading them. Thank you to all the authors of this genre who work so hard to spin the magic of happily ever after.

Louise McBain
August 2020

CHAPTER ONE

The Coming-Out Party

"Don't call me Amelia."

"But you're my wing woman, Charlie."

"Don't call me Charlie either."

Daniel wrapped an arm around his taller, broader-shouldered twin sister. "Okay, *Charlotte*. But without your hand on the throttle, none of my adventures would get off the ground." He squeezed her arm. "Thanks for coming tonight."

Charlotte looked down at her brother and smiled. Their nearly identical hazel eyes met and held. "First of all, you know I never touch anyone's throttle. Ever." She paused as Daniel let out an appreciative cackle. "And second, can we please pick another pilot? Amelia Earhart went down in the South Pacific."

"Sounds like heaven to me," Daniel deadpanned then flicked a finger toward the stage at the back of the bar. "We're on next, by the way. Want any water? Another bourbon?" Without waiting for her answer, he motioned to the waiter for another round.

Charlotte glanced at the small stage where a man was finishing a comedy routine about nude grandparents on Skype. "I can't believe you talked me into this."

"Talked you into what?" Daniel raised his cosmopolitan in a toast. "We're the Charlie Daniels Band, remember? The devil's just down in Washington, DC, now." He took a sip of the pink cocktail and grimaced.

Charlotte shook her head and a few pieces of dark hair fell loose from the bun at the nape of her neck. "We called ourselves the Charlie Daniels Band exactly once, in middle school," she reminded him. "And why do you drink cosmos when you clearly hate them? It doesn't make sense."

"I'm trying to grow, Charlotte," he said, and for a moment looked like the little boy who'd been so scared of thunderstorms he'd slept under his bed. "You know this."

Charlotte felt guilty. Daniel had been very open about his goal of wanting to become more sophisticated. It was his stated reason for leaving their hometown of Portland, Maine. *There had to be more to life than lobster rolls and L.L.Bean.* Who could empathize with this sentiment more than she could? Known as Charlie her entire life, Charlotte had only recently made the switch to her proper name. New town, new name. It made sense. What didn't compute was how drinking a cocktail you despised counted as personal growth. But it wasn't fair to press the point. It had been nice of Daniel to let Charlotte tag along on his life adventure.

"I'm sorry. I'm just nervous about performing," she lied.

"Don't start that." He took a stoic sip of the cosmo. "You're a professional singer."

"I am *not*."

"You've been paid."

"It's not the same thing."

"Isn't it?"

"Definitely not." Writing and recording a catchy jingle for her ex-girlfriend's bakery to help pay for nursing school was not the same thing as being a professional singer. It had been a trade-off, nothing more, a means to an end.

"I respectfully disagree," Daniel said. "You've got a great voice and you know it. I have to shake my tallywacker to get anyone to notice me."

"You mean your money-maker?"

"I mean whatever it takes."

"Stop it." Charlotte waved away his anxiety. "You don't need me to tell you that you're fabulous."

Daniel handed the waiter his empty glass and accepted a refill. "Yes, I do." He took a sip and shuddered.

"Okay, you're fabulous, you're fabulous, you're fabulous. How's that?"

"Better." He directed her attention to the comic now taking a series of small bows. "Showtime at the Apollo, Amelia."

Charlotte rose from the table and followed him obediently through the crowded room. Though in a new bar in a new city, this wasn't a new scenario. It was as Daniel had said earlier. They were a duo. Daniel fueled the fun but Charlotte insured safe passage. She'd always served as either his cohort or support staff. The dynamic had developed in early childhood out of necessity and continued because it worked.

Their father, who'd been head of the science department at Bates College, had died suddenly of a heart attack when they were infants leaving their mother to support the family. Charlotte had no memory of him and very few photos. Sarah Kincaid was also on faculty at Bates. A research scientist, she specialized in insect pathology. Though always physically present in family life, her mind rarely left the lab. After long hours on campus, she'd continue writing up experiments and planning new ones late into the night. Charlotte and Daniel had turned to each other by default. Charlotte loved her mother, but if she needed to ask an embarrassing question that she was too scared to Google, she called Daniel.

Tonight was supposed to be about him. Charlotte still wasn't sure what had changed. For weeks, Daniel, an enthusiastic amateur pianist and singer, had been plotting his DC coming-out party. It was open mic night at Birdie's piano bar in Georgetown, the perfect place for him to shine. He'd carefully chosen an outfit, practiced a song and then another song in case someone else sang his first song. Every detail had been planned. Why, at the eleventh hour, had he suddenly asked Charlotte to sing a duet?

She couldn't remember the last time she'd been on stage. She'd often performed with Daniel in high school. They'd participated in every school production and twice scored parts in community theater. But Daniel had been the driving force. Daniel had picked their audition pieces, chosen their clothing, guided their talent. Charlotte still loved to sing but now, aside from karaoke and Christmas carols, she rarely did so outside of the car.

The emcee steered them toward a baby grand piano positioned in a spotlight. Charlotte took a seat next to Daniel at the polished bench. "Tell me again. What happened to your solo?"

He swiveled his head in a practiced gesture of surprise she remembered from their ninth-grade improv class. The hazel eyes were all innocence. "Oh sweetie, I'm still doing my solo. This duet is for you, Charlie Pie. I'm not the only Kincaid twin who needs a coming-out party."

"Daniel!"

He was saved by the emcee who was back in front of the crowd. "Hello my little birdies. Can we have another round of applause for the comedy stylings of Sami B?" He stroked his uneven beard. "Next time, maybe don't give Nana the Wi-Fi password, Sami." The crowd laughed and he tipped his porkpie hat. "Up next, we have a real treat. They're a delicious duo. A brother and sister who've just moved here from Portland, Maine." The crowd started whooping.

Someone yelled "Rock Lobsters!"

Charlotte glared at Daniel. "What did you tell him?"

"Not too much." He kept his gaze on the piano as the emcee shouted the last of the introduction.

"They're twins, they're gay, they're single and looking! Please give a big Birdie's welcome to the Charlie Daniels Band!"

"I can't believe you." Charlotte jabbed an elbow into her brother's ribs.

"Sure, you can." He smirked and began playing the short introduction to the song "Summer Nights" from the musical *Grease*. The crowd's reaction was instantaneous and loud. After the opening bars a woman in a tiara gave a guttural shout and rushed the stage followed by a gaggle of her friends wearing matching pink T-shirts. They were mostly drunk and mostly gorgeous. It looked like a bachelorette party. Charlotte locked eyes with a curvy blonde at the edge of the group and missed the opening lyrics.

It was Daniel's turn to throw an elbow. "Pay attention," he hissed and played the introduction again.

"Sorry," Charlotte stammered and tried to focus on the performance. It was a well-rehearsed piece. They'd developed it years ago when Daniel was conspiring to audition for *American Idol*. The hook was that Charlotte sang the Danny Zuko part and Daniel sang Sandy. The gender-bender routine never failed to bring down the house. The fact that everyone in the room had screamed the words into a hairbrush at some point in their lives did not lessen its appeal. Nostalgia mixed with alcohol was a potent combination. Daniel knew his audience.

When he played the intro a second time, Charlotte was ready. She exploded into the lyrics, her rich alto expressing the joy and wonder of first lust while Daniel answered back all coy-boy, sweetly owning a newfound infatuation.

The crowd loved it. More people left their tables to collect around the stage but the sexy blonde from the bachelorette party maintained her position in front of the piano. Every time Charlotte looked up she found green eyes watching her. After the fourth or fifth time, Charlotte couldn't help it and blushed. The woman noticed and started blushing too. Moments later, to Charlotte's disappointment, she disappeared into the crowd.

Daniel was working the room like a seasoned cruise ship performer. When a beautiful young man with gorgeous ebony skin began singing along, Daniel motioned him onstage to be part of the chorus. In no time, half the bar was crowded around the piano begging Charlotte and Daniel to tell them more. When Daniel slammed into the penultimate verse in teetering high falsetto, Charlotte didn't hold back. Trading lines with her brother, she dug deep into her lower register and brought home the brazen innuendo of the lyric.

As the chorus screamed their back-up Daniel turned to Charlotte and grinned. "Take us home, Amelia."

Her spirit lifted as she moved upward toward the crescendo. Where John Travolta had taken the pitch high and tight, Charlotte squared up and knocked it over the fence. The crowd roared their approval. When the song was done, the twins were beset with enthusiastic applause while the emcee snapped his fingers from the side of the stage. "Show some love for the Charlie Daniels Band!"

The crowd cheered again and Daniel kissed Charlotte on the cheek. "Thank you."

"Anytime."

"I'll hold you to that."

"I know you will."

The weight on the bench shifted as the young man with the beautiful ebony skin slid in next to them. Charlotte took it as her cue to leave. Slipping off the bench she stepped down from the stage onto the dance floor where a tall man in a gold, sequined T-shirt pulled her into a hug.

"Love a duet. Love! A! DUET! And twins! I could eat ya'll up."

"Thanks." Charlotte smiled politely but stepped away from the embrace. She didn't like to be rude but generally reserved hugs for people she knew.

"I'm going to be singing that song all night. Tell me more! Tell me more!" he hooted and spun off into the crowd.

Charlotte turned and caught a pair of electric green eyes watching her. The bachelorette-party woman was back. In closer proximity Charlotte found her gaze even more unsettling. She was exceptionally pretty, but it was more than that. She looked at Charlotte as if she knew a secret. When Charlotte looked pointedly back at her, the woman colored but did not look away. Maybe it was the confidence of a successful performance, or the anonymity of being in a new city, but Charlotte felt uncharacteristically bold. She took a step forward.

"Hey," she said quickly.

"Hey," the woman responded. Her lips tipped at the corners but the smile didn't reach her eyes. "You were great, really great," she said begrudgingly and then seemed to hear herself. "I mean that. I do," she asserted, though her expression was still oddly forlorn. Charlotte wondered at her attitude. Did she know this person?

"Thanks," Charlotte said as she tried to match her familiar demeanor. "I thought you'd left."

The green eyes widened a fraction but didn't lose their intensity. "You noticed that?"

"I noticed you." Charlotte doubled down. She now felt as if she was acting a scene. Whatever was going on with this enigmatic beauty she wanted to see how it played out. "I have to ask, have we met before?"

The question seemed to surprise the woman and she jerked her head back. "I don't think so. No. But I noticed you too."

Once again, Charlotte was struck by her air of resignation. "Is that a bad thing?" she asked and the woman's face softened.

"No, it's just that I haven't noticed anyone in a long time," she said. This time when she smiled it reached her eyes. "You can tell that I'm off my game. Listen to me, blabbing all my secrets." She lifted a finger and pointed to the woman in the tiara who was now standing on the stage adjusting the microphone. "And for the record, I didn't leave. I went to get the bride a drink."

"I wondered if it was a bachelorette party," Charlotte said. As interested as she was to discuss being noticed, the look in the blonde's eye said it was a story better left for quiet conversation. She let her eyes drop to the woman's chest. Her T-shirt had an illustration of two women tied around each other in a heart-shaped knot. The design was provocative but couldn't compete with the soft swell of the woman's breasts. Charlotte allowed her gaze to linger a fraction longer than polite before looking into the emerald eyes again. "The shirts are cool."

"Yeah, I love Gowear. Cost more but they're worth it."

Charlotte shook her head. "I meant the illustration. Gowear gear is great but that design is wonderful."

"Thanks." The woman gave a shy smile and leaned in to be heard. Charlotte caught the scent of her perfume. *Whoa.* "The design is actually mine."

"You're an artist?" Charlotte was thrilled to have stumbled onto a valid talking point.

"Not a professional." The woman shook her head. "It's just something I do for myself, and friends when I get the chance." She looked down fondly at the illustration on her shirt then back at Charlotte. "Right now, visiting galleries and museums is about as close as I get to real art. But that's the great thing about living in DC." Her smile broadened. "There are so many great venues."

"Do you go often?"

"Almost every Sunday."

"What makes art real?" Charlotte asked.

"When someone pays you for it." The woman laughed. "Right?"

"That's one way to think of it." Charlotte smiled. It was not lost on her that she and Daniel had just had the same conversation. "What else do you do for yourself?" Oh, God. Had she really just said that?

The woman gave a tiny start but rebounded quickly. "Not enough. Making the shirts was the most fun I've had in a while. They're my wedding gift to the bridal party. I'm also designated driver tonight. I don't go out much so I was happy to volunteer."

"Very cool." Charlotte tried to put her at ease. She wanted to ask her why she rarely went out but opted for a safer subject. "How do you know the bride?"

"I work with Sheen," she said and her eyes flicked toward the door. "In about two minutes the other bachelorette party is going to be here."

"Who's the other bride?"

"Beth. She's an active duty Marine. Been home for about a week from a six-month tour in Afghanistan. Sheen is going to serenade her. It's all terribly romantic. They're getting married this weekend." There was a wistfulness in her voice that made Charlotte's heart squeeze.

"Thanks for telling me." Charlotte flashed her warmest smile. "It'll make Sheen's performance so much better. I'm Charlotte, by the way." She offered her hand.

"Hi Charlotte, my name is…"

Feedback from the onstage microphone drowned out the last word but Charlotte was too caught up in the feel of warm fingers clasping her own to care. At the first moment of contact she knew she was in trouble. It wasn't just that the heat of the woman's hand matched the blush on her face. It was how Charlotte's body reacted to it. She knew if she were to look in a mirror her pupils would be dilated and her cheeks flushed. If they were naked, other things would give them away. Naked? Was Charlotte seriously already thinking of getting naked? Though it was a normal response to being near someone you were attracted to, this level of reaction usually didn't happen in the first two minutes. It certainly never happened to Charlotte. But so far, everything about the encounter felt decidedly abnormal. The woman stroked her thumb lightly across Charlotte's hand and then let go with a squeeze.

"You're the gal who put the Charlie in the Charlie Daniels Band," she said softly and Charlotte released a breath. The tables had definitely turned. The woman seemed to have made up her mind about something and was now on the offensive. Though Charlotte found nothing offensive about it.

"That was not sanctioned. My brother can be a real rascal."

"Rascal?" The woman smiled, revealing perfect white teeth. "You make him sound like a raccoon."

Charlotte laughed. "That's not too far off."

"Are you really twins?"

"We are."

A cheer went up in the room as a group of women wearing purple turbans entered the bar and began snaking their way toward the stage. One turban was twice the size as its counterparts making its occupant look like a swami. In one hand she held some kind of bejeweled stick and in the other an oversized wineglass.

"Is that Beth?" Charlotte said.

"That's her." The woman nodded. Charlotte still didn't know her name. Before she could ask, the emcee was at the microphone again calling for the crowd's attention.

"Love is in the air tonight, my little birdies! In two days' time this lovely lady will marry the woman of her dreams. Please welcome Sheen!" The crowd screamed as the guitarist began to strum a slow song. Charlotte vaguely recognized the tune but couldn't pin it down. The lights dimmed to a spotlight on Sheen. Her tiara winked at the crowd as she cradled the microphone in her hands.

"Would you like to dance?" The blonde was now at Charlotte's ear. Warm breath tickled her skin and her nipples tightened reflexively.

"Yeah, okay."

Two more chords and Charlotte had the song. Sheen was singing "At Last," the torch song immortalized by the late Jazz singer Etta James. She'd never heard it performed with a single guitar, but it worked. And Sheen was giving it her all. The song started strongly and so did her dance partner. Slipping her arms around Charlotte's neck, she pressed their chests together causing Charlotte's already fevered body to pulse even more hotly. Charlotte was a few inches taller but their bodies fit like puzzle pieces. The woman seemed to enjoy this and pushed herself decisively against Charlotte. She smelled like a perfume sample from a fancy fashion magazine. Charlotte was seized with the impulse to drive a thigh between her legs but willed herself to relax. When Daniel told Charlotte to put herself out there, dry humping a stranger in a Georgetown bar was not what he had in mind. She was almost sure of it.

The song came to a close and Beth joined Sheen on stage as women in both bachelorette parties wept and shot video. The blonde released her arms from Charlotte's neck but kept one slung low around her waist so their bodies remained in contact. Charlotte leaned into the touch.

The emcee tipped his hat. "Mazel tov! Ladies! Mazel tov! That was beautiful. But I'm not sure who wants to follow that?"

"Me!" A familiar voice shouted somewhere to the left. Charlotte didn't have to turn her head to know who it was.

"Wonderful!" The emcee gushed. "My Maine man, Daniel!"

The brides exited the stage to another thunderous round of applause. The emcee repositioned the microphone into the stand by the piano and Daniel bounded back into the spotlight.

"Your brother is adorable," The blonde whispered into Charlotte's ear as Daniel started playing the opening notes of an Elton John classic.

"He claims I cannibalized him in the womb," Charlotte replied, earning a laugh. "Would you like to dance again?"

"I would." She looped an arm around Charlotte's waist and they moved to the song. "You don't look that much taller than him."

Charlotte shrugged. "It's only about three inches, but my shoulders are so much broader people think I'm his mother."

"One hot mother."

"Thank you." The fact that she was larger than Daniel had never bothered her. But it was nice to hear that this lovely woman found her attractive. She looked down at her lips and wondered if it was okay to kiss someone when you didn't know their name. "Listen carefully to the chorus," she said instead as Daniel finished the first haunting verses of the song "Don't Let the Sun Go Down on Me."

"Okay." The green eyes danced with anticipation as Daniel built to the crescendo.

Charlotte held a hand to her ear. "Wait for it..."

"Please let your sons go down on me!" He sang and the crowd roared with laughter. Charlotte couldn't hear the blonde's reaction but she had a hand over her mouth and her eyes were streaming. Everyone around them was smiling. The man with the beautiful ebony skin was in front of the stage with his hands swaying in the air. The turbaned ladies had their arms around each other and the brides were dancing. Daniel milked it for everything it was worth. If this was his coming-out party, he'd definitely arrived. When the song concluded he executed one tight bow and did a high guitar kick off the stage. Not stopping to sign autographs he made a beeline for Charlotte.

"Great job!" The blonde was enthusiastic. "You were so funny."

"Thank you!" Daniel flashed her a brilliant smile but then grabbed Charlotte by the hand and began tugging her away. "Time to go."

"Hey!" She tried to shrug him off but he tightened his grip and pulled harder. Charlotte looked apologetically back at the beautiful woman who, until a minute ago, had been nestled in her arms. "What are you doing?" she hissed at Daniel.

"We need to make our exit. Like now."

"But why?"

"Because it's time to go."

"Why?"

"Because you always leave them wanting more."

"But what if I want more?" The woman, now surrounded by other members of the bachelorette party, suddenly seemed very far away.

"Pace yourself, Amelia, it's a long flight."

CHAPTER TWO

North, South, East and Wellesley

Daniel unlatched the alley gate behind their Aunt Wellesley's Georgetown townhouse. It was just before midnight and Charlotte was still fuming about their untimely departure from the bar.

"Please explain why you made us leave," she said.

Daniel swung open the decorative iron gate allowing his sister to pass through first. Ignoring her question, he addressed their musical performance instead. "I thought our song went well, all things considered."

"What's there to consider besides the fact that you dragged me away from the prettiest girl in the room?"

"The acoustics for one, which sucked. But the baby grand had a wonderful tone. Don't you think?" Daniel continued on the theme.

"I think you made me look rude."

"But the crowd seemed to like us. Or am I being overly generous with myself?" He flashed Charlotte an uncertain smile and she felt a pang of conscience. This evening was supposed to have been about him. Caught up with the mystery blonde, she'd forgotten that she'd been invited along as wing woman. Her job was to have Daniel's back, not to wander off and pick up girls. Idly, she wondered if this is what had happened to the real Amelia Earhart. She certainly hoped so.

"Of course not," she reassured him. "The crowd loved you. Your solo was great. But I thought you were going to do 'Pocket Man.' What happened?"

"I wasn't feeling it." He paused by the door to a small carriage house at the back of the property. "I'm sorry I made you leave. There is a reason." He closed his eyes. "But you're going to hate it with the fire of a thousand suns." He turned the key in the lock.

"Oh, goodie." Charlotte pushed past him into the cottage and called for her dog. Whatever Daniel needed to tell her, whatever situation needed sorting out, it would have to wait. Rhianna was more important. "Rhi?" She looked around for the long-haired silver dachshund but there was no sign of her. The dog had yet to acclimate to their new home. Charlotte feared Rhianna was in genuine distress. When the dog didn't appear, Charlotte turned to Daniel for help. "Check the living room?"

"Of course." Daniel said and walked quickly down the short hallway. "Rhianna?" he called with a small note of panic in his voice. There was every reason to be worried. In the three weeks since they'd moved to DC, the dachshund had been so anxious that her appearance had significantly altered. Large patches of hair had fallen out of her normally silky coat, giving her the look of a mangy stray. This was unfortunate as nothing could be further from the truth. Charlotte was such a devoted pet owner that her mother held Rhianna responsible for Charlotte's decision to change her career focus from scientific research to nursing.

"Rhi?" Charlotte looked around the kitchen but saw no sign of the animal. It was out of character for her not to greet Charlotte at the door. Besides her alarming appearance, Rhianna hadn't eaten anything in two days apart from her favorite dog treats. Charlotte had run out of the specialty biscuits earlier that morning and wasn't sure what she was going to do. Replenishing them was tricky as the treats came from a bakery in Maine owned by Charlotte's ex. Reordering meant interacting with Madison. It was the last thing Charlotte wanted to think about. "Rhianna?" She called again and scanned the carriage house for her dog.

"She was in the cupboard over the refrigerator earlier today."

"Again?" Charlotte began to fling open the high cabinets. Rhianna's low-slung physique belied an uncanny ability to parkour her way to geography above the ambition of the average dachshund. Most of her life had been spent in the shared company of their mother's cat, Taco. The feisty Siamese had instilled in the little dog an appreciation of high places and raw tuna.

"She was chewing on the business end of an old flyswatter." Daniel scanned the top of the highest bookcases.

"Why didn't you tell me?" Charlotte finished searching the kitchen and went to look in the two back bedrooms.

"Because you wouldn't have come to Birdie's," he shouted after her.

A cry from Charlotte's bedroom announced that the dog had been discovered. There was a series of plaintive barks followed by the sound of Charlotte's soft murmuring. Moments later she reappeared in the living room with the dachshund tucked under her arm. In her free hand, she held a badly chewed shoe.

"Oh no." Daniel took the shoe from Charlotte. Pinching the damaged item between two fingers he held it up for inspection. "Not the new Dansko work clogs."

"She just ate one. She's not greedy." Charlotte rubbed Rhianna's belly and the dog released a heavy sigh. Shoe chewing had clearly taken a toll. "I found her on the dresser."

"She was starving, poor thing." Daniel dropped the clog on the floor and collected Rhianna from his sister. "Hasn't had anything to eat all day but an old fly swatter." He stroked the dog's ears, and she licked his hand.

Charlotte sat down heavily on a green vinyl couch that, along with the rest of the décor, was significantly older than she was. It was as if Aunt Wellesley had closed the door one day in 1963 and opened it three weeks ago when the twins had shown up. "Tell me why we had to leave the bar early. I didn't even get that girl's name."

"Laurel Jaguar?"

"You know that isn't her name." Charlotte leaned her head back on the couch. After leaving the bar, Daniel had realized he'd left his cell phone on the piano. Circling back to retrieve it, they'd seen the blonde driving off in a hunter-green Jag with a group of the bachelorettes. The car dealer's name, Laurel Jaguar, had been visible on the license plate frame. Daniel had seized the title and assigned it to the mystery woman. Charlotte wished she knew her real name, but she had to admit Laurel Jaguar had a nice ring.

Rhianna squirmed out of Daniel's arms to join her mistress on the couch. More hair was missing from her coat and Charlotte worried she'd soon be completely bald. "What am I going to do with you?" She scooped the dog into her lap.

"A wig?" Daniel offered and wandered into the kitchen. "Seriously, I saw a store down the street that sells all sorts of pet notions. If they don't have a wig they'll know where to find one."

"I'm not buying a dog wig," Charlotte said. She stroked her fingers through what was left of Rhianna's coat.

"You know what the problem is?" Daniel asked, but the question was rhetorical. The reason for Rhianna's distress was not a secret. It was a classic case of heartbreak.

"Taco," Charlotte agreed, chagrined. Her pride was a little bruised that Rhianna was more attached to their mother's temperamental Siamese cat than she was to Charlotte. "I knew they were close, but I had no idea it went this deep."

"It's your fault for moving in with Mom." Daniel pointed out. "You threw them together."

"I was saving money while I was studying!" Charlotte argued. At the time, it had seemed like an excellent idea. Their mother was far too busy mulling over the genetic mutations of insect larvae to pry into Charlotte's personal life. Happily, she was not too busy to make dinner or do Charlotte's laundry. Sarah Kincaid also refused to accept rent, an excellent quality in any landlord. Except for an occasional lecture about how Charlotte was underutilizing her brain by changing her career direction to nursing, it had been the ideal living arrangement. Charlotte had no idea she'd lose her dog over it.

"If it's any consolation, Mom says Taco is depressed too." Daniel filled two glasses with water from a stoneware jug in the refrigerator.

"How can she tell? Has he killed fewer birds?" Charlotte stroked Rhianna's ears.

"More." Daniel picked up the water and walked into the living room. He handed a glass to Charlotte. "It's been like the end of a Tarantino movie. Mom's been burying the bodies in the backyard."

"No way. When did you talk to her? I thought she was locked up in lab trials with those Swedish guys."

"Sven and Jens."

"Right."

"She called me this morning. I think she has a crush on Jens. Or maybe it's Sven. I can't keep them straight. Mom wanted to know how to get on Facebook so she could friend him." Daniel made quote marks with his fingers and Charlotte nearly choked on her water.

"Mom has a crush?" Charlotte was shocked. To her knowledge their mother had not dated anyone since their father's sudden death more than twenty years ago. Long hours had yielded Sarah tenure at Bates and the seminal professional paper on gnat influenza, but never romance. Daniel liked to say that Sarah had prematurely donated her body to science.

"I think so. Mom has a yen for Jens."

"Or Sven."

"It might be Sven," he agreed.

"Why didn't she call me?" Charlotte was hurt. If their mother had suddenly decided to share her resurrected personal life, why had she chosen to confide in Daniel? Was Sarah angry with Charlotte for moving to DC so abruptly? The job offer at Children's Hospital had come at the last minute and been contingent on her immediate relocation. Maybe Charlotte should have turned it down, given the decision more time? They'd only recently healed the rift caused when Charlotte left research.

"Mom didn't call you because you don't know anything about social media, dummy."

"Oh, good point," Charlotte said and felt instantly better. She made a note to call her mother to ask about the crush. Because Daniel was right. Charlotte knew nothing about social media beyond her reluctance to participate. Human interactions were difficult enough in person without adding a cyber component.

"It's not like Mom gave me any details. She just grilled me for Facebook tricks and then hung up to nuke a Lean Cuisine."

"Facebook has tricks?"

"My point exactly." Daniel fidgeted with the cuff of his shirt. It was a bad sign. Daniel only made public wardrobe adjustments when he felt guilty. He took a deep breath as if preparing to jump in the lake. "After I hung up with Mom, I called Madison and asked her to send more dog treats."

"You did what?" The house got very quiet.

"I called Madison."

"What the fuck, Daniel?" Charlotte glared at her brother. She'd dated Madison the last two years of college and one beyond. It had taken an entire year and more guts than Charlotte knew she had to extricate herself from the relationship. When she'd finally mustered the courage to end it, Madison had not gone quietly. Every encounter with her since had felt like beating back the tide.

"Why would you do that?" she asked him again. Contacting Madison directly, after months of careful avoidance, was like ordering drama from a menu of potential horrors. Daniel knew this better than anyone. Charlotte couldn't imagine why he would have done it. He bowed his head and she braced herself for the worst. Surely whatever damage he'd done could be corrected. How bad could it be?

"When I found Rhianna chewing on the flyswatter, I panicked. We were out of treats so I left Madison a voice mail.

I don't know where to get CBD dog treats around here. I didn't think."

Charlotte's fair skin went a shade paler. "Wait. Rhianna's treats have CBD in them?"

Daniel rolled his eyes. "Don't pretend you didn't know."

She gave him a hard look. "I didn't. The bag Madison gave Mom wasn't marked. She said it was a taste trial or something. No one mentioned cannabidiol."

Daniel shrugged. "Well, it's no big deal. People get their panties in a twist because CBD, or cannabidiol," he air-quoted the word, "is extracted from marijuana but it doesn't have psychotropic effects. That's THC. CBD alleviates anxiety and pain." He cocked an eyebrow. "Surely they taught you this in nursing school?"

"Yes, of course they did." Charlotte punched his arm. "I just wasn't aware we were dosing the dog!"

"You had to know something was different," Daniel challenged her. "The minute those treats were gone, Rhianna went from mellow to hell-no."

Charlotte scratched the dog's head. "I thought it was about Taco. The heart is a powerful organ."

Daniel nodded. "Maybe it's Madison who needs some CBD."

"No maybes about that."

Madison's inability to let Charlotte go had been paramount in Charlotte's decision to take the last-minute job and leave Maine. "Did she call you back?"

"She texted."

"What did she say?"

"She said *on the way*."

"What does that mean?" Charlotte nearly shouted. "Is she sending more CBD biscuits?"

"That's what I wondered too, but then…" Daniel pulled his phone from his pocket. "When I texted back to say thank you, I got this." Scrolling down the screen he tapped on a message and showed it to Charlotte. It was an automated reply saying the owner of the phone was driving.

"You think she's coming here? It's a nine-hour drive!" Charlotte tried to make sense of what Daniel was saying.

"I do."

"That's crazy."

"That's Madison."

"But she could be going to the store or something. She eats ice cream late at night. Maybe she's going to get ice cream."

"Or she could be driving here." Daniel tapped the screen a few more times and brought up Snapchat. A bitmoji of Madison marked her as seen two minutes ago in Washington, DC.

"Fuckity-fuck." Charlotte took the phone and stared intensely at the screen.

"I'm so sorry," Daniel said.

"Why isn't the dot moving?" Charlotte wanted to know.

Daniel looked over her shoulder. "I think it means the person is stationary."

"Can you scan in any closer, to see exactly where she is?" Charlotte asked, but a loud knock on the cottage door rendered the action unnecessary. Rhianna gave a reactionary bark and skittered off Charlotte's lap. Flying across the small living room, she flung herself at the front door. Charlotte rose from the couch. "I can't believe this."

The knock sounded again. Charlotte leveled a look at Daniel before placing her hand on the knob. But it wasn't Madison. Standing on the doorstep, dressed in a long, colorful kimono with a paint-stained sponge in her hand was their Great-aunt Wellesley.

"Aunt Wellesley!" Charlotte scooped Rhianna into her arms so the little dog wouldn't twist herself into the folds of the elaborate robe.

"Good evening, Charlotte, or should I say good morning?"

"Oh right, good morning."

Wellesley looked around the carriage house. Spotting Daniel on the sofa she nodded her head. "I was working in my studio when a distraught young woman appeared. She's in the kitchen now, crying. Lovesick I'd imagine." Wellesley stared hard at Daniel. "Shall you come sort her out?"

"Me?" Daniel squeaked. The look on his face suggested someone had asked him to nurse a baby giraffe from his own bosom. "The lovesick lady belongs to Charlie."

Aunt Wellesley turned her attention back to Charlotte. Until this moment, Charlotte had met her exactly once. The day of their arrival, Aunt Wellesley had walked them through the backyard and given them a set of keys to the carriage house and a brief speech about keeping the gate shut. Charlotte thought it a marvel this exotic person was related to them though she'd never really been in their lives. Wellesley Kincaid was their late father's paternal aunt. The family received a handwritten holiday card every year and owned a self-portrait Wellesley had done in college. It hung proudly in the living room over their mother's display case of Victorian scarabs. On the back of the portrait was a provocative if enigmatic inscription: *north, south, east and Wellesley*.

To enable his life change with a move to DC, her brother had waged a relentless campaign to win over their reclusive great-aunt. Using a calligraphy set and a wax seal on the envelope, he wrote her a letter once a week for a year before she responded. Their mom had thought there would be no response. She'd only met Wellesley once herself and it was a long time ago, before their father had died. But one day, out of the blue, Wellesley wrote back and offered Daniel the carriage house, rent-free.

Thus far, Charlotte had seen no sign of familial interest or attachment, though Daniel was intent on manufacturing one. Having a famous, reclusive artist aunt in the family fit nicely into his new self-image of a sophisticated man about town.

And Wellesley Kincaid was indeed famous. A celebrated Georgetown socialite from the Kennedy era, she'd used her divorce settlement from a Texas oilman to finance a career in modern art and the gambit had paid off. Fiercely talented, she had work hanging in museums and galleries all over the world. For the past three weeks, Daniel had lolled about the garden trying to catch her in conversation. Thus far he'd had no interaction with her beyond one brief encounter when she'd asked him to coil the garden hose. And now she was standing in the living room quizzing Charlotte about her sexuality.

"Madison is your lover, Charlotte?" Wellesley dropped the sponge on the kitchen table. The forearms peeking out through the colorful robe were long and strong but her body had the spare look of someone who didn't think too much about food. She was not tall but had a statuesque poise that drew the eye and a confidence about her person that inspired curiosity. Her hair was a beautiful silver-gray that was not that far from Rhianna's.

"Yes, I mean no. I mean she was. Madison is my ex-girlfriend," Charlotte clarified and then blushed. She wasn't worried about Wellesley judging their sexuality. She was certain her famous aunt had experienced far racier things than two twenty-five-year-old Maine lesbians. But disturbing her at work was unforgivable. Daniel had yet to breach the front door of the elegant Georgetown townhouse, yet Madison had stampeded the fortress and was now sobbing within.

"Well, you better come along." Wellesley gestured for Charlotte to follow her. "I left her with an open bottle of Sancerre and the girl had a thirsty look about her."

"Okay." Charlotte handed Daniel the dog. "Take Rhianna out for me please?"

"Sure." Daniel jumped from the couch to get the leash. Charlotte knew the pep in his step was for Wellesley's benefit but was thankful he didn't protest. Spying the sponge on the kitchen table he snatched it up and chased Aunt Wellesley out the door. "Don't forget your sponge."

Wellesley looked at the discarded item with disdain. "Do me a favor, pretty boy, and add it to the trash. I'm quite done tonight." Without another word, she opened the cottage door and slipped out into the night.

"She thinks I'm pretty," Daniel mouthed and did a little dance.

Charlotte gave him a wan smile. "Thanks for walking Rhi." She blew a kiss toward Rhianna. The dachshund was squirming happily at the sight of the urban-camouflage leash Daniel had produced from a hook on the pantry door. Daniel clipped the leash to her collar and then took the gauzy silver scarf from his neck and wrapped it artfully around the dog's bald spots. Tying the ends together in a neat knot at the top of her neck, he created a functional sarong. The outfit, together with the dachshund's silver coat and the tufts of hair on her ears, combined to give her the appearance of an eighties' rock star.

"She looks like Madonna," Charlotte said and held the door open for them.

"It could be much worse," Daniel replied and set Rhianna down on the brick path leading to the street. Charlotte closed the door behind them and started the other way.

"Good luck, Charlie," he called over his shoulder.

"It's Charlotte," she answered back. She heard him unlatch the gate followed by the happy sounds of Rhianna's paws clattering against the asphalt. She wished she could go with them. Though curious to finally see the inside of Wellesley's townhouse, this was not the circumstance she'd imagined. Or wanted.

Charlotte followed the path around a bend and noticed two iron sculptures of great blue herons in full flight. The figures took her breath away and she stopped to get a better look. Had Aunt Wellesley made these? Was their aunt a sculptor as well as a painter? There was so much Charlotte didn't know. She wanted to pause and inspect the statues properly but knew she couldn't inconvenience her aunt any longer. Madison was waiting. *Oh, God.*

She exited the backyard through the gate on the side of the house and walked around to the front porch where she was surprised to see two older gentlemen sitting in high-backed rocking chairs. They were drinking out of teacups. "Oh hello," she said and mounted the flagstone steps. It was now well past midnight. What were two old men doing on Wellesley's porch?

"I'm Charlotte, Wellesley's niece from Maine."

The men stood and offered their hands. The shorter of the two had thinning gray hair and a dapper mustache. He was wearing a kimono similar to Aunt Wellesley's over a pair of pajamas. Covering Charlotte's hand with his own he smiled. "A pleasure to finally meet you, dear. I am Stefano." His accent was thick and Italian, his fingers warm and dry.

"And I'm Jacob," the taller man said. His hair was darker than Stefano's but he also had a warm handshake and wore a colorful robe. "Your aunt is inside." He didn't offer more information about why they might be sitting on Wellesley's front porch after midnight wearing bathrobes and Charlotte was too polite to ask. She knew Daniel would have no such qualms.

"Thank you." She twisted the brass ringer inset into the giant oak door and a bell sounded shrilly from inside the house.

"There's no need to ring the bell," Jacob said.

"They're expecting you, dear." Stefano gave her a kind smile and Charlotte noticed there were a pair of glasses and a book next to him on the rocking chair. Jacob was wearing slippers. *These men lived here.* Charlotte felt a blush stain her cheeks. Not only had Madison interrupted Aunt Wellesley in her studio, but her roommates as well.

"I'm so sorry for the confusion," Charlotte started to explain. "My friend didn't know how to get to the carriage house. I think she may be upset."

Stefano held up a finger. "*Was* upset. I gave her sambuca. I think Madison is much better now."

"Oh." Charlotte swallowed hard. It was clear these men had been the first responders to Madison's meltdown. Her blush deepened. "I'm really sorry to have disturbed your evening."

"It is nothing." Stefano waved his hand.

"And I think it's your evening that's in trouble." Jacob nodded his head toward the door.

"I think you may be right," Charlotte said. Turning the handle, she went inside.

CHAPTER THREE

Charlie Pie

The interior of Aunt Wellesley's townhouse was dimly lit and smelled of freshly baked bread. Lamps in large rooms opening off the entrance hall cast just enough light to reveal an eclectic grandeur. Even to her untrained eye there appeared to be what Laurel Jaguar would classify as real art on every wall. It wasn't a surprise, exactly. Wellesley Kincaid was rich and famous. Classes on her work were offered at major universities around the world and there were websites dedicated to her achievements.

While Charlotte had expected the home to reflect a certain level of success, she'd not expected to be affected by it. She took a minute to look around. It was uplifting. Her mother kept a clean house but gave little thought to decoration. Wellesley's self-portrait was the only piece of art in the house. Wellesley's decor made Charlotte feel as if she was in a museum or on the set of a period film. *But people actually lived here.*

Voices in the back of the house drew her through an impressive library down a dark hallway toward a closed door. Backlit from the light in the kitchen, the door looked like a floating rectangle at the end of the passage. Charlotte imagined it was a portal to a past dimension. It was the last place she wanted to visit. But she couldn't abuse Wellesley's hospitality any longer. Daniel would never speak to her again if she jeopardized their living arrangement. The fact that he was responsible for their current predicament would not count for much if they were forced to look for new housing. Pushing the door open, she entered the kitchen.

"Charlie!"

A human projectile slammed into Charlotte knocking her backward against the pantry. She had no time to react. Landing hard against the wood she felt the small body pressed tightly to her chest and knew it was Madison.

"I can't believe you moved and didn't tell me," she said, and she burrowed her face into Charlotte's neck.

"What are you doing here?" Charlotte patted her lightly on the back. It felt weird to be holding the slender body again after so much time apart. It felt weirder to be holding her in front of Aunt Wellesley, who was standing by the sink watching them.

"Daniel said Rhianna was out of her special biscuits." Madison's voice was muffled in Charlotte's hair.

"You could have mailed them," Charlotte told her and gently detached from the embrace. "I can't believe you drove all the way down here." Looking into Madison's hopeful brown eyes she was at a loss for words. What did Madison expect to happen? Did she think Charlotte would be happy to see her? They were no longer a couple. Hadn't been in months. Charlotte wasn't sure they were even friends. There was an awkward silence broken only when Wellesley opened the cabinet to take out a glass.

"I'll give you ladies some privacy." She placed a clean wineglass on the counter next to the bottle of Sancerre and indicated that Charlotte should help herself. With a firm click she closed the kitchen cabinet.

"You don't have to go," Charlotte blurted and then felt stupid. Of course, Aunt Wellesley didn't want to stay and listen to Charlotte and Madison squabble about dog treats.

To Charlotte's surprise, Wellesley cocked her head to one side. "It's tempting, I confess." She paused as if truly considering the invitation before deciding against it. "No, I need to get to bed. Big day tomorrow, but thank you for offering." She nodded to Madison. "Good luck with the new baker, I hope Melanie works out."

"Oh, thank you!" Madison said. Flying across the room she threw her arms around Wellesley's neck and hugged her like lost kin.

Charlotte was mortified. She hoped Wellesley wasn't offended by impulsive body contact, but she honestly had no idea what her aunt liked or didn't like. At this point, Madison had spent more time with her aunt than she had. Thankfully, Wellesley didn't appear to mind. She even seemed to return the embrace before stepping away and opening the door.

"Good night, ladies." She waved her hand and disappeared.

"Wow, she's so nice," Madison said. She smiled at Charlotte and took a tentative step forward. "I can't believe I just met Wellesley Kincaid."

"What are you doing here?" Charlotte winced when she saw the hurt look on Madison's face but didn't move to comfort her. Madison was the one intruding, she reminded herself. It was something she was really good at. Give her an inch and she'd take over your entire life.

"I missed you, Charlie Pie," Madison started but Charlotte held up a hand.

"Please don't call me that." Walking over to the counter, she filled her wineglass to the rim. White wine was not her go-to beverage but the warm glow of the bourbon at Birdie's was long gone and Charlotte was ready to drink bathtub gin if it would buffer the shock of seeing Madison in her aunt's kitchen. Holding a glass would have the added benefit of occupying her hands. Because, right now, Charlotte wanted to pick up Madison and shake her like a martini mixer. Seriously, what was she thinking coming to DC on the pretense of delivering dog treats? And what was up with her T-shirt? Charlotte pointed to it now.

"Is that a new design?"

"Do you like it?" Madison pushed out her small breasts to better display the familiar logo of her bakery, MadSnax. Charlotte scanned the image. It was the same scripted font from the previous logo with the added words "Home of the Original Charlie Pie." She closed her eyes.

"I told you how I feel about that name."

"I know." Madison sounded sincere. "But we can't get away from it now. The Charlie Pie has really taken off. We've placed it with a national distributor."

"You did?" Despite the unfortunate name of the treat, Charlotte couldn't help feeling a tiny bit impressed. Madison's rich parents might have bankrolled the bakery as a college graduation gift, but the ensuing success all belonged to Madison. "That's great."

"Thank you." Madison looked pleased.

Her genius did not lie in baking, though she hired excellent bakers, but in marketing the business through social media. Funny ads, cupcake giveaways, the Madsnax jingle she'd talked Charlotte into singing—Madison tried everything to get customers in the door and it worked. It was uncanny. Both her skill and her success were undeniable. Now it seemed she was taking things to the next level.

"We've had to rent a small factory in South Portland to keep up with the demand." Madison allowed herself a smile. "We're shipping to five states. You might even start seeing them around here."

Charlotte's jaw dropped open. She closed it again and then shook her head. "I'm not sure what to say. I mean, congratulations. But the name, the name really bothers me."

"I know, I'm sorry." Madison lifted her shoulders in a not-my-problem gesture. "But I can't change it now. We'd lose all the momentum."

Charlotte blew out a breath. "I get that. But you see why it might make me uncomfortable?"

"No one knows," Madison promised her.

"*I* know."

"I'm sorry," Madison said again. Apparently, it was all she had to offer.

The situation was beyond ridiculous. Three years ago, Madison had named the bakery's signature blueberry pop tart in secret tribute to her favorite part of Charlotte's anatomy. It had been their joke. Their very private joke. Charlie Pie after Charlie's pie. Fresh Maine blueberries baked into a delicious confection coated with lemon-sugar frosting. The dessert had been an instant success. The fact that it was also a sexy, inside joke had only made that success sweeter, until things had soured. Now it just felt weird. Super weird. Making matters worse, the jingle Charlotte had recorded for the bakery played in a seemingly endless loop on local radio. There was no getting away from it. This was the primary reason she'd moved to DC. Now it was following her here?

"When did all this happen?"

Madison rolled her eyes. "If you'd answered a single one of my texts you might know what was going on in my life."

"That's not fair," Charlotte replied, but then she felt a stab of guilt. Following the breakup, it had been necessary to distance herself from Madison who wasn't used to being told no. Sometimes, too many times, Charlotte had seen Madison at a club and given in to temptation. One look at the sculpted cheekbones and naturally bronzed skin and she succumbed to baser instincts. But sex had never been their problem. It never fixed anything either. Each time they'd reconnected, Charlotte had had to break up with Madison all over again. It had become a vicious cycle. Rinse. Repeat.

"Moving without telling me is fair?" Madison put a hand on her hip and Charlotte flashed to a memory of being chastised for buying tampons with the wrong type of applicator.

"It's none of your business where I live." The statement, though true, was harsher than she intended, and Madison looked as if she'd been physically struck. Fortunately, Charlotte was well-acquainted with all of Madison's facial expressions. Daniel called this one "diva 911". Charlotte let it pass.

"I'd like to think we're still friends." Madison tried again.

"O-kay." Charlotte took a long sip of wine and then another. The glass was soon empty so she poured herself a second. Friends? Who was Madison kidding? Even when they'd been a solid couple, the relationship had revolved more around sex and alcohol then a true connection. Their dynamic had been great in college. Completely pussy-whipped, Charlotte had been only too happy to follow Madison around southern Maine. They'd had a great time together, traveling with Madison's parents to Europe twice and vacationing with them on their yacht at every chance. But once out of school, things had fallen apart.

Or maybe Charlotte had just grown up. You couldn't shoot tequila until two in the morning when you had patients the next day. They'd been over the whys of the breakup too many times to count. Charlotte didn't want to do it again. She chose her words carefully. "I'm sorry if you were hurt. The housing opportunity with Aunt Wellesley came up pretty quickly. I didn't have time to tell anyone."

"I'm not just anyone," Madison said. She retrieved her wine from the kitchen table, took a sip, then held it out to Charlotte for a refill.

"You sure you want more? You had a long drive. You must be exhausted."

"Trying to get me into bed?" Madison flashed a hopeful smile and kept her glass aloft.

Charlotte took in the near-perfect features. The only child of a Nordic father and Greek mother, Madison had never been hard to look at. But Charlotte didn't want to look at Madison, or talk to her, or have sex with her, not anymore. She'd expressed this opinion numerous times. It had been painful. But it was over. How were they suddenly here again? She poured her another splash.

"I'm not trying to sleep with you," she said firmly and set the bottle down on the table. "But I do need to sleep. I have to work early tomorrow."

"How's the new job?" Madison pivoted quickly from the rejection. "Daniel said you were working at a hospital."

"Yes, because I'm a nurse." Reluctantly, Charlotte told Madison about her job at Children's Hospital. The position had been arranged through a doctor Charlotte had worked with in Portland. It had all happened so quickly that Charlotte had barely had time to discuss it with her mother, much less alert Madison. Given their estrangement it seemed preposterous anyway. Charlotte's vocation had always been a sore point between them. Madison didn't seem to understand that Charlotte had a calling. It was the one thing Madison had in common with Charlotte's mother. When Charlotte had realized, halfway through senior year of college, that she wanted to switch her focus, both women had tried to talk her out of it. Sarah Kincaid had taken it personally while Madison had openly disparaged her. Why would Charlotte want to be a nurse when she could be a doctor? *Because it's a completely different job.* Things had gone downhill from there.

"Do you like it?" Madison asked incredulously. She just didn't get it.

"I love it."

"That's great," she said her expression reading the opposite. "Tell me about it?"

Some things never changed. Though they'd dated during Charlotte's first year of nursing school and part of the second, Madison had never once asked Charlotte about her training. She claimed to be squeamish, and maybe that was true, but she was also selfish and generally bored with any subject that wasn't about her. If it wasn't about Madison, it wasn't worth talking about. At least, not unless she wanted something. Like now. Charlotte took a calming breath. Sharing the precious details of her three-week-old job, thoughts she'd yet to process herself, felt like a betrayal of her new life. But it was easier than talking about their breakup again. So, Charlotte gave her a watered-down version of a day on the job at Children's and then served up Daniel like a hot Sunday buffet. It was only fair.

"Daniel now is working as an event coordinator for the Human Left." Charlotte explained the group's mission to support the legal representation of undocumented citizens and political refugees. "He's planning their annual gala. They're trying to book Bono."

"No way." Madison's eyes grew wide making Charlotte smile. Her own reaction had been similar when Daniel had casually dropped the fact a few days earlier. It was exciting. Washington was home to countless political and media celebrities, and other famous people filed through on a regular basis to lend their name to various causes. Daniel called it Hollywood for Ugly People and claimed to have run into Woodward and Bernstein at Whole Foods. The only famous person Charlotte had seen so far was Aunt Wellesley.

"Will he get to meet him?" Madison asked.

"What do you think?" Charlotte cocked an eyebrow making Madison laugh. She put their wineglasses in the sink and Madison picked up a backpack from the counter. "Come say hi to Daniel then we'll find you a hotel room."

"Oh," Madison said, in a small voice. "Can't I stay with you?"

"No," Charlotte said and held open the door.

Stepping down into the yard they were suddenly alone in the moonlight. Madison tried to catch her eye but Charlotte looked away. Once upon a time she would have jumped at the opportunity of having Madison in her bed. But this wasn't once upon a time. Sleepovers were a thing of the past and would send entirely the wrong signal. Whipping out her smartphone, Charlotte activated the flashlight while Madison picked at the thread of a more agreeable conversation.

"Of course, Daniel is going to meet Bono. Forgive me, I forgot who we were talking about." She forced a laugh. They'd all gone to college together and Madison had borne witness to some of Daniel's most uninhibited antics, including the time he'd gotten onstage to dance with Lady Gaga. "By Christmas they'll be best friends, skiing in Utah."

Charlotte nodded. "It's a safe bet. He really puts it out there." She smiled hesitantly. She knew better than to let Madison back in her life, even as a friend. If she needed proof that her ex-girlfriend hadn't changed, all she had to do was look at her. No one had invited Madison to DC, yet here she was assuming Charlotte would take her in. But the familiarity was so comforting it was difficult to resist. It was nice talking to someone from home, someone who knew her, someone who knew Daniel. Her co-workers at the hospital were friendly enough, but she didn't know them. Against her better judgment, she dropped her guard. "I worry about him sometimes. His job is really challenging. He's putting so much pressure on himself to succeed."

"Party planning?" Madison sounded incredulous. "When has party planning ever been a challenge for Daniel? Remember the time he had a pancake dinner for two hundred people? On a boat? What was the name of that thing?"

"The *Aquaholic*," Charlotte answered automatically. She also remembered fucking Madison in the bathroom below deck. She wondered if Madison was intentionally trying to put this image in her head. The tactic was entirely successful, though, if her goal was seduction, counterproductive. The bathroom of the *Aquaholic* had been cramped and smelled of hand sanitizer with a hint of bilge water. Thinking about it now made Charlotte feel sick. She changed the subject. "Daniel's job has a fundraising component too. The competition for nonprofit money in DC is tough." She stopped outside the carriage house and pulled open the screen door. "He's going crazy trying to find sponsors."

"Maybe my dad can help," Madison said eagerly and Charlotte wanted to kick herself. She hated to deprive the Human Left one penny of potential funding, but she couldn't afford to have Madison back in her life. She hurried to shut it down.

"Oh Maddie, no, please don't get involved."

Hearing the old nickname, Madison's eyes grew moist and she tilted her head expectantly. Charlotte swallowed hard. She didn't want to hurt Madison's feelings but she didn't want to kiss her either. All she wanted to do was crawl into bed and fantasize about Laurel Jaguar. Fortunately, she didn't have to make a decision. Her exit strategy came in the form of a nearly hairless dachshund.

"Rhianna!" Madison dropped to the ground and allowed the dog to cover her face with kisses. "What happened to you?" she asked. Scooping Rhianna into her arms she let the dog nuzzle her neck. The visual impact of the dog's semihairless state coupled with Daniel's scarf had not diminished in the forty-five minutes since Charlotte had last seen her.

"She hasn't adjusted well to the move," Charlotte said. It sounded defensive but it was all she had. She was also ninety-five percent sure it was true. She held open the door for Madison. "We think she misses Taco."

"Poor baby, misses her baby." Madison stroked Rhianna's ears but kept her eyes trained on Charlotte. "I can relate."

Charlotte ignored the comment. They entered the house and found Daniel waiting for them in the kitchen. Hands on hips and with guarded affection, he regarded Madison.

"What the Helvetica Font are you doing here?" He extended his arms for a hug and Madison stepped forward into the embrace, pinning Rhianna between them.

"You said Rhi was out of treats," she said. Pulling away from him she held the dog out to examine her better. "Poor thing looks like Stephen Tyler."

"She prefers Madonna," Daniel corrected her. "Have you ever heard of the US Mail?"

"You know I'm only into women," Madison quipped and then steered away from the subject. "Have you taken her to the vet?" Putting Rhianna down on the hardwood floor, she fished around in her backpack until she found a bag of dog treats.

"No, I haven't found one yet," Charlotte admitted, and she again felt defensive. She knew Madison was only looking for common ground but she'd touched a nerve. Charlotte hadn't had time to find a vet. It was on her list of things to do but they'd barely been in town three weeks. "I think she's just stressed over the move." She repeated and then frowned. "I didn't know the treats she'd been eating were medicinal."

"I thought I told you that?" Madison batted her eyes.

"No, you didn't. But they seem to be working. She was doing okay until we ran out. But she hasn't eaten anything since." Charlotte sank into a kitchen chair.

"I can fix that." Madison offered Rhianna a dog treat. To Charlotte's relief the dachshund gobbled the biscuit down in one gulp and licked Madison's hand asking for more.

"May I?" Madison looked to Charlotte for permission.

"Sure." Charlotte didn't know how much CBD Madison's baker put into the treats, but it had to be better for Rhianna than an old flyswatter or a Dansko clog. Rhianna ate another treat and then another before Charlotte decided she'd had enough. The dog wagged her tail and trotted to the back door.

"I got it," Daniel said and followed Rhianna into the yard.

There was a moment of silence and then Madison cleared her throat. "I should probably go find that hotel." The look on her face suggested this was the last thing she wanted to do.

"It's fine," Charlotte lied. "You can stay here." It was decidedly not fine but she couldn't send Madison to a hotel in the middle of the night. The wine and the late hour must be impairing her judgment. Too late now. "It was nice of you to bring Rhianna treats. I just wish you'd called first."

"You'd have told me not to come."

"That's true." Charlotte filled two glasses with water and handed one to Madison. "But it's okay that you're here now," she lied again. "I do need to get some sleep though. I've got an early day tomorrow. You can have my bed. I'll take the couch."

Madison frowned. "Really? We shared a bed for almost three years. Nothing has to happen."

Charlotte hesitated. It would be really nice to sleep in her own bed. The mid-century modern couch, adequate for a Netflix snooze, was iffy for a whole night's sleep. It was four inches too short for her extra-long body. Charlotte could curl up but she couldn't stretch out without having her feet hanging over the edge. Madison pressed her.

"We'll build a pillow wall in between us. You won't even know I'm there. I promise." She held up two fingers. "Scout's honor."

"You were never a scout," Daniel interrupted, returning with the dog.

"I was a Brownie."

"Brownies have no honor. They make you fat and give you zits," he teased. "Some are nut jobs."

Madison clapped her hands together. "I should have brought you our new Choco Loco. They're THC-infused. Our new baker, Melanie, is fantastic. She's got so much in the works."

Listening to their banter, Charlotte was reminded of their senior year in college when they'd all been roommates. It was bizarre. Did Madison think they could just pick up where they left off? Didn't she understand that Charlotte had moved on? Literally. Moved on. If relocating to DC hadn't gotten the message across, she wasn't sure what would. What would it take? Charlotte didn't have any answers tonight. She just wanted to go to bed so the night would be over and Madison could get back into her shiny blue Mercedes SUV and go back to Maine. The quickest way to accomplish this was to share the bed. Pillow wall it was.

"Okay, we can share," Charlotte said, surprising everyone. She knew it was probably a huge mistake but was too tired to argue anymore. Patient care was challenging even when you had all your wits about you. Madison had caused enough trouble already. Charlotte wouldn't let her affect her job performance.

Madison looked pleased but had the sense not to gloat. "Can I borrow some PJs?"

"Absolutely."

Leaving caution, common sense, and a gawping Daniel behind in the living room, Charlotte followed Madison into the bedroom.

CHAPTER FOUR

Clan of the Cave Bear

The staff lounge on the recovery ward at Children's Hospital was not designed to be a place of rest. There was a coffee station, usually stocked with sugary, homemade offerings from grateful families, and a small refrigerator for perishables, but no upholstered surface that might facilitate a nap. Charlotte thought of the room as an oversized closet. It was certainly not a proper lounge. This was unfortunate as this morning she could barely keep her eyes open. She'd been up late again texting with Madison. Since her surprise visit two weeks ago, it had become almost a nightly routine. And now it was catching up with her. Charlotte wished she had a place to close her eyes, if only for a few minutes, but then took it back. Working in a pediatric hospital she knew better than to squander wishes.

"Those blueberry things are the truth," a voice said from the open doorway. Charlotte recognized the West Virginian drawl of the senior ward nurse, Laura Minor. "The family of that five-year-old brought 'em in."

"Chiara?" Charlotte said automatically. The young daredevil had ruptured her spleen jumping off her swing set. Charlotte had been her nurse for two days on the recovery ward. Chiara would spend two more days in a step-down ward before being discharged. "How's she doing?"

"Chiara, yes." Laura walked into the room. "She's doing fine. Her mom sent us these heavenly confections and wrote a very nice note." Laura picked up a greeting card propped behind a bakery box. On the cover of the card was a photo of a nightingale. Laura held out the card for Charlotte. "She mentions you by name, calls you the singing nurse. What's that about? Did you sing to her child?"

Charlotte froze. "Is that okay?"

"Of course!" Laura nodded enthusiastically. "This is a healing center. Any way you can forge a connection with your patient helps the process along. I think it's wonderful. But I'm curious. How did it happen?"

Charlotte tried to reconstruct the moment. "I'm not sure. I didn't plan it. The poor love was just so uncomfortable. I remember thinking she really needed to rest. Her mom was outside the room on a call or something. I wanted Chiara to go to sleep, so I sang her a lullaby I used to sing to my brother." Charlotte smiled remembering the furrowed brow relaxed in sleep. It had felt like a professional victory.

"That's really nice."

"I didn't know the mom heard me."

Laura handed Charlotte the card. "She did. And she wants you back to sing again tonight."

Charlotte was dumbstruck. "You're joking."

"Nope."

Charlotte scanned the carefully worded note. Chiara's mother hoped "the nightingale nurse" would have time to pay her daughter another visit.

"Do you think I should go?" Charlotte asked. Laura Minor was as small as her name suggested but she commanded a huge presence on the ward. In the nearly six weeks Charlotte had been working under Laura's supervision, she'd seen Laura perform every task from showing a transport engineer how to correctly lower an older model hospital bed, to catheterizing a mortified fifteen-year-old boy. Her opinion meant a great deal. "Do you think I should do it?"

Laura frowned. "That's up to you, Charlotte. I can't tell you what to do in this case. It's a tricky vocation. We all have to decide how much of ourselves to give. There's endless need, but not always endless energy."

"What room's she in?"

Laura laughed. "Seven-B." She gave Charlotte a warm look. "You've got the calling, girl. I knew it the moment I saw you."

"Thanks, Laura," Charlotte said, and unexpected tears pricked the back of her eyes as the compliment hit the edge of her exhaustion. She filed it away to tell her mother the next time Sarah questioned her decision to become a nurse. Charlotte hadn't made a choice—she'd followed her calling.

Laura moved to open the bakery box and Charlotte did a double take. The logo was painfully familiar. Madsnax, Portland. *Holy shit.* Laura selected two lemon-frosted blueberry pop tarts, carefully wrapped them in wax paper and stuffed them into her purse. Lifting a third, she offered it to Charlotte. "I promise, they're the truth."

"No thanks." Charlotte did her best to keep a blank face. Madison had not exaggerated the success of the Charlie Pie. Good for her. But this was just too weird to process. Having a dessert named after your vagina was bad enough. To have it find national distribution and show up in the staff lounge at work—well, there were no books written on how to handle the situation. Charlotte shuddered. "I'm not hungry."

"I'm not hungry either," Laura said and shook a pop tart at Charlotte. "But I will be later when the cafeteria is closed and my blood sugar is downtown like Julie Brown. Take a treat. You've earned it. It says so right here on the card." She slapped her free hand down on the picture of the nightingale.

"Okay, fine." Reluctantly, Charlotte took a bite of the pop tart. It was delicious. There was no argument. Charlie Pies were fantastic. These were the flavors and the tastes of Maine, of home. Charlotte just wished they were called something else.

Laura beamed at her enjoyment. "What did I tell you? These things are the truth!"

Charlotte took another bite and then another. Soon she was staring at an empty napkin in her hand. When was the last time she'd eaten?

"You want another one?" Laura asked, her hand poised over the Madsnax box.

"No, that was perfect." Charlotte used the napkin to wipe her mouth and then tossed it into the recycling bin.

"Feel better?" Laura asked.

"I do."

"Great, because there's something else you need to deal with." An odd look formed on Laura's face.

"What?"

"A balloon installation arrived earlier today for you. I'm not sure why, but they sent it to long-term care. You'll need to go up there and sign for it."

"Excuse me?" Charlotte wasn't sure she'd heard Laura correctly. Perhaps she was more exhausted than she realized. "Did you just say balloon installation?"

Laura shook her head. "That's what the security guard said. His name is Ethan and he's called twice. Mind going up there?"

"I'll do it before I check on Chiara," Charlotte replied and then fled before Laura could task her with something else.

The last hour of her shift passed by in a blur. Though the Charlie Pie had provided a nice pick-me-up, Charlotte's head felt light and she wondered if she might actually be in a state of shock. She still didn't know quite how it had happened. More than a year ago, she'd gathered up all her courage and ended her relationship with Madison. It had been painful, emotional, and horrible in every way.

How were they back together again? How had Charlotte let Madison back in? Daniel pointed out Charlotte might have avoided the predicament had she been more vigilant in maintaining the integrity of the pillow wall, or at least put Madison in a hotel. Georgetown had at least a dozen, and it wasn't like Madison couldn't afford it. But Charlotte was only human and Madison had been relentless. The end result had been awkward reunion sex that had given Madison the wrong impression. When Charlotte tried to explain that nothing had changed, Madison had turned a deaf ear. Since then, boundaries had become murky. But what did Charlotte expect? Drag a toe in the bottom of the creek, and the bottom completely disappeared.

Daniel claimed to see things more clearly. When he'd spotted Madison wearing Charlotte's bathrobe, he'd snidely welcomed Charlotte to the *Clan of the Cave Bear* and then sashayed out the door. But not before accepting Madison's generous offer to ask her father to underwrite the cost of the Human Left Gala dinner. It was a mere formality as Felix Hagen owned half of southern Maine and never denied his daughter anything. Daniel knew Charlotte was wildly against the idea but had agreed out of principle. He'd coached Charlotte through each stage of the breakup with Madison. If Charlotte was allowed to get back in bed with her, Daniel was too.

It didn't help Charlotte's emotional state that Rhianna had returned to Maine to live with Taco and Sarah. Sending the dog back to Portland was one of the hardest things Charlotte had ever done. In the end, concern for Rhianna had won out and she'd put the dachshund in the car with Madison on her return trip. Her mother had congratulated her on making an adult decision, which felt nice, and Rhianna was eating again which was everything. It stung a bit, but the dog was happier in Maine where a pet door gave her unlimited access to a fenced-in yard and a fat Siamese who made her heart go pit-a-pat. Sarah sent regular photos so Charlotte knew some of Rhianna's hair had grown back, though the dog still looked like Madonna. The most important thing was that Rhianna's behavior was back to normal without needing CBD biscuits—if normal meant climbing onto the porch roof to sun her belly with Taco.

Charlotte scanned her hospital ID on the monitor outside the ward elevators. Though she had two more tasks inside the hospital, she was now officially off the clock. This was an important distinction because it meant she was allowed to use her phone. Slipping it from her backpack, she powered it on. A text message from Daniel popped up followed by another and then two more. Charlotte tried to make sense of them.

Did you bring your glove to DC?
I need you to play for me, Charlie!
Be my foxy-proxy?
Pretty please?

Charlotte smiled at the messages. Daniel had dropped all the Michael Jackson songs from his repertoire years ago. So, the mention of a single glove had to mean softball. Despite her exhaustion, she felt her spirits lift. An All-State pitcher during her last year of high school, Charlotte was still an excellent player. She'd competed on an intramural team in college and had been on a rec team in Portland. Yes, she did in fact have her glove. But where had Daniel found a team?

Yes, I have my glove.
What team?
When is the game?

She fired off the texts and then stepped into the elevator to go up to long-term care. Hopefully Ethan from security would still be on shift and he could help her sort out the balloon installation, whatever that meant, and she could move on to the next task. Charlotte was more than a bit suspicious the offering had come from Madison whose love language was aggressively retail. Though so far she'd practiced remarkable restraint. Perhaps it was all a mistake. Charlotte Kincaid was not that uncommon a name. Maybe the balloons were for someone else.

Positioned on the top floor of the hospital, the long-term care ward received the best natural light in the building and immediately made Charlotte feel more cheerful. The feeling turned to dismay when she saw the balloons. A giant rainbow-colored rectangle with a big red heart in the middle, it looked like an inflatable Valentine's Day card. Charlotte put her hand over her mouth. She could certainly understand why Ethan from security had declared it an installation. It had to be over eight feet long. What on earth was she going to do with it?

"There it is!" A voice squealed, pulling Charlotte from her thoughts. She turned to see a small girl, attached to a portable

IV drip, dragging her parents across the lobby. The only thing bigger than the installation was the excitement on the girl's face.

"Wow, that's awesome!" exclaimed the mother. Her happiness was not in the balloons, as impressive as they were, but in her child's delight.

"Can we take a picture?" The little girl wanted to know. "I want to send Katie a picture."

"Of course," the father said and pulled out his phone.

Out of nowhere, a tall, blond man in a guard's uniform stepped forward and offered to be the photographer. Charlotte supposed this must be Ethan. She watched as he expertly positioned the little family in front of the balloon heart. He might have been in an elf suit attending Santa at the mall. When the family turned to go, Ethan met Charlotte's eye.

"May I help you?" He automatically scanned her hospital ID. "Oh wow! You're Charlotte Kincaid!" He gave a happy, horsey laugh. "I've been waiting for you all day. What's going on with these beautiful balloons?"

"I'm not sure," Charlotte said. She walked closer to the installation to get a better look as Ethan fished a card from his breast pocket. He handed the envelope to Charlotte. "Maybe this will help."

"Thanks." Charlotte started to open the envelope but stepped aside when another family wandered into the lobby to have their photo taken. As Ethan took their picture, Charlotte scanned the card.

To the girlfriend with the biggest heart, thank you for letting me back in yours. M.

Charlotte read the note twice and then shoved it inside the front pocket of her uniform. She looked up and found Ethan watching her closely. In one hand he was holding a small packing box.

"Any help?" He raised an eyebrow.

Charlotte didn't make a practice of discussing her private life with random security guards, but this situation was anything but normal. Ethan had been baby-sitting this absurdity all day. He deserved an explanation. "The balloons are from my ex, who thinks we're back together, because I kind of said we were back together. But we're not..." The answer came out far more garbled than Charlotte intended. When she tried to clarify Ethan held up a hand. The gesture made him look like a traffic cop from a children's book.

"I get it," he said.

"You do?"

"We get to keep the balloons." He smiled broadly.

Charlotte blinked her eyes. "Yes, I guess you do." She paused. "But are you sure you want them?" Positioned in front of a wall of framed photographs, the balloons blocked the images from view. "Is there enough room?"

"Of course, we want them." Ethan acted as if Charlotte had suggested throwing away his grandparents' engagement rings. "They make the kids happy. And they're only obscuring the Administrator's ego wall. What are people going to say? Move the balloons that make sick children happy, so people can see our fat, smug faces?" He gave his horsey laugh again.

"I guess not," Charlotte agreed. She was thankful Ethan had taken ownership of the balloons. Also that she was not in administration. She looked back at the giant heart and had the mad impulse to throw it to the ground and stomp it to death. What could Madison be thinking? Calling Charlotte every night was bad enough. Sending an eight-foot balloon installation was crossing a line.

Ethan handed Charlotte the box he was holding. "This came with the balloons. Let me grab a pen and you can sign the delivery slip."

"Thanks," Charlotte said. She looked down at the box. What else had Madison sent? It could be anything. As the only child of wealthy, generous parents, money was not a consideration—unless you were considering how to spend it. And Madison was never lacking ideas. Inside the box could be an expensive silk scarf or even a diamond necklace. Instead she found more Charlie Pies. Was there no escaping these things? Charlotte closed the box and sealed the lid shut.

Ethan handed her the delivery slip and a pen. "If your ex sends anything else you don't want, you know where to find us."

Charlotte signed the slip and handed it back to Ethan along with the Charlie Pies. "How do you feel about blueberry pop tarts?"

Ethan smiled at the box. "I love them."

"Great." Charlotte turned to leave and he waved his hand at the installation. "Wait! Don't you want your picture taken with the balloons?"

"I do not." Charlotte pressed the button to summon the elevator. The door opened to a couple with a new baby. The mother held the child carefully against her chest as the father steered them directly over to the balloon heart. The infant couldn't have been more than a day old.

"Well, you're the only one," Ethan replied and happily stepped forward to take the family's picture.

Charlotte watched their smiling faces as the elevator door closed. She was glad Madison's giant balloon heart could provide joy to so many people. In Charlotte's actual heart she knew this display of affection was more about control. Madison was not in love with Charlotte. How could she claim to love her when she had no respect for her boundaries? Charlotte resolved to tell her this tonight. She hoped she had the fortitude to push home the point once and for all.

Her phone buzzed and she checked the screen to find a text from Daniel.

The softball game is tonight. You are playing first base for the Human Left, yes?

Charlotte tapped back a quick affirmative. As tired as she was, softball with Daniels's co-workers sounded infinitely more exciting than popping Madison's love balloon. First base wasn't particularly taxing for a player of Charlotte's caliber and it would be nice to get some fresh air after being inside all day. The more she thought about playing softball the more her spirits lifted. The conversation with Madison could wait. By the time she arrived at room 7B to sing Chiara to sleep, she was trying to remember where she'd stashed her mitt.

CHAPTER FIVE

Rounding First

"Don't be a dick, Steve!" A woman shouted at her teammate from the bench but the batter ignored her. Kicking at the dirt like a cartoon bull, he squared his shoulders and cocked the bat. The first pitch was high so he took a step back and spat in the dust.

Ball one.

"What are you doing, dude? You're not even a lefty!" The woman on the bench, a lanky redhead, continued to voice her displeasure loudly.

The hitter didn't engage. Pulling at the crotch of his old-school baseball knickers, he looked away. Charlotte tried to catch the eye of the runner standing next to her on first base. The attractive blonde had earned the bag when Charlotte's teammate, an Englishman in a winged unicorn hat playing right field, had woefully mismanaged a pop fly. Though apparently nationally ranked at snooker, this was Colin's first time playing softball. The man at the plate was trying to capitalize on Colin's inexperience by batting left-handed. Anything he hit was likely to go in the Englishman's direction. Charlotte agreed with the redhead's assessment. It was a dick move.

"You're being an asshole, Steve!" The redhead's yelling caused the woman on first base to titter. She shot Charlotte a conspiring smile.

"Steve's my boss, so I can't chime in. But I agree. He's being a complete asshole."

"I hope he's not *her* boss." Charlotte nodded toward the redhead on the bench.

The blonde beamed. "No, that's my wife, Hannah. She's our biggest client and can say whatever the hell she wants. Plus, she's an awesome shortstop. So, steer clear of the middle."

"Good to know," Charlotte said and put herself in the ready position as the pitcher launched another offering.

It was the top of the first inning and she was already having fun. Being on a softball field always had this effect on her. The fact that this particular softball field lay in the shadow of the Washington Monument only enhanced the sensation. Charlotte had been stunned when the Uber driver deposited them at the polo fields along Independence Avenue. When she and Daniel had visited Washington on their fifth grade Lion's Club trip, she'd not noticed there were ball fields adjacent to the National Mall. She smiled at the sensation of feeling familiar in an unfamiliar place and wondered what other secrets DC had in store for her.

Another reason for Charlotte's happiness was that Laurel Jaguar was on the opposing team. Daniel had spotted the curvy blonde immediately upon arrival. Her brother didn't miss a trick. When he'd seen the green Jaguar, he'd almost done a backflip but Charlotte had dismissed it as coincidence. Then he'd pointed out the driver. It was definitely her. Charlotte was eager, more than eager, to resume the conversation they'd begun at Birdie's but faced the small problem of not knowing her name.

The next ball was hittable but the umpire called it deep. Ball two.

"This is a beer league, Steve. Swing the bat!" Hannah yelled from the bench. But the man was not to be rushed. When he bent over to tighten his shoelaces Charlotte took a chance and questioned the woman on first base.

"Do you know the woman's name on the left end of the bench?" It was a gamble to query a complete stranger. This might be Laurel Jaguar's sister, who knew? There was a slight resemblance that had Charlotte curious. Chatting her up was risky, but it was Charlotte's best option.

The woman narrowed her eyes. "Green hat?"

"Yeah."

"Her name is Lillian. Why?"

Charlotte tried to look nonchalant but couldn't hide a smile. *Lillian.* It was such a pretty name. "I danced with her a few weeks ago at Birdie's."

"You danced with Lillian?"

Charlotte felt her confidence slip. "Yeah, she probably won't remember me."

"Oh, she'll remember you." The woman looked Charlotte up and down. Her brow furrowed into a thoughtful expression. "She'll definitely remember you."

Charlotte wasn't sure how to respond, so she said nothing. The woman seemed genuinely surprised that Charlotte had danced with Lillian. She also seemed more interested in the conversation than in the next pitch.

"What's your name?" she asked, now sounding a little protective.

Charlotte kept her eye on the batter. "Charlotte."

"Ball three!" the umpire shouted.

"I'm Camille. Lillian and I work together and she's a great girl."

"Nice to meet you," Charlotte said and stepped back into the ready position. The pitcher dropped the ball perfectly across the plate and the conversation was over. Steve teed-off like Tiger Woods at the Masters, knocking a high, line drive down the first base line. It was sure to be a base hit, possibly more. Colin would truly have to be Pegasus to have any chance of stopping it.

Camille started for second base just as Charlotte left the ground. Leaping high into the air, she extended her body to full vertical capacity and snatched the ball clean out of the sky. Punctuating the moment, she landed with one foot on the bag, doubling Camille off and ending the inning.

Daniel gave a series of little shrieks from the bench. "That's my sister, bitches! That's my sister!" And both teams cheered loudly, acknowledging the beautifully executed play. This was Charlotte's favorite thing about recreational softball. Steve's bad sportsmanship aside, opposing teams were generally supportive, interested more in the game than in the win.

"You're out!" The first base umpire stuck her thumb at Camille who swatted playfully at Charlotte's arm.

"Nice catch, LeBron!"

"Thanks." Charlotte accepted the compliment, smiling as the pitcher from her team, a plump woman named Olive, came to give her a high five. Colin joined the celebration. Crowning Charlotte's achievement, he placed the winged unicorn hat on her head.

"Look who's coming." Camille gestured to Lillian who was now walking toward them across the infield. "I think she might remember you."

Charlotte swallowed. Lillian was indeed coming their way. Dressed in running shorts and a softball jersey, the firm musculature of her body was on full display. The name Laurel Jaguar was particularly apt. God, she was hot. The easy grace of her stride reminded Charlotte of a sleek cat. She walked closer, and Charlotte remembered their dance, the press of Lillian's breasts against her own. She tried to stop a blush but was unsuccessful. She felt infinitely better when she noticed Lillian was having a similar problem.

"Are you by any chance the famous Charlie, from the Charlie Daniels Band?" Her eyes were shy when she peeked up beneath the brim of the green ball cap. She still looked at Charlotte as if she knew a secret, but she no longer seemed annoyed about it. This was good news, very good news.

"I am indeed her," Charlotte said and took it as a positive sign that Lillian had chosen a reference that took them immediately back to the dance floor. "You're Lillian, right? The saintly designated driver and talented designer of bachelorette party T-shirts?" She glanced at the graphic on the sporty Gowear softball jersey and noted a similar whimsical style. A frog was snatching a fly ball out of the air with its tongue. "Did you make these too?"

"I did, yes. But please, call me Lily, okay?"

"Okay, sure. Lily. That's so pretty." Charlotte wondered why Camille had said her name was Lillian. She looked to catch her eye but somehow, probably when Charlotte was staring at Lily's breasts, Camille had made it to the opposing bench. "And I'm Charlotte."

"I remember," Lily said softly, the sparkle back in her eyes. "I also remember..." she began but was interrupted by Hannah, who was indeed playing shortstop.

"Take your position, Lillian!" Hannah shouted and fired a practice ball toward the catcher. Charlotte was impressed with her arm but wondered why she'd called her Lillian. Hadn't she just said she preferred to be called Lily? That thought and all others flew from her mind when soft fingers brushed her forearm.

"It's nice to see you again," Lily said, then hesitated. "I wasn't sure I would. You sort of ran off the other night." She touched her again and Charlotte's knees grew weak.

"Lillian!" Hannah shouted again and Lily took a step back.

"Maybe I'll run into you after the game?"

"Sure," Charlotte replied. Feeling slightly dazed, she float-walked back to the Human Left bench positioned along the first base line. Teammates congratulated her on the double play but she barely heard them. There was one thought in her head. *Laurel Jaguar's name is Lily.* Colin took back his unicorn hat and she tried to smile at him. *Lily, it was such a nice name.* Someone gave her a cup of water—she couldn't say who—and she took a sip. When Charlotte finally sat down Daniel pounced on her like she was the last beer left in the cooler. Draping his arms over her shoulders, he purred loudly into her neck.

"Laurrrrrel Jaguarrrrrr."

"Her name is Lily." Charlotte tried to brush him off but he only clung to her more tightly.

"I preferrrrr Laurrrrrel."

"You don't get to choose."

"What did she say?"

"That it was nice to see me again."

"Does she want to see *more* of you?" Daniel tugged at the collar of Charlotte's T-shirt and she slapped his hand away.

"Please be quiet."

"Could she be a final cure for the Madness?" He put a hand over his heart.

"Stop." Charlotte punched his arm. Madness was the not-so-subtle but spot-on word Daniel used to describe Madison or any drama involving her. He'd coined the term in college and, sadly, there'd never been a reason to retire it. But Madison was the last thing Charlotte wanted to think about right now. It was all ridiculously complicated. Daniel had locked down her father's sponsorship with an official email, but the check wouldn't come until after the caterer presented the bill. There wasn't much Madison could do to sabotage the donation now, but Charlotte didn't like to chance it. The breakup conversation needed to be handled with extreme precision. Do it tactfully, and Charlotte might be able to preserve both the friendships and the donation. Handle it poorly, and hell hath no fury. Either way, calling her names wasn't helpful.

"Please don't call her that," Charlotte said and pushed him off her back. "She's our friend. And she's sponsoring your event."

Daniel shook his head. "Her dad is sponsoring the event. That has nothing to do with your relationship and the fact that you're letting her hold you hostage. Again."

"It still isn't nice."

"How about we call her Ba-loonie instead?" Daniel said and Charlotte cursed herself for telling him about the balloon installation.

"No."

"Because she's a balloon-atic!" he sang.

"Talk about something else, please."

"Okay, fine." He gave her a saucy smile. "Did you know the winning team gets to pick the bar tonight?"

"I did not," Charlotte replied. Her brother loved tiny organizational details the way most people loved french fries. This characteristic served him well as an event planner. No piece of information was below his notice. Charlotte often benefitted. Like today, when he'd spotted Lily's car.

"That's why we have to let them win," Daniel continued. He kept his voice low so his co-workers didn't overhear.

"What? Why?" Charlotte was pulled from her reverie by the unorthodox request.

"Be quiet, and listen," he whispered. "If we win, we go to Birdie's and that can't happen."

"Why not? I thought you loved Birdie's."

"Yes, but Birdie's may have a Geoffrey Problem tonight," Daniel explained and Charlotte started to clue in. For reasons yet to be explained, her twin disliked a new co-worker and referenced him only as the Geoffrey Problem.

"He and no-Shoshanna had a late meeting with the Irish Embassy," Olive chimed in. The pitcher was shamelessly eavesdropping but Daniel didn't seem to mind. "Word is they are backing out as the gala venue."

Daniel pressed a hand over one eye. "Can we please not talk about it?" The gala was their biggest fundraiser of the year. Daniel was the assistant on the project. A venue change, four months out from the event, would complicate his life dramatically. Olive mimed zipping her mouth closed.

"Who's no-Shoshanna?" Charlotte asked Olive. The nickname had Daniel's fingerprints all over it.

"Our first baseman," Olive explained. "But she almost never comes and we always have to find a sub. That reminds me, what are you doing next week?"

"I'm not sure," Charlotte said and lifted her head to center field. She wasn't positive but it seemed like Lily was looking in her direction.

Olive didn't get the hint. "Okay, Charlie. Let me know. You've got a great glove. We'd love to have you play with us again."

"Let's see what happens," Charlotte said, keeping an eye on Lily. "And please call me Charlotte."

The game was once again underway. The leadoff batter for the Human Left was up. A wiry woman named Sheila, she looked good for a base knock. The outfield was betting against her strength and had stepped in a few yards. Charlotte shook her head. It was common practice in co-ed ball to play shallow against women hitters. It wasn't a bad strategy, but it was sexist and annoyed the hell out of Charlotte. She hoped they made the same calculation when she came to bat.

Steve, the switch-hitting asshole, was pitching. In addition to old-school baseball knickers, he wore high socks and had a rosin bag next to him on the mound. Charlotte had used the chalky substance playing fast-pitch in high school and found it very effective for drying out sweaty hands. She didn't see how it was necessary in slow-pitch ball. But everything about Steve's softball persona was overkill. Under the baseball pants he was probably wearing a cup.

He intentionally pitched the first two balls inside trying to get Sheila to swing. But the scrappy gal from the Human Left was having none of it. Each time the ball left Steve's hand she stood back from the plate as if she were waiting on a bus. Her attitude was perfect. It came with the added benefit of annoying Steve who slapped at the rosin bag as if it were to blame. He placed the next pitch in the strike zone and Sheila liked what she saw. Squaring up, she swung the bat and sent a beautiful line drive over Hannah's head. There it was gobbled up by Camille who was playing left field in her wife's back pocket.

Olive recorded the out in the stat book. "You're on deck Charlie," she said and picked up a bat.

"It's Charlotte," she corrected her again, and she picked up a bat. Watching Olive approach the plate, Charlotte took a few practice swings and let her gaze drift back to Lily. Despite the complicated situation with Madison, her heart felt light. Was it the adventure of living in a new city, being back on a ball field, or was it *this girl?* Charlotte thought of their dance at the club and the flirty banter just now. There was no denying Lily had an effect on her. She wondered if she planned to go to the bar after the game. Lily had said she'd hoped to see Charlotte later. Did that mean tonight? Charlotte didn't give a Fig Newton which team won, as long as she got to look into those green eyes again.

"Ball four," yelled the umpire and directed Olive to first base.

The plump pitcher tossed her bat toward Charlotte. "Good luck, Charlie."

Charlotte didn't bother correcting her this time. Eyeing the defense, she approached the plate. She might not care who won the game, but she wasn't above showing off a little. Especially when Lily had a front-row seat. But Camille had taken Charlotte's measure and directed the rest of the outfield back. Charlotte wondered if it was her athletic build—at five foot eleven she cut an imposing figure on any ball field—or the front row seat to the double play that made Camille cautious. It would make Charlotte's task more difficult but not impossible. She warmed to the test.

"That's right bitches, you best show some respect. That's my sister at the plate! Smack it, Charlie," Daniel yelled from the bench.

Charlotte smiled. Daniel knew better than anyone how she responded to a challenge. The farther the other team backed up, the harder she'd hit the ball. It was as simple as that. She glanced once more at Lily in center field. Poised with her feet apart, she was ready to spring into action should Charlotte send the ball her way. Charlotte was very interested in watching her body move, but the best chance of clearing the outfield was targeting the left side. If Baseball Knickers gave her the pitch she wanted, she could pull the ball onto a neighboring field and send everyone scrambling. With any luck she'd make it to third base before the ball was back in play. She stepped into the batter's box and tapped the bat to the bottom of both cleats.

"We got a player!" Hannah yelled and waved at the outfield to move back an additional few paces.

Charlotte cursed the ritual that signaled her experience but knew she was powerless to stop it. Knocking the dirt from the bottom of her cleats before the first pitch was muscle memory.

It was no more easily edited from instinct than brushing her teeth before bed. Squaring her shoulders, she put it out of her mind and focused on the pitcher. Steve was looking at her as if he knew something. Charlotte found the smirk almost as annoying as his pants. Where did a grown man find polyester baseball knickers anyway?

The first pitch came high and inside, barely missing her elbow. Charlotte adjusted her position. It didn't suit her plans to get struck by a pitch. Steve pulled at his crotch and she thought about hitting the ball directly at his head but then quickly dismissed it. If she knocked him out, she might have to give him mouth-to-mouth.

The next pitch was high and away. A little lower and it would be in Charlotte's sweet spot. Squaring up, she tapped her cleats again. Olive had walked in four pitches, but Charlotte wanted to hit the ball.

"Give her a damn pitch, Steve!" Hannah yelled, echoing the thought in Charlotte's head.

The next offering was on target. Arching high in the air the ball dropped over the plate in the very center of the strike zone. It was not the exact pitch Charlotte had hoped to hit but it was too good to pass up. Waiting just a beat, she lifted the bat off her shoulder and met the ball with a mighty blast. At the moment of contact Charlotte knew she'd struck it perfectly. She also knew it was going to center field.

CHAPTER SIX

Sweet Emotion

The opposing team's bar of choice was a pool hall in Dupont Circle called Buffalo Billiards. Olive, who'd begged a ride in their post-game Uber, informed Daniel and Charlotte the bar had been a fixture in the neighborhood for more than thirty years. Walking through the basement space, Charlotte understood why Daniel had been so keen to move to DC. The crowd was young, urban and hip. She felt like an imposter moving among them. Miraculously, no one had called her out.

"Can I get you a drink?" Daniel wanted to know.

Charlotte nodded. "Big glass of water, please."

"Splash of bourbon?" he added.

"Later," she replied, and she scanned the room. Somewhere in this crowded pool hall Lily might be waiting for her. The desire to see her pulled at Charlotte much more strongly than the need for alcohol.

"It's now or never." Daniel cocked a hip. "I'm not waiting in that line twice, Charlie."

"Water please," she repeated.

"How about a soda?" he pressed her. "Your blood sugar has got to be low after that outstanding display of athleticism."

"It was outstanding," Olive gushed. "You're an amazing softball player, Charlie." Her eyes shone with such alarming appreciation that Charlotte took a step back.

"Thanks. I had a lucky night and please, *please*, call me Charlotte." She shot a look at Daniel. "Seriously, I just want a glass of water."

He pursed his lips but said nothing. Charlotte ignored him. One of the best and worst things about being Daniel's twin was his assumed responsibility for her physical well-being. His endless fussing more than compensated for their mother's absentminded care but it could be trying. It didn't help that he was nearly always correct.

"I'm getting you a ginger ale," he said finally and turned to Olive. "Drink?"

"Stella Artois, please." Olive pointed to the far end of the pool hall. "Come find us over that way. Colin is still wearing his hat. You can't miss us."

"Got it. Keep an eye on my sister," Daniel said, feigning concern. "She's new in town and easily led astray."

"I am not," Charlotte protested but Olive looked worried.

"I'll watch her. I promise," she agreed and, to Charlotte's astonishment, latched onto her forearm. The unexpected contact was nothing like the brush of Lily's fingers a few hours earlier. Where tingles had erupted at Lily's touch, Charlotte now felt only dead weight. She wanted to break free but couldn't move. Daniel read her body language but, apparently annoyed that Charlotte was neglecting her blood sugar, continued to punish her.

"Thank you, Olive." He put a hand to his temple. "This means so much."

"No problem." Olive clutched Charlotte's arm more tightly. "I'll stick close."

"Back in a flash." Daniel winked at Charlotte and skipped off into the crowd.

Charlotte looked down at the woman holding her arm. She wanted to shake her off like she might a bug in the woods. It wouldn't be difficult. Charlotte had at least six inches on Olive. The only consideration beyond manners was liability. If Charlotte shook the pitcher too hard, she might launch her across the room.

"I would hate for anything to happen to this arm." Olive ran her hand up Charlotte's bicep. It was overt flirtation and not a huge surprise. The look of admiration Olive had given Charlotte after the double play had blossomed into adoration when Charlotte hit the ball onto a neighboring field. When Charlotte had done it a second time, Olive had asked for her cell number. Though flattered by the older woman's interest, Charlotte knew it wouldn't be fair to encourage her. Not when Charlotte was still technically dating Madison and thinking only of Lily.

"Thanks, Olive," she replied and gently pulled away from her touch. "I hope I can play with you guys again next week. But right now, I need to check on my dog." It was a weak excuse but not untrue. She didn't bother to mention that Rhianna was in Maine. Charlotte had been too preoccupied looking for her softball gear to call her mom after work. She knew Rhianna didn't notice or care, but the call made Charlotte feel better. She also didn't want her mom to think that she was dumping Rhianna on her. Charlotte was still a responsible pet owner. It was just now via Skype.

Olive looked concerned. Her mass of short red curls bounced with alarm. "You're not leaving?"

"No," Charlotte held up her phone, "I'm going to call my mom. I should have done it in the Uber."

"No."

"No, I can't call my mom?" Charlotte eyed the smaller woman. Without her ball cap she looked a bit like Annie from the Broadway musical. The dusting of freckles across her nose made the resemblance even more striking. Charlotte had played the role in middle school and knew all the songs by heart. The one that came to mind now was about making a stray dog go away.

"I'm sorry, Charlie," Olive replied, not looking sorry at all. "Of course, you can call your mom. You just can't do it here. There's no reception in the basement. You'll have to go outside. But let's find Colin first. He's waiting for us."

Before Charlotte could protest, Olive had reclaimed her arm and was pulling her through the crowd. Charlotte felt like a steamship to her tug and wondered if anyone in the bar noticed. She wasn't insecure about her appearance. The combination of slim hips and broad shoulders attracted equal numbers of women and men. But tethered to Little Orphan Olive was not the way she wanted to encounter Lily who could be walking around the next corner.

They wound their way into a semi-private room and she saw the winged unicorn hat. "Colin!" she said with more enthusiasm than she'd normally give someone she barely knew. But right now, Charlotte was actually thrilled to see the Englishman. Lifting her hand to wave she freed it from Olive's.

"Charlotte!" Colin cried with equal fervor.

Other teammates from the Human Left greeted Charlotte with a round of applause.

"Your brother said you were a ringer. But damn, girl," Sheila swore respectfully.

"Thanks, I had a lucky night," Charlotte repeated the phrase that had been her mantra since little league. Because it wasn't untrue. Charlotte had been lucky tonight. Just as she'd been lucky the night before and the night before that. Physicality was mostly good fortune. Charlotte did her best to maintain the body nature had given her, but she couldn't take any credit for it. And she didn't take it for granted.

Moving in behind her, Olive joined the conversation. "Charlie says she'll play for us next week."

"There's a game next week?" Colin tweaked the bill of his hat. "Sign me up. I think I was quite getting the hang of it toward the end."

"You were great, Colin." Sheila punched his arm. "And your hat was the perfect antidote to that numb-nuts in the baseball pants."

Charlotte laughed. "What was up with that guy?"

"They're lawyers from Walker and Jenkins. Their offices are down Mass Ave on the other side of Dupont Circle," Olive informed them. As team manager she kept the schedule as well as the roster.

Charlotte perked up at this new information. Was Lily a lawyer? She tried to imagine the curvy blonde in a courtroom and found that she could. Not that this meant much. Charlotte found that she could imagine Lily in a myriad of places, not all of them professional. She did a quick scan of the room. Members of the opposing team were playing pool at the table in the back. She recognized Camille and Hannah, but didn't see Lily.

Charlotte had been playing *Where's Waldo* with the green baseball ball cap since arriving at the pool hall. It occurred to her now that Lily may no longer be wearing it. Charlotte had removed hers in the Uber. Her long dark hair now fell freely around her shoulders. Having it down made Charlotte feel less exposed but the chill of air-conditioning had goose bumps pricking her arms and chest. She suddenly hoped Daniel had ordered her a bourbon instead of the water. Damn him for being right.

"Lawyers? That doesn't surprise me," Sheila said, running a hand through her spiky black hair. Tattoos snaking up both arms completed a style that Daniel called urban lesbian. It was a bold statement of identity she executed very well and Charlotte envied the self-confidence. Sheila wore her sexuality like a blinking rainbow billboard. "That pitcher was a douche. I can totally see him as a lawyer."

"They picked a great bar." Colin eyed the pool tables affectionately.

"Daniel told me you're a nationally ranked snooker player," Charlotte said. "Isn't that like pool?"

"What?" Olive and Shelia both yelled at the same time as Colin's face split into a goofy grin.

"I can't believe Daniel told you that!" he said, though clearly thrilled he had.

"Is it true?" Olive demanded. "How did I not know this?"

"I'm sorry, Colin." Charlotte was mortified that she may have revealed a confidence. Daniel was relentless in his pursuit of information but once in his possession he wasn't always careful where he left it. "Was it a secret?"

"Of course, it's not a secret." Colin looked indignant. "You don't walk three miles to the boy's club each day for ten years and become England's junior champion to hide the news under a bushel."

Sheila punched his arm again. "That's fucking awesome. Are you any good at pool?"

Despite Charlotte's early heroics, the Human Left had not won the softball game. After Charlotte's second home run, the pitcher had walked her intentionally each time up. He pitched everyone else inside to draw ground balls.

"Would you like to see?" Colin looked slyly at the table of lawyers surrounding the pool table and the awkward right fielder completely disappeared.

"Let's do it!" Sheila hooted but Little Orphan Olive was not enthusiastic. Charlotte suspected her manager's sensibility was chagrined at not having the full scouting report on her right fielder.

"Why didn't I know this?" she complained and the red curls bounced angrily around her head. Charlotte knew that if Daniel were there, he'd tell her to stick out her chin and grin.

Where was Daniel? Charlotte looked around for her twin but didn't see him. Another scan for a green baseball hat came up empty. The game had been over for more than an hour. Maybe Lily wasn't coming after all. Maybe she'd gotten into her sexy, hunter-green Jaguar and gone home. Charlotte felt herself deflate. Her analytic brain marveled at the immediate physical response to the emotional letdown. Lily was definitely having an effect on her.

Charlotte tried to focus on Colin's snooker tutorial but her mind began to wander. It had been a long day. Tomorrow would be another one. She still had to talk to Madison, set new boundaries. She needed to check on Rhianna.

"Sorry I'm late." Light fingers brushed the back of her arm and all her worries faded. She didn't have to turn her head to know who it was. It was as if someone had turned on a space heater.

Lily had arrived.

"I found this one prowling around the bar," another voice said. It was Daniel. "You did say you wanted a tall drink of water." He laughed at his own joke.

The group expanded to include the newcomers and Charlotte introduced Lily to Daniel's co-workers. The blonde had indeed removed the green hat and now wore her hair back in a loose bun. Missing also were the shorts and tank replaced by a sundress and sandals. She smelled incredible. When Charlotte looked into the green eyes she fell headlong into the warmth.

"You look great," Charlotte told her. Holding back the compliment was impossible, like failing to comment on a snowstorm in the desert.

"Thank you." Lily blushed hotly and for a moment it seemed like they were the only two people in the room.

Daniel gave Olive her beer and pushed a bourbon with ice into Charlotte's hand. "Lily insisted on buying."

"You did?" Charlotte said. She was absurdly touched that Lily had bought her a drink. It was silly. Attaching significance to it was setting herself up for a letdown. She let it wet her lips. "Thank you, Lily."

"You're welcome," Lily replied. "You deserve a drink after that game."

Olive watched the exchange with alarm. "I thought you said you wanted water, Charlie." She put a hand on her hip accusatorily.

"Yes, but this is delicious," Charlotte replied, her eyes on Lily's face.

"Don't you need to check on your dog?" Olive tried another tactic. "I'll go with you. I just wanted to find Colin first."

"Rhianna's in Maine," Daniel informed Olive but Lily cut him off.

"I'm taking Charlotte to check on her dog," she announced as if arrangements had been made weeks ago, notices sent out. Everyone within earshot knew it was complete bullshit but that only made it sexier. Charlotte's heart fluttered. She couldn't take her eyes off Lily and she didn't try. She heard herself respond.

"Yes, yes, I'm going with Lily to check on Rhianna."

"You ready?" The look in Lily's eyes was one of unmistakable desire. Charlotte had studied pheromones in physiology and knew Lily was having an involuntary physical response brought on by sexual attraction. The idea that Lily could be reacting this way to Charlotte was a powerful aphrodisiac. It was also about as necessary as pouring kerosene on a bonfire.

"You can't take your drinks outside," Olive warned.

"At least wait until Colin snookers that asshole," Sheila suggested.

But their words fell on deaf ears. They were leaving together, now. Charlotte took a last sip of her drink and threaded her fingers through Lily's as if it was an everyday occurrence.

Daniel's eyebrows shot up but he raised his cosmo in salute. "Stay in touch." He took a sip and almost succeeded in not making a face.

"I'll text you," Charlotte said roughly. The feeling of Lily's fingers entwined with her own was making it difficult to speak.

"Nice to meet you, Lily," Colin said.

Lily smiled. "Thanks, Colin." She leaned forward. "And please, kick Steve's ass?"

"On the docket, counselor," he replied and tipped the unicorn hat.

Lily tugged on Charlotte's hand and they moved through the crowded pool hall. Did Lily really think they were going to check on Rhianna? It didn't seem to matter. She pulled Charlotte up the steps to street level. Suddenly they were on an empty sidewalk. After the crush in the bar, the empty pavement felt like open pasture.

"Thank you," Lily said and filled her lungs with air. She squeezed Charlotte's hand and they began walking toward Dupont Circle.

"You're welcome." Charlotte returned the squeeze. "But I have no idea what I'm being thanked for."

"Oh." Lily's pretty face knitted into a serious look. "I guess I just really wanted to get out of there." They stopped in the crosswalk before the traffic circle and waited for the light to change.

"Why did you come in the bar if you were going to leave the minute you arrived?" Charlotte blurted and then worried she'd crossed into sensitive territory.

Lily didn't answer right away but seemed to be carefully considering her answer. The light changed and they crossed the street into the urban park within the large traffic circle. Benches rimmed the inside perimeter and Lily steered Charlotte toward a vacant space. They sat down, close enough that their knees touched. Lily didn't let go of Charlotte's hand.

"I came back because I wanted to see you," Lily said. The blush was back on her cheeks.

"Oh," Charlotte stammered, now blushing herself. "I'm glad you did. I wanted to see you too." She squeezed Lily's hand. "I was worried you weren't going to come."

Lily smoothed the fabric of her dress. "I almost didn't. But you seem to have this effect on me." She let the words sink in before raising her free hand and pointing to her face. The blush had now settled into a deep pink. "I haven't had this reaction to a woman in a long time. It feels fantastic, but sort of out of control too. I don't even know you."

"I'm really nice," Charlotte said softly. "You can ask anyone. I have outstanding references."

Lily giggled. "I can't wait to find out." She stared quietly at Charlotte for a few moments and then shook her head. "I don't know what it is. You have a beautiful singing voice. Maybe it did something to me. And you were right. I did run away at the end of your song."

"Really?"

"You scared me."

"But then you came back," Charlotte reminded her.

"I came back." Lily smiled. "And tonight. Watching you play softball?" She inhaled sharply. "I can't describe it."

"Describe what?" Charlotte was confused.

"There's something about you that makes me sure I want to get to know you better."

"Is that why you asked me to call you Lily? Everyone on the team calls you Lillian."

She nodded. "Those are my work friends. My ex called me Lillian so they do too. But people close to me have always called me Lily. I spell it like the flower. Just one L."

"I like that." Charlotte squeezed her hand. She also liked the implication of being factored into the demographic of people who were close to Lily. Because Lily wasn't the only one feeling a connection. Powerful feelings of attraction were at play. Feelings Charlotte wanted to explore further. Her eyes dropped to Lily's lips. Kissing was imminent. They both knew it. Charlotte moved her face nearer to Lily's but didn't close the gap entirely. They were now breathing the same air and the anticipation was delicious. Charlotte wished it could go on forever until she felt Lily's fingers cup her face.

"I'm going to kiss you," she said and brushed her lips against Charlotte's so softly it might not have happened at all.

Charlotte began to hum and the hand snaked into her hair, drawing her nearer. She opened her mouth to meet Lily's tongue and tiny bursts of light exploded behind her eyelids. It was the first taste of something special and they both knew it. *God in heaven.* Charlotte wanted to lose herself and never be found. They clung to each other for several minutes exploring the electricity of the connection until Lily pulled away gasping.

"Okay, wow." She pressed her forehead against Charlotte's. "That was even better than I imagined."

"You imagined?" Charlotte said and they both laughed.

"You have no idea." Lily gently released Charlotte and pushed back on the bench. Looking around the park she seemed aware of their public surroundings for the first time. "I've thought about you a great deal," she admitted and began to fuss with her hair. Charlotte couldn't be sure but it looked like her hands were shaking.

"I've thought of you too, Lily," she said quietly.

"Good," Lily replied. The beautiful green eyes were feverish, the blush still out in force. "But I have to be honest. This energy scares me a bit." She waved a finger between them. "The last time I had this reaction to someone was a couple of years ago and I was hurt pretty badly."

Charlotte thought of the flash of pain on Lily's face at Birdie's. "I'm so sorry." She stroked Lily's blazing cheek. Her caregiver's need to comfort, coupled with her carnal desire to possess, made it impossible not to touch her. "I mean, I'm not sorry that we like each other." She smiled shyly. "I'm sorry someone caused you pain." She leaned in and kissed Lily's eyelids. "We can take this slow."

"Thank you," Lily said.

"You're welcome," Charlotte replied. Waiting was the responsible thing to do. Lily was dealing with some powerful emotions and there was still the issue of Madison. Those thoughts and all others flew from her mind when Lily's mouth crashed against hers once again.

CHAPTER SEVEN

Boxed In

The next morning Charlotte broke up with Madison. It had to be done. The feelings Lily inspired in her made the idea of going along with the farce a moment longer preposterous. It was like comparing a black-and-white film to technicolor. Lily struck a chord in her. An intense energy surrounded their connection. There was so much there. Charlotte wanted to explore all of it.

Madison had put up a fight, which wasn't a surprise. She'd never been comfortable with the word "no." After their first fight, Charlotte had bought reconciliatory bath bombs for a month before Daniel had pointed out that her girlfriend had a pathological need to win every argument. Madison couldn't let Charlotte go because the breakups had never been her idea. But Charlotte had persevered and ended the conversation with a promise to check in when she was home for Christmas. She was relieved but not proud of herself.

She walked out of her bedroom to find Daniel adjusting a paisley bowtie in the hall mirror. He'd bought the vintage item at an overpriced thrift store in Georgetown. It cost twenty-seven dollars and smelled like mothballs but it was a perfect match for his polo shirt.

"Is it done?" he asked Charlotte's reflection as she passed behind him.

"It's still a little crooked," she teased.

"I'm not talking about my bowtie."

"You're not?" She put on a pair of sapphire stud earrings and a silver link bracelet. They'd been summoned to Great-aunt Wellesley's for brunch. At last. They'd lived in the carriage house for almost two months and aside from the day they'd arrived and the night Madison had shown up uninvited, they hadn't interacted with their famous aunt or her dapper housemates at all. Charlotte had no idea what prompted this sudden invitation, but it seemed important to make an effort.

"The conversation with Madison?" Daniel was trying his best to look annoyed but the extra wattage in his smile made this impossible. He was beyond excited. He'd been plotting private access to Wellesley Kincaid since he was twelve years old. The moment he'd realized the famous artist in *Vogue* was his paternal grandfather's sister, he'd claimed her as his people. Daniel was convinced that if he could get past her door for five minutes, she'd invite him in forever. "How did the breakup go? Did you pull that mad weed? Make room for a Lily in your garden?"

"I did." Charlotte smiled back at him. Thinking of Lily in her garden conjured up all sorts of wonderful images. Like the kisses they'd shared the night before, and Lily's confession.

"Good. I don't like thinking of you as a cheater."

"So glad you approve." Charlotte swallowed a snort. Daniel was infamous for his ability to have up to four relationships simultaneously. He'd once referred to it as the stovetop approach to dating, and it fit. You kept all the burners on and adjusted the heat as warranted. Charlotte was impressed that her brother seemed to manage this without getting burned. But he'd also never had a relationship that lasted more than two weeks.

"You're a Charlotte, not a harlot," he continued, warming to the theme.

Charlotte frowned but didn't respond. Daniel had developed a new habit of reciting her personality traits as if she was a character in a book. It was mostly supportive but also limiting. How could she be herself when he kept telling her who she was? What if she felt like being a harlot? If Lily hadn't put the brakes on during the make-out session, Charlotte would have followed her home. This was a fact. Part of her, mostly the part seated on the bench, had hoped when Lily had mentioned she lived close by that this was where the evening was leading.

She opened the refrigerator and took out the Lambrusco Daniel had purchased. He'd read about the sparkling red wine in *GQ* magazine and thought it sounded more interesting than champagne or Prosecco. Aunt Wellesley had said it was a celebratory brunch. They didn't know the occasion, but Daniel was keen to make a good impression. He'd even dictated Charlotte's outfit. Fortunately, for both of them, she liked the gray linen sundress he'd selected. She'd liked it even more when he'd offered to iron it. Black ballet flats completed a polished look that was both classic and comfortable. Daniel had dressed himself as if he later might be going to Nantucket. In addition to his vintage bowtie and polo shirt, he wore Madras pants, happily informing Charlotte the fabric was known as preppy vomit. It was typical Daniel to go all out. In high school his senior quote had been "halfway leaves you nowhere."

"What are you doing with that?" He eyed the Lambrusco as if he hadn't spent the better part of an hour deciding which label best matched his shirt.

"It's time to go. I don't want to be late," she told him firmly. Just as he had her number, she had his.

"Put it away," he instructed and waved his hand at the wine. Picking up a magazine, he sat down on the couch with a definitive plop. "Aunt Wellesley is Posh Spice. We can't be on time. It's bourgeois. We'll leave in twenty minutes." He crossed his legs and flipped through the pages.

"*You* can wait twenty minutes," Charlotte informed him. "I'm leaving now." Starting for the door, she called his bluff. Daniel was less concerned about being déclassé than showing up to a party alone.

"Fine." He slapped the magazine down on the coffee table, scaring himself. "But if Aunt Wellesley pegs us as tacky, low-rent relations, the stink is on you."

Charlotte unlocked the door to the carriage house and held it open for her twin to pass. "The stink, Daniel? Really?" She sniffed his shoulder. "You know you smell like Mom's hope chest."

The comment cost her twenty minutes. Waiting for Daniel to choose another outfit, Charlotte thought about Lily. Was it too early to text her? They'd exchanged numbers the night before and made a plan to visit the National Portrait Gallery the following Sunday. Charlotte frowned. Their night had ended too abruptly when Daniel had texted from outside the bar. He'd tracked Charlotte with "find my phone." No-Shoshanna had shown up with bad tidings. The Geoffrey Problem had not been successful in booking the Irish Embassy for the gala venue. The event team would have to work overtime to secure a new location. Despite the fact that Colin had trounced Baseball Knickers at eight ball, the news had ended the party.

With a long embrace and a promise to text tomorrow Charlotte had left Lily. Now it was tomorrow. But was it too early to make contact? She wondered what Lily did on a typical Sunday morning. She'd mentioned going to museums. Was that her plan today? Charlotte had meant to send a sweet dreams text the night before. She'd even composed a message in the Uber, agonizing over the exact wording and tone. But then she'd become caught up strategizing the breakup conversation with Madison, and never pressed send.

"Let's go," she yelled to Daniel. It was now almost half past the hour and they were in danger of being rude.

"Hold your horses, Seabiscuit," he said and walked casually into the room. He was now wearing a perfectly tailored dark-green suit, complete with purple silk tie and matching pocket square.

Charlotte blinked. "What is that?"

Daniel shot his cuffs and knocked an imaginary piece of lint off one sleeve. He gave her an impish grin. "Too much?"

"You know you look amazing," Charlotte said and meant it.

Daniel did a slow spin to display the fine lines of the suit. "I bought it to wear to the gala. It would have been perfect."

"Because it's green?" Charlotte asked, already knowing the answer. Buying a natty green suit to wear to an occasion at the Irish Embassy was exactly something her twin would do.

Daniel sighed. "Now I have to find another venue and another outfit." She noted a hint of anxiety in his voice and knew it didn't concern the suit. Her brother did not have shopping issues. But finding a new venue was another story. If the gala was in southern Maine, he'd fix the problem in three phone calls. But, new to DC, he had no connections. It had to be frustrating. Working for a nonprofit, he also had scant funds. Fortunately, the problem did not rest entirely on his shoulders.

"Do you have any leads?" Charlotte picked up the Lambrusco. Crossing the room, she held open the door.

"I've hit all the stores in Friendship Heights but I'm thinking of driving out to Tyson's Center. Want to come? No-Shoshanna says it's epic."

"I'm not talking about your outfit."

"Then let's change the subject." Winking at her, he walked through the door. "Come to the mall with me?"

"Pass." Charlotte pushed the door closed and followed her brother into the yard.

"Are you sure?" Daniel stopped and picked a flower on the path to thread through his lapel. "I know you don't love shopping but No-Sho says it's hot. You gals might hit it off. She's really cute."

"Don't you think I have enough women in my life?"

"One fewer today," he said.

"True."

They rounded the path toward the main yard. Charlotte saw movement behind the hedge and wondered if they were having brunch outside. She'd noticed the back patio many times. Beautifully paved in Potomac flagstone, it sat sadly neglected and covered in leaves. Its fancy ornate wrought-iron chairs without their cushions looked like wealthy neighbors who didn't want you to visit.

"I think our guests have arrived," a male voice said.

"What gorgeous creatures," said another.

They turned the corner and Charlotte saw that the patio had been transformed. It was as if a designer had come in and created a set for a European garden party. A wooden trellis draped in flowering vines now sat above the patio table and chairs. The flagstone had been power-washed and there were large potted trees adding splashes of color. Wellesley was seated at the head of the table. In an embroidered cotton tunic of the lightest violet, she matched both the flowers and the china. Charlotte was suddenly very glad that Daniel had insisted on ironing her dress.

"Well, they are *my* family," Wellesley said, and giggled. She remained seated while both Jacob and Stefano rose to their feet.

"Good morning, Aunt Wellesley." Daniel leaned over and kissed her cheek. Removing the flower from his lapel, he held it forward.

"Good morning," she said and nodded at his outfit with approval. "Smashing suit."

Daniel repeated the spin he'd done in the guesthouse. "Thank you for noticing. It's brand new and I love it."

Stefano clapped his hands with delight. "Bravo Daniel, the suit is very nice."

"And Charlotte, what marvelous hair you have." Wellesley turned her attention to her niece. "It's glorious."

"Thank you, Aunt Wellesley," Charlotte replied and handed the Lambrusco to Stefano. She stood back as Jacob pulled out a chair for her. "I'm sorry we're late."

"Late?" Stefano repeated as if he couldn't have possibly heard her correctly. "My darling, this is a celebration! We've only just begun." He nestled the Lambrusco into an elegant silver cooler situated below the table. Charlotte could see other bottles of wine already chilling and wondered how many guests were expected. There were only five place settings at the table but enough alcohol in the cooler to satisfy a rugby team. In addition to the wine, there was a very fancy bottle of vodka open on the table. Before sitting, Jacob poured them shots.

"Wellesley has finished another masterpiece," he said and handed the tiny glasses around. When everyone had one, he held up his glass in toast. "Nine months of ecstatic expression have yielded a masterwork, *Valkyrie as Mother Nature*. She is honest. She is beautiful. She is brutal. But most important..."

"She is finished!" Stefano shouted. "We are free to live!" He knocked his glass against Jacob's and both men downed their shots in a gulp.

Wellesley giggled again. It was a light girly sound that made Charlotte smile. Tilting her glass in salute, the artist drained the contents. "Certainly, I wasn't that bad?"

Stefano raised his eyebrows but didn't answer.

"You were focused," Jacob told her. "It was impressive, as always. It may be the best work you've ever done."

"Yes, I agree, your *Valkyrie* is spectacular," Stefano said sincerely. "The museum will be overjoyed."

"Thank you, darlings," Wellesley said, accepting their compliments. She turned to Charlotte and Daniel. "I can be quite the bitch when the muse is on me."

"No way," Daniel protested but Jacob and Stefano both nodded.

Wellesley giggled again.

"It's the price you pay to live with genius," Stefano said.

"That's why we only live here for half the year," Jacob quipped. He picked up the Lambrusco and removed the protective seal.

"Where are you the other six months?" Daniel asked.

"Miami. We retired there but couldn't stand the summers so we come back here each year and live with Wellesley."

"You are needed," Wellesley put her hand on Jacob's and they shared a smile.

"How do you know each other?" Daniel continued to quiz them like a talk show host.

"They were my attorneys," Wellesley explained. "I've used them for all my divorces." She nodded to the house behind them. "They helped finance my home. It's only fair that they get to live here too."

"I bet living with Wellesley is amazing," Daniel said and the men laughed.

"Most of the time," Jacob said. "When she's working, things can get interesting."

"Valkyrie was like her new, mad lover. She could think of nothing else until the woman was out of her system," Stefano explained.

"Really?" Charlotte was curious. She knew what it was like to become absorbed in hard work but not to the exclusion of the outside world. She'd certainly never felt love like that. She imagined she could feel it with Lily.

"Oh, yes." Stefano popped the cork and tipped the bottle into the crystal flute to his right. "Let me prove it."

"Stefano, don't," Jacob warned but Wellesley pounced on him.

"What dirt have you got on me, Stef? What have I done? Forgotten your birthday?" she teased, and then her face paled. "Have I?"

"No, darling," Stefano assured her. "Jacob made reservations at Fiola Mare. You had the cod and wore your Chanel suit."

"Yes! I do remember that. Thank God." She smiled at Charlotte and touched her hand. "I would hate to be a diva bitch *and* have dementia."

"You are not a diva bitch," Jacob argued. "You are a focused artist at the height of her powers. The world must wait while you spin gold from straw."

"Jacob is absolutely right," Stefano agreed, and Charlotte was certain the two men were lovers. They'd not been introduced as such, but something in the way Stefano said Jacob's name made her sure.

"I want to know what dirt Stef has on me," Wellesley said. She was not to be put off.

"Me too," Daniel chimed in and Charlotte smiled. Her brother was so caught up in Wellesley's charms he would have co-sponsored a petition to give voting rights to ferrets.

"We must go inside the house to see," Stefano said, enigmatically.

"Is it alive?" Wellesley wanted to know.

"Bigger than a breadbox?" Daniel asked.

"It's mail," Jacob said curtly, putting an end to the guessing game.

"Sign me up," Daniel quipped and raised his hand.

"Not a male. Mail, from the post office." Jacob smiled at Daniel's joke but continued. "There are packages, lots and lots of packages, all for Charlotte. I'm sorry dear, but we only discovered them this morning. Wellesley was stuffing them in a hall closet. I was looking for an umbrella and nearly lost an eye."

"Those packages are for Charlotte?" Wellesley said in stunned surprise.

"They're addressed to her, yes," Jacob said but not unkindly.

"I had no idea." Wellesley turned to Charlotte. "I saw Kincaid on the label and just assumed they were for me. I did wonder at the volume, though."

"You were thinking of other things." Stefano patted her arm.

"Well, I do apologize, Charlotte," Wellesley said sincerely. "I hope you weren't expecting anything important."

"No," Charlotte said slowly. She had a bad feeling that Madison was involved.

"The packages may have been collecting for weeks." Jacob shook his head.

"That's impossible," Wellesley said. "The twins have only been here..." She narrowed her eyes trying to calculate the time.

"Almost two months," Jacob said.

Wellesley's blue eyes pulsed wide and then began to twinkle. "An entire month! Well it's about time we had a party. Don't bogart the Lambrusco, Stefano."

He laughed and poured a flute for Wellesley. "Bogie was never my cup of tea, Welly, but Gregory Peck..." His eyes drifted to Jacob. On closer inspection, Charlotte saw the taller gentleman looked remarkably like the golden era film star.

Wellesley was nodding. She also now seemed to be talking about Jacob. "A very beautiful man, Stef." The two men were definitely a couple.

Daniel, who was not paying attention, spoiled the tender moment with an ill-timed joke. "I'd let Atticus Finch take me to court anytime. Or bust up *my chifforobe.*"

There was a second of stunned silence as Jacob paled and then Stefano and Wellesley burst into raucous laughter. Daniel shot Charlotte a look of alarm and she shook her head, a signal she would explain later. Jacob rose from the table as Wellesley and Stefano continued to titter into their napkins.

Addressing Charlotte, he cleared his throat. "Would you like to inspect the packages now, Charlotte? You must be curious?"

"Of course," Charlotte answered, lying. The last thing she wanted to do was to confront love offerings from Madison. The sound of her ex fake-sobbing into the phone was still fresh in her ears from earlier that morning. But Gregory Peck needed to exit the stage and had requested her assistance. Taking his arm, she went into the house.

CHAPTER EIGHT

Daniel in Distress

Charlotte let her voice linger on the last note of the song. She loved the Tom Petty lullaby, "Alright for Now," but continuing to sing it would be counterproductive. Her audience of one had fallen asleep. Stepping away from the bed, she backed carefully out the door and almost knocked over Laura Minor.

"Sorry!" the senior nurse stage-whispered. She tugged Charlotte out of the room and closed the door behind them. "Is he out? Did you get him to sleep? Poor little guy." She wiped a tear from the corner of her eye and tucked a cell phone into the pocket of her scrubs.

"He's down," Charlotte confirmed and stared hard at the pocket where the phone disappeared. Had Laura been taping the lullaby? She frowned. Not only was it against hospital rules to have a phone out during a shift, taping Charlotte without her consent was decidedly uncool. Not that she felt she could chastise her supervisor. The previous week Charlotte had made the colossal mistake of forwarding Daniel a lullaby that was shot by grateful parents and he'd shared it on Facebook without asking. The clip had generated a lot of unwanted hoopla. Charlotte didn't want a repeat performance but she didn't call Laura out. "That was a tough one."

"Yeah."

Typically, it took no more than three songs to soothe an anxious child to sleep. Charlotte's velvety alto when paired with the right song had a miraculous somnolent effect on children. It was as if they fell into some type of trance, often fading to sleep with beatific smiles. Umberto had been a particularly challenging case. Charlotte had sung for nearly an hour before the tiny patient had capitulated. Though gratified, she was exhausted and not happy with the notion of being captured again on video. Daniel's post had been shared ten times before Charlotte made him take it down.

"You sing like an angel."

"Thanks," Charlotte said, her voice tight. She had tremendous respect for Laura but the video felt like a violation.

Laura seemed to pick up on the discomfort and rushed to fill the silence. "Are you visiting anyone else this morning? You're in high demand around here. Especially for the morning nappers. It's important to keep the little ones on their schedules."

"Umberto was the last one." Charlotte looked over Laura's head at the clock. She'd sung to three other children that morning before taking on the challenging three-year-old.

"That's fantastic." Laura bobbed her head with enthusiasm. "Just great."

"Thanks," Charlotte said and stifled the urge to chastise the senior nurse.

Soothing children to sleep with lullabies felt oddly private. Outside the bounds of traditional care, it gave Charlotte a unique sense of satisfaction and went beyond anything she'd studied at school. There was nothing more peaceful than a sleeping child. She'd made the discovery singing to Chiara nearly a month ago. Now, it was almost a daily thing. Calls came in from every quarter of the hospital requesting a lullaby from Nurse Nightingale. Laura Minor's fingerprints were all over it. The senior nurse only called Charlotte herself when the stakes were high. Treating Charlotte like an ace closer in the bullpen, she counted on her to deliver. Like this morning. Umberto had been awake all night. His parents, recent immigrants from Honduras, worked the night shift and could only visit in the late afternoon. It broke Charlotte's heart to see the stoic little face hold back tears as he waited for them to appear. He'd shown little reaction when she'd started her first song. But working her way through the set list, she'd put together with help from Daniel and Google, his eyelids began to flutter. It wasn't until the Tom Petty song that he'd finally drifted off.

"I shot a video," Laura blurted, confirming Charlotte's suspicions. "I hope you don't mind."

"Actually, I do." Charlotte was frank. She didn't mind being known around the hospital as Nurse Nightingale but Internet notoriety was another story. Madison had courted it like mad. The social media surrounding Madsnax and Charlie Pies was ridiculous. Charlotte had only experienced it from the periphery. To be the center of something similar did not interest her in the slightest. Laura looked stricken.

"I'm sorry!" she said and pulled her phone from her pocket. "I just keep telling my wife how amazing you are. She's a huge music fan, makes me go to concerts every weekend. I told her you were better than the last show she dragged me to. I wanted her to hear for herself. I'm so sorry. I'll erase it right now." She began to tap the buttons on her phone but Charlotte stopped her.

"You can show your wife." She smiled to let her know all was forgiven. Making an unsanctioned video was not cool, but it was fine if Laura was only going to show it to her wife. "Just please, don't post it anywhere."

Laura touched the crystal pendent at her neck. "I won't," she promised and crossed her heart. She slipped the phone into her pocket and picked up the clipboard on Umberto's door. "Who has time for that stuff anyway?"

"Not me," Charlotte replied. And she didn't. Lulling babies to sleep, as fulfilling as she found it, was a definite time suck. Charlotte couldn't reconcile taking time away from her patients so she only performed the service off the clock, as a volunteer. Like this morning. Sunday was supposed to be her day off. She'd be late for Wellesley's weekly Sunday brunch, but it couldn't be helped. Laura had called with the SOS and Charlotte had come to the rescue.

An hour later she was walking through Wellesley's backyard. The beautifully landscaped outdoor space contrasted sharply with the sterility of the hospital and Charlotte stopped by the heron sculptures to take a moment. Surrounded by art and nature, Charlotte should feel exalted. But something was off. A picture of Lily popped into her head and she pushed it away. She wasn't ready to dissect the disappointment.

She heard the brunch group before she saw them.

"She's pimping out Charlotte's dog!" Daniel was shouting. There was a chorus of laughter and Charlotte stopped to listen. Her twin was telling the brunch group about Rhi-Treats. Wonderful. Exactly what she wanted to discuss on her first Sunday off in weeks. She kicked at a stone on the path and considered going back to bed.

"Is that legal, Jacob?" Wellesley asked. "Do animals have a right to privacy?"

"I'm not that type of attorney," Jacob replied.

"Yes, we all know that you're a very important man," Wellesley teased.

"I think she should sue," Daniel said. "Charlotte is too nice. If it were me, I'd have Madison arrested."

"Didn't you just say her father was sponsoring your event?"

"Okay, I'd wait until the check cleared, then I'd have her arrested."

There was more laughter.

"We still don't know if it's a criminal offense," Wellesley reminded him.

"Have you seen the ad campaign?" Daniel replied. "Someone needs to be punished. Poor Rhianna looks like a ragamuffin."

"I thought you said she looked like nineteen-eighties Madonna," Wellesley said.

"There's a difference?" Daniel responded to more laughter.

Despite the unfortunate subject matter, Charlotte couldn't help smiling. Her twin had a knack for finding the humor in every situation. But Madison's latest ploy was decidedly unfunny. She'd reached a new low. Branding her CBD dog snacks as Rhi-Treats and pairing it with a photo of the dog looking nearly hairless had crossed a line. It was possibly actionable. Charlotte wanted to confront Madison but had yet to muster the energy. She hadn't spoken to her ex since the breakup call four weeks ago. Reengaging meant cultivating drama, inviting Madness. The Rhianna stunt was obnoxious, but what did the dog really know? How much were Rhi-Treats affecting her life? This was the question Charlotte used to soothe her guilty conscience.

She resumed walking and Wellesley's patio came into view. Sitting around the glass-topped table were Wellesley, Jacob, and Daniel. Today, her twin was dressed casually in Bermuda shorts and a polo shirt. Sprawled in a chair, he looked a far cry from the nervous Nellie he'd been at Wellesley's celebratory brunch. Had an entire month really passed? It was hard to believe though Charlotte saw evidence everywhere.

This morning, when she'd left for the hospital, Daniel had been backing out of the driveway in Wellesley's vintage Saab. Stefano had happily relinquished the position of resident chauffeur and now Daniel took their aunt on her errands. The two had become thick as thieves. That morning they'd been off to see a new mural of Ruth Bader Ginsburg on U Street. Daniel had been wearing a black leather driving cap and matching gloves Wellesley had found him at Neiman Marcus. They made him look like a movie star from the sixties. He spent increasingly more time at the main house but Charlotte didn't begrudge him. She noted his bare legs crossed at the ankle and smiled. Her brother was perfectly at ease.

She looked down at her own shoes and frowned. Beneath a sleeveless, cotton sheath-dress she wore Dansko clogs. But she'd somehow paired the new shoe Rhianna hadn't chewed with one from the older set. The contrast wasn't noticeable unless you looked closely. But it felt odd. Like having one foot in the past and one in the present. Given Charlotte's current circumstances, it seemed entirely appropriate.

"Here's our songbird!" Wellesley was the first to notice her. Flying from her chair, she rushed to greet Charlotte with a quick peck on each cheek. She clasped Charlotte's hands in her own. "We are honored to have you join us on your precious day off. How is the famous singing nurse?"

"She's happy to be here," Charlotte said, shooting a look at Daniel who'd either forgotten or ignored her directive to keep her volunteer activities to himself. She didn't mind the group knowing, but she didn't want it to be their focus of conversation. The FB video had been quite enough.

"Come sit down, dear. Fix a plate." Wellesley ushered Charlotte to the patio. The food today, though as plentiful as the morning of their first brunch together, was more casual. In addition to fresh bagels, there was cream cheese, lox and a plate of assorted pastries. Jacob stood and pulled out a chair for Charlotte while Daniel remained sprawled in his seat.

"We were just talking about you." Daniel picked up an onion bagel, smeared it with cream cheese, then loaded it with lox. "I think you need to take action against Madison. The Balloon-atic has gone too far this time."

"So, I gathered." Charlotte sat down in the chair. "Thank you, Jacob."

"You're welcome." Jacob gave her a fatherly smile. "How goes Christmas in October? Are the packages making it to the hospital okay?"

"Yes, thank God," she told him, causing Daniel to snort.

The pile of packages in Wellesley's dining room had not been a one-off. In a haze of reunion delirium, Madison had signed Charlotte up for ten different weekly themed gift services: books, flowers, fruit, herbal tea, jam, candy, pretzels, candles and chocolate, each from a different specialty boutique. The excess was unconscionable. She'd been mortified until Jacob had come up with the brilliant plan of rerouting the items to the long-term care ward at the hospital. The idea had been an instant success. Charlotte had donated everything but the fruit, which Stefano begged to keep for his smoothies. The rest went to sick children or their parents in most need of a pick-me-up. The only negative was that Nurse Nightingale had been linked to the gifts making her even more popular, her lullabies even more in demand. Charlotte wanted to be known at the hospital for her nursing skills, not as a singing Santa Claus.

"It never would have occurred to me to donate the stuff to the hospital," Charlotte praised the lawyer. "Thank you so much for thinking of it. We channel the gifts to the kids who have no visitors. It really couldn't be more perfect. Though Ethan in security may have developed a little crush on me."

"Tell him to take a number." Daniel handed Charlotte the loaded bagel. "Everyone wants a slice of my Charlotte russe."

"They do not," Charlotte disagreed and took a bite. She certainly didn't feel very popular. Madison was harassing her through dog biscuits and Lily had stopped answering her texts after she'd had to postpone their date to the Portrait Gallery. Charlotte still couldn't believe it. The night of the softball game she thought she'd had an accurate read on the beautiful lawyer. In fact, she'd never been more certain of anything in her life. But when Charlotte had pulled a double shift and needed to reschedule their date Lily had abruptly stopped communicating.

"Hello?" Daniel sang. "No-Shoshanna asked for your number last night in front of the entire softball team. I thought Little Orphan Olive was going to punch her in the neck."

Charlotte glared at her brother. She'd known better than to have told him the unkind nickname. Just because you thought of clever things didn't mean you had to say them out loud.

"Really? Tell us everything!" Wellesley commanded. After the first brunch, it had become quickly apparent that when not singularly possessed by her artwork, their reclusive aunt had an enormous appetite for life, and even more so for gossip.

"There's not much to tell," Charlotte hedged.

"I'll be the judge of that," Wellesley said and settled in to listen. Brunch was never a hurried affair. Their first gathering had lasted well into the afternoon. They'd eaten every scrap of food, drained all the bottles in the fancy silver cooler while Wellesley had regaled them with stories. It had been fascinating. In the sixty years Wellesley had owned the Georgetown home, she'd been married three times. Unable to have children, she'd given birth to art instead. She'd rubbed shoulders with numerous celebrities and *bon vivants*. According to Daniel, the patio had once hosted a wedding party for a Zulu prince. Charlotte had begun to think of her aunt as an exotic bird, beautiful but ravenously carnivorous. Currently, she was eying Charlotte like a choice morsel.

"Daniel's exaggerating." Charlotte was firm but Wellesley didn't look convinced.

"Is he?" she asked and the intelligent blue eyes burned with curiosity. "How many lovers do you have, Charlotte?"

"None!" she replied and Daniel cackled.

"Really?" Wellesley challenged and stared at Charlotte as if she expected her to map out the chaos of her personal life on the tablecloth.

"Leave Charlotte alone," chided Jacob from behind the *Washington Post*. But it was too late. The great artist was focused on her niece. The big blue eyes probed Charlotte like lasers, making her uncomfortable. She attempted to change their trajectory.

"I'll tell you who I'd like to punch in the neck," Charlotte said and looked pointedly at Daniel.

"Me?" He put a hand to his chest. "What have I done?"

The back door opened and Stefano walked onto the patio. In one hand he carried a pitcher of cocktails and the other a plate of fresh orange slices. "Charlotte is here! *Ciao bella!*" He set the items on the table and leaned in to kiss her cheeks. "How is our beautiful singing nurse?"

"Violent," Wellesley said with relish. "Charlotte wants to punch someone."

Stefano filled Charlotte's glass from the pitcher and dropped an orange slice on top. "Tell me. Who are we fighting? I will be your lieutenant."

"The Italian Lieutenant's Woman?" Jacob shook his head. "Doesn't have quite the ring."

"Don't joke." Charlotte picked up the drink and took a sip. "I may take him up on it. This is delicious by the way."

"It's an Aperol spritz." Stefano gestured to the plate. "Oranges were our Madison fruit this week."

Charlotte shuddered. "Please don't say her name."

"Is that why you're angry?" Wellesley pounced. "Are Madison's gifts annoying you?" The empathy in her voice suggested she'd had personal experience with unwanted love offerings.

Charlotte nodded though she knew it was more complicated. Madison was not the only thing weighing on her mood. Work had been tough lately and she missed Rhianna terribly. Lily's face flashed in her mind and Charlotte was surprised to feel the sting of tears. Maybe she was just exhausted. Daniel was quick to notice.

"You're really upset!" he said with concern.

"Poor Charlotte." Wellesley petted her arm. Waving off the spritz, she poured herself a shot of vodka.

"I'm also emotional about Rhianna." Charlotte decided to go along with the thread. It was easier to vent her anger toward Madison than to probe the fresh wound of Lily.

"What's happening with your dog?" Stefano asked and Jacob filled him in.

"Madison is using Rhianna in a marketing campaign for her bakery."

Stefano looked confused. "A dog in a bakery doesn't sound like good marketing."

"Unless you're selling CBD dog treats," Jacob said.

"Rhi-Treats!" Daniel corrected.

"It could be very profitable," Jacob acknowledged. He put down the newspaper and picked up his glass.

"She's making bank!" Daniel exploded. "It's plastered all over social media. She's rebranded her CBD treats as Rhi-Treats after Rhianna and using an unsanctioned picture of Charlotte's dog. They might be more successful than Charlie Pies. Another time Madison took advantage of Charlotte. I saw them at Whole Foods, by the way," he informed Charlotte.

"Great."

"I wonder if CBD would help me," Wellesley mused. "I've seen it advertised as a miracle cure."

"Absolutely." Daniel nodded. "I don't know what your problem is but CBD is good for everything. Right, Charlotte?"

"There's no evidence against it," she said but he was already talking over her.

"It helps with anxiety and depression." Daniel counted out the benefits on his fingers. "It reduces pain, helps your heart, clears up your skin." He shrugged, "We should all be taking it. They put it in everything. You can get CBD-infused lip balm, lotion, gummie bears, dog treats, of course. Let me get you some tincture."

"Tincture?" Wellesley looked intrigued. "Sounds witchy."

"A few drops under your tongue. It's supposed to be the best method," Daniel said. "It's not hard to find. They sell it at Whole Foods just like Charlie Pies." He cut his eyes back to Charlotte.

She gave him a wan smile. The pop tarts now showed up with some regularity in her orbit. There was no getting away from them. The brunch group had tried them the week before and declared them delicious. Charlotte did her best not to think of their origin. She reminded herself that no one knew the truth but she and Madison. Right now, Charlie Pies were the flavor of the month. Be patient and their popularity would fade like cupcakes and doughnuts.

Daniel tapped the screen on his phone and pulled up the advertisement for Rhi-Treats. He handed the device to Stefano. Jacob passed over his reading glasses.

Stefano looked at the photo for several seconds then gave Charlotte a worried look. "Is this dog sick?" he asked.

Charlotte shook her head. "All her hair fell out from the stress of moving to DC. That's why I sent her back to Maine. She looks much better now."

"Despite the fact that Madison is exploiting her," Daniel reminded them.

Wellesley took both the phone and the glasses from Stefano and studied the image. "This looks nothing like Madonna," she announced. "But the poor thing does look exhausted. Rhi-Treats, it's quite brilliant. What's tied to the dog's head?"

"Daniel's scarf," Charlotte said as she took the phone from Wellesley. Madison must have taken the photo on the drive back to Maine when Rhianna's hair had looked its worst. Charlotte smiled. Even in her semihairless state, the silver dachshund was adorable. It was understandable why Madison had wanted her in the marketing campaign. It would've been nice if she'd asked Charlotte's permission first.

Jacob took the phone from Charlotte and the glasses from Wellesley. He studied the image. "Very clever," he said.

"Can we sue?" Daniel wanted to know.

"We're not suing, anyone." Charlotte shook her head. "I just want her to go away." Threatening a lawsuit would be counterproductive to her goal of moving forward, akin to poking a bear. Charlotte wanted Madison in the rearview mirror not sitting next to her in court. With any luck she'd soon get tired of this stunt and move onto something else. Hopefully she'd move past Charlotte once and for all.

"Two minutes ago, you said you wanted to punch her." Wellesley pointed out the contradiction. "To me, that demonstrates a persistent passion."

"Indeed," Jacob murmured and ducked back behind his newspaper.

"Do you still love her?" Stefano asked.

"No!" Charlotte said, and then thought of Lily again. To her surprise, tears that had threatened earlier now began to fall. She did her best to hide them but it was no use.

"Oh, my dear," Stefano said and covered her hand with his own.

The display of emotion seemed to satisfy Wellesley's predilection for drama. She poured Charlotte a shot of vodka and pushed it into her hand. Only Daniel seemed skeptical. He eyed Charlotte suspiciously over his spritz but said nothing. Jacob thoughtfully changed the subject. Putting down his newspaper, he artfully flipped the spotlight.

"How goes the hunt for a venue?" he asked. Charlotte shot him a thankful look while Daniel sucked in a dramatic breath.

"Dismal," he started and Charlotte tuned out as he relayed the details of the ongoing search for a place to host the event. She swiped at the remaining tears on her face. What was up with the waterworks? It was hard to believe it was all due to disappointment about Lily. She barely knew the woman. But there it was. Each time Charlotte pictured Lily's face she felt like crying. It was just such a letdown.

"Must your gala be in town?" Wellesley was asking Daniel now.

"I'm not sure," he replied, perking up like a meerkat. So far, Wellesley had gifted him free rent, use of her car and natty driving apparel. There was no telling what she might offer next.

"I bet Sid would let you have Quarry," she mused, looking thoughtful. "If I ask him nicely," she corrected herself modestly, though her tone had the confidence of a woman who'd charmed three men to the altar. "When's the date again?"

But Daniel hadn't heard her because he'd fallen out of his chair.

Quarry was the ultimate get. A new museum fashioned of glass and steel, it was located twenty miles outside Washington in Potomac, Maryland. Built inside the cavern of an old stone quarry, it was an architectural marvel. The place was so famous even Charlotte had heard of it. *Valkyrie as Mother Nature* had been commissioned to hang in the entrance gallery.

"Don't make promises you can't keep," Jacob cautioned as Daniel crawled across the patio and laid himself at Wellesley's feet.

"I would do anything!" Daniel said and then repeated the word for emphasis, "Anything!"

Wellesley ran her fingers through his hair like he was a lap dog. "Drive me out there this afternoon? I'd like to see *Valkyrie* in public. You can talk to Sid about the event." She said all this as if it were completely normal. Had Daniel not already been on the ground, he might have fallen again.

His eyes slid to Charlotte who gave him a nod of encouragement. "Of course," he said carefully. "I'd love to go to Quarry with you, Aunt Wellesley."

"May I come too?" Stefano asked. The Italian man was not going to be left behind. Going with Wellesley Kincaid to Quarry to see *Valkyrie as Mother Nature* was like checking out street art with Banksy. Notoriously reclusive, Wellesley was never photographed with her work and did not make public appearances. *Valkyrie* had been installed in the middle of the night with a small team of engineers flown in from New York City. Daniel had seen the piece with Stefano and Jacob and declared it a masterpiece. Charlotte had been too busy singing to babies.

"Let's all go," Wellesley said, and her blue eyes twinkled. She was clearly enjoying the effect she was having on the group. "You'll come too, Charlotte?"

"I'd love to," Charlotte said without hesitation. Though tired, sad and a bit tipsy from the spritz and vodka, declining the invitation was unthinkable. It was an experience she might one day tell her grandchildren about.

"Who are you? And what have you done with my friend Wellesley?" Jacob asked and the artist giggled her girlish laugh.

"This isn't about me," she said. "There's a Daniel in distress."

"And you're his knight in shining armor?" Jacob said. He lifted an eyebrow and Stefano let out an appreciative chuckle.

"No, I'm the fairy godmother," Wellesley shot back.

"I accept!" Daniel leapt in the air like the high-school cheerleader he'd once been. "You can be this fairy's godmother any day."

Everyone laughed. Daniel bent to embrace his aunt and then sank into a chair.

"How do you know Sid will be there today?" Jacob challenged.

Wellesley's smile grew wider. "I may have spoken with him." She looked at Daniel fondly.

"Did you mention the gala?" he whispered.

"Yes, and I'm afraid you'll have to use their catering people."
The blue eyes narrowed.

"Sid signed a contract with some organic vendor. He went
to Brown with the owner's mother. The man is a pushover for
old lovers."

"Good news for you, Daniel," Stefano said and took a sip of
his drink.

"Indeed," Jacob agreed.

"What time can we go?" Daniel squeaked.

"We'll leave at four." Wellesley checked the man's Rolex she
wore like a bangle on her thin wrist. "That will give us all time
to nap and for Charlotte to change her shoes."

Charlotte looked down at the mismatched Danskos and
then up to gauge Daniel's reaction. But her brother wasn't in his
chair. Once again, he'd fallen to the ground.

CHAPTER NINE

Saab Story

The ride to the museum was surprisingly calm. Daniel navigated Wellesley's silver Saab through the DC suburbs as if the biggest meeting of his career were not on the line. Charlotte detected no anxiety in her brother whatsoever and considered that his confidence might be a by-product of Wellesley's influence. The woman's success was such that it made you believe in your own.

Charlotte wriggled her toes in the low-heeled, black ankle boots she'd subbed in for the mismatched clogs. Madison had given her the custom-made footwear for Christmas the previous year. Gorgeous Italian leather. They raised Charlotte's height to more than six feet, but she didn't mind. Every time she wore the boots, she felt like a Bond girl. Today she'd paired them with fitted black jeans and a sleeveless wool sweater of the same color. Daniel thought she looked like a hottie biker babe. Wellesley had proclaimed her chic.

The further outside the city they traveled, the bigger the houses. Single-family homes transitioned from modest to affluent to ostentatious. Once in Potomac everything was enormous. Architectural designs varied to a distracting degree. They drove past a chalet, a hacienda, a castle. One house looked like a cruise ship. Charlotte wondered what kind of people lived in houses this size. What if they lost their keys? Or a child?

"I would go mad out here," Wellesley announced and looked out at the countryside as if it were a burning hellscape. "All this land, nothing to feed your mind."

"You could invite your fans over," Stefano teased her. "Host weekend lectures."

Jacob chuckled while Wellesley swiveled her head and glared at them. Stefano glared back. Wedged in the backseat with Charlotte and Jacob, he could not be comfortable.

"We'll be there in two minutes," Daniel said, checking the GPS on his phone. He had a bad habit of consulting the device while driving. Charlotte had chastised him many times to no avail. Right now, the phone was resting on the console between the front seats. When he glanced at it again, Charlotte snatched it away.

"Give that back!" Daniel demanded. He took his hand off the wheel and swatted at Charlotte in the backseat.

"You'll get it back when we get to the museum." She held on tightly to the phone.

"Give it back!" Daniel screamed and continued to hit her.

"Careful!" Jacob said when Daniel's black chauffeur's cap fell off into Stefano's lap.

"She's got my phone!"

"But you've still got your brain," Wellesley reminded him. She pointed to a sign on the side of the road. The Quarry was ahead on the right. They had arrived.

"I'd like my phone back, please." Daniel was not backing down.

"When you park the car," Charlotte said resolutely. She slid the device under her leg and focused her attention out the tinted window of the Saab. They were now inside the gates of the property where rocky outcroppings foretold the quarry ahead. The museum was not yet visible but the surrounding grounds were impressive. Verdant and wild, the landscape was in its natural state. On the left side of the road a small creek followed their progress. Winding across fallen logs and moss-covered stones it beckoned them forward. After another mile or so, they rounded a bend into a freshly paved parking lot. The surface was large and empty. By Charlotte's estimate there were at least three hundred spaces. Surprisingly, only about ten were occupied.

"What time does it close?" Jacob asked.

"Does it matter?" Wellesley asked.

"I thought you wanted to see *Valkyrie* with the public."

"No." Wellesley frowned at Jacob as if he'd suggested she streak naked through the Library of Congress. "I said, I'd like to see *Valkyrie* in public, not with the public," she clarified. "The museum closes in ten minutes. Pull up here, Daniel." She pointed to a spot next to a green car. Daniel parked the Saab as directed. But when he started to open the door Wellesley clawed at his thigh. "Not yet," she said, and she checked her Rolex. "Ten more minutes." Daniel held his hands up where Wellesley could see them but Stefano was unclipping his seat belt.

"You're welcome to stay in the car," he said, unlocking the door. "But we're packed in here like saltines."

"Sardines," Wellesley corrected, but Stefano was already in the parking lot. Wellesley slipped on a pair of large sunglasses but not before Charlotte saw a hint of anxiety in the vibrant blue eyes. Despite her bravado at brunch, a public foray was a big leap. Jacob, too, seemed to notice the change.

"Why don't the twins stay here with you?" he suggested. "Stefano and I will find Sid. Let him know you've arrived."

"Great idea," Charlotte and Daniel replied at the same time. Wellesley was clearly uncomfortable. No one ever discussed the reasons behind her reclusive nature and Charlotte now wondered if it was anxiety. It would certainly explain her interest in CBD.

"Thank you." Wellesley surveyed the nearly empty parking lot. "We'll be right here, next to the Jaguar."

Charlotte jerked her head around but Daniel was way ahead of her.

"Oh my God, it's her! How did I miss that?" he wailed.

"Who?" Wellesley wanted to know but Jacob was blocking the open window.

"We'll text you when the museum is empty. Take the elevator down and meet us." He adjusted his hat in the side mirror. "There's no need for us to come back up here. The twins can escort you inside."

"Wonderful." Wellesley waved them off and the two older men started across the parking lot toward the elevator lobby. Housed in a small building at the back of the parking lot, the lifts would take them down to the museum inside the old quarry.

Daniel was quizzing Charlotte. "Do you think it's her?"

"Who?" Wellesley demanded. Slipping the Chanel sunglasses down her nose, she took a careful look at the Jaguar. "Do you know who owns that car?"

Charlotte thought about the question. If the Jag were indeed Lily's, it would be difficult to answer.

Thankfully, Daniel spoke up. "One of the gals marking up Charlotte's dance card drives a car exactly like this." He craned his head out the window. "Lily's has a Laurel-Jaguar dealer frame around the license plate. But I can't see the back from here."

"Well, get out and check!" Wellesley yelled, as if the claw marks she'd left on his thigh were not still visible. "Charlotte must know."

She didn't have to say it twice. Daniel was out and back before Charlotte could weigh in.

"It's definitely her." He slid back into the driver's seat grinning.

"It has the Laurel-Jaguar frame?"

"And an NYU Law sticker."

"Oh," Charlotte stammered, "then it's probably her."

"It's definitely her," Daniel said and pointed to a blond woman walking toward them across the parking lot.

Wellesley nodded with approval. "Well done, Charlotte, very attractive."

"She's not…" Charlotte stopped herself. There was no way to explain her feelings for Lily without risking more tears. The one thing she did know, was that she didn't want to talk about it. Her best hope of avoiding a scene was to avoid being seen. The tinted windows of the Saab made this entirely possible. She ducked her head behind the seat.

"Are you kidding? Lily's totally hot. And she's totally hot for you!" Daniel flung his hand out the window. He didn't know yet that Lily had stopped texting Charlotte. Fiercely loyal, he was likely to take the slight personally and make things more difficult.

"Stop waving! And roll up the window!" she said with more force than she intended.

Daniel gave her a surprised look. "Why? I thought y'all were vibing?"

Charlotte's answer was cut off by the sound of a Sherwood-Forest trumpet blast coming from beneath her leg. The ringtone was Daniel's special text notification for the Geoffrey Problem. His eyes went wide.

"Give me that."

Charlotte passed over the phone but not before glimpsing the picture on the screen. A gorgeous young man, incongruent with the monster her brother had conjured in describing him as the Geoffrey Problem smiled back at her. What was going on? It was something to consider later. Currently, a gorgeous young woman was occupying Charlotte's thoughts. As Daniel scrutinized the incoming text, Charlotte watched Lily approach. God, she had a sexy walk. Her curvy body moved in a graceful rhythm that warmed Charlotte's blood. Lily approached the driver's side door of the Jag and fumbled with her keys. For a moment, it looked as if Charlotte may get her wish. Then Daniel's phone rang.

"Lucifer," he muttered and answered the call quickly. His voice was cheerful, just short of fawning. "Hi, Geoff?" He opened the car door and stepped into the parking lot.

Lily noticed him immediately. She raised a hand but Daniel waved her off as if seeing her in a remote museum parking lot was a daily occurrence. Pointing to the phone in his hand, he stalked off toward the elevators. Lily looked back at the Saab.

Through the open door, she found Charlotte. Their eyes met and held.

"You've been spotted," Wellesley whispered dramatically.

"Yes," Charlotte agreed. Her heart felt tight. She'd kissed Lily on the bench nearly a month ago. They'd shared a moment of real passion and Charlotte had allowed herself to hope. It was risky—a real leap of faith, and Charlotte had fallen flat. She was still falling.

Lily stood still for a long moment as if she was deciding something. Her eyes looked sad, but there was a flicker of something else too that Charlotte couldn't read.

"She's blushing!" Wellesley exclaimed. "How perfectly sweet."

"Yeah, she does that."

Lily walked toward the Saab. The blush was indeed back. But what did it mean? Charlotte didn't want the question answered in front of Wellesley. The eagle-eyed artist would report everything back to Daniel who would act as judge, jury, and executioner before Charlotte had time to consider the case.

"I'm going to say hello," Charlotte said. With a shaky hand, she unbuckled her seat belt.

"Take your time, dear," Wellesley said and cracked the window.

When Charlotte exited the car, Lily was standing outside the door. "Hi," she said, and she ran a hand through her dark blond hair. It looked a little shorter, and Charlotte wondered if she'd had it cut.

"Hi." Charlotte shut the door, and leaned back against it. "It's nice to see you."

"It's nice to see you too," Lily said, her eyes searching. "How've you been?"

Charlotte hesitated. How candid should she be? Should she tell Lily how adding the volunteer component to her job had her feeling like a worn dishrag? Should she mention that she had cried that morning at brunch? Telling Madison half-truths had never worked. Charlotte decided to be honest. "I've been better." She shrugged. "I've missed hearing from you, actually."

Lily's blush deepened. "I'm sorry about that." She let out a bitter little laugh. "I was too busy lying to myself to text you back."

"I don't understand."

She gave Charlotte a sad smile. "When you broke our date, I told myself that I didn't care."

"Oh," Charlotte said and looked down at her feet. "I'm sorry about that." Lily hadn't given her a chance to explain earlier. Why should Charlotte bother now? "I had to work."

"But that was a lie."

"Excuse me?" Charlotte was incredulous. "You think I'm lying about having to work?"

"No." Lily put a tentative hand on Charlotte's wrist and Charlotte felt a wave of heat enter her bloodstream. "I know you had to work. The lie was that I told myself I didn't care."

"Oh," Charlotte croaked. Though Lily's touch was light, Charlotte could feel it in every part of her body.

"I'm really sorry. I should have let you explain."

Charlotte's smile was hesitant. How much should she say? She'd suffered a significant letdown when Lily had stopped texting her. Seeing her now was painful. Again, she decided to go with the truth. "I hated to break our plans, Lily. But they asked me to cover an extra shift at the hospital. Two nurses are out on maternity leave right now. I'm new on staff and trying to make a good impression. And honestly?" She struggled not to show the emotion welling inside her. "I thought you'd understand. I thought we'd have another chance."

Lily flinched and drew back her hand. "I know. And I'm sorry. I want us to have another chance too." She smoothed her hair, nervously. "I'm sure you're making an excellent impression at work. I'm the one being an idiot. I tried to tell myself the spark between us was no big deal, that the broken date was a sign that things weren't supposed to work out. But seeing you again I know I was wrong. There's just something about you."

Charlotte studied her. "Tell me this, if we hadn't run into each other today would I have heard from you again? Be honest."

Lily hung her head. "I've wanted to call you, I have," she said. "I think about you constantly, believe me but..."

"So, the answer is no?" Charlotte wanted to believe Lily was not filling her head with more rainbows and unicorns but found it difficult. What if this was just a line too? What if she disappeared again?

"But now you're here," a voice said from inside the car. Lily took a surprised step back as Wellesley rolled down the window and poked her head out. "Sparks are special. They're rarer than diamonds and don't last nearly as long." She opened the door.

To her credit, Lily acted as if the appearance of a Chanel-clad sage was completely normal. She even had the presence of mind to offer Wellesley a hand getting out of the car.

"Thank you, my dear." The artist gave Lily's hand a firm shake before letting it go. "I am Charlotte's great-aunt, Wellesley Kincaid."

"Lily Chapman," Lily said automatically. Her voice sounded strangled and Charlotte knew that she'd made the celebrity connection. Wellesley's sparkling blue eyes told Charlotte that she knew it too.

"It's an honor to meet you, Ms. Kincaid. I'm a big fan, huge." She gave Charlotte an incredulous smile.

Wellesley laughed her sweet girlish laugh. "Are you an art lover, Lily Chapman? An artist yourself?"

Lily shook her head as if she couldn't believe she was having this conversation. "I'm both, Ms. Kincaid. But I came here today specifically to see *Valkyrie as Mother Nature*. It's magnificent."

"I like this girl, Charlotte." Wellesley patted Lily's arm. "Would you like to join our little tour?"

"Um…" Lily looked at Charlotte who nodded her assent. No matter what happened between them, Charlotte would not deny Lily this opportunity. "I'd be honored," Lily answered and smiled again.

"Wonderful, because Daniel just texted and Sid is ready for us. I'll meet you by the elevators. Don't be too long."

"Okay."

"Wellesley Kincaid is your aunt?" Lily whispered as they watched her walk away. "I can't believe I just met her. I mean, I *love* her work."

"She's wonderful," Charlotte agreed. "But she doesn't get out too much. We should probably stick close."

Lily hesitated. "Are you sure it's okay for me to join you?" she asked. "I hate to intrude."

"You were just personally invited by the artist," Charlotte said lightly, prompting Lily to blow out a breath.

"I mean, is it okay with you, Charlotte? I don't want to overstep."

Charlotte was quiet for a moment. It had hurt her feelings when Lily stopped answering her texts. More than she cared to admit. But Lily was obviously still recovering from something traumatic. She'd apologized for her bad manners and she looked amazing in the sundress. Didn't everyone deserve a second chance? "Promise not to disappear in the museum?" she teased.

"I promise," Lily said and they started across the parking lot after Wellesley. "You look really pretty, by the way," Lily said shyly. The blush had subsided but only a fraction. "I love those boots."

"Thank you," Charlotte said and then added. "Did you get your hair cut? It looks nice."

"I did." Lily touched the back of her neck as if she'd forgotten. "Thank you."

"You're welcome," Charlotte said and wondered if Lily knew how much she affected her. Aunt Wellesley seemed to have some idea. Inside the elevator lobby, she met them with a knowing look and a million questions.

"When you're not sparking with Charlotte, what kind of art do you create, Lily? Do you exhibit your work?" She pressed a button with a capital letter Q on it.

"I'm an illustrator, Ms. Kincaid," Lily explained. If she was flustered, she didn't show it. "I haven't exhibited since before law school but I keep notebooks."

"Notebooks," Wellesley repeated. She made no effort to hide her lack of enthusiasm, but Lily didn't falter.

"Yes, notebooks," she said. Her eyes flashed with confidence. It was sexy as hell and Charlotte gave her an encouraging smile. "The notebooks feed an installation I'm creating in a spare room."

"An installation," Wellesley cooed as if she were hearing about a new baby. Lily now had her complete attention. "Are you marking directly on the walls?"

"No, I've tacked up strips of paper."

"Mulberry?"

Lily nodded. "The long fibers make it the best surface for ink. I started with one forty-two-inch roll." She smiled. "I think there are seventeen now."

"Mulberry paper is archival too. Smart girl!" Wellesley enthused. "Once on a peyote interlude in Peru, I made the mistake of painting directly on the walls of my hotel suite. The piece was inspired but the bastards charged me a thousand dollars for damages and now they rent the room at a higher rate."

Charlotte and Lily both laughed.

"It didn't occur to me to draw on the walls. I never thought of it as something permanent. It all started as therapy," Lily said. "I didn't expect it to be anything else, really. It was just supposed to be for me. But then..." she paused as a dreamy look came over her face.

"The muse found you," Wellesley finished her sentence.

"I like to think so, yes."

"How marvelous," Wellesley enthused. "I'd love to see it when you're ready."

"Thank you, Ms. Kincaid. I'll let you know." Lily shot Charlotte an incredulous look that morphed into another blushing smile. Charlotte could get addicted to them. She really could.

CHAPTER TEN

Quarried

Valkyrie as Mother Nature was the focal point of the museum's main lobby. Ten feet square, the painting was as evocative as it was grim. A young woman dressed in classical battle armor was shown plucking animals from a burning planet. Freed beasts floated in the air around her while animals left on the surface writhed in agony. Charlotte had seen photos of Wellesley's latest work but wasn't prepared for the impact of being in its physical presence. The environmental statement was devastating. Daniel had proclaimed the painting a masterpiece. Lily had called it magnificent. The superlatives were not enough.

"Aunt Wellesley, it's just, wow," Charlotte said simply. The painting moved her in ways she couldn't articulate. She wondered if having a personal connection to the artist intensified her feelings. Or maybe it was because Lily was standing next to her.

"Yes, it's brilliant," Lily murmured.

Wellesley laughed her girlish laugh but something was off. "The judgmental bitch plagued me for years. I couldn't rest until I'd gotten her out of my system."

"I'm so glad that you did," Lily said, and smiled at Wellesley who tapped her shoe against the concrete floor.

"Once I signed a contract with Quarry, I didn't have a choice," she said and Charlotte wondered if her aunt was nervous. A few straggling patrons lingered here and there but no one paid them any attention. The only person they'd encountered since exiting the elevator was a security guard who'd been awaiting their arrival. Was the open space making Wellesley anxious?

They heard loud voices coming from the central gallery and Charlotte knew something was wrong. Daniel was speaking in his take-no-prisoners, do-not-fuck-with-me, serious tone. The last time she'd heard him use this voice Taco had peed on his cashmere overcoat. Had something gone wrong with the meeting? Wellesley had acted as if booking Quarry for the gala location was a done deal. Maybe she'd been premature. Jacob's voice had now joined Daniel's and he wasn't happy either. What was going on?

"This sounds promising," Wellesley said and tapped her foot harder.

"I'm sure it's nothing," Charlotte lied and took her aunt's hand.

Wellesley slid the Chanel sunglasses back over her eyes. "Don't be so sure. People are horrid."

"They really are," Lily agreed.

The voices grew louder and Daniel, Jacob, and Stefano emerged from the main gallery. Behind them a very tall man in a light gray suit was explaining something. Wildly gesturing with his extra long arms and legs, he looked like an agitated insect.

"There is a back exit, you know. I'll drive her out myself. There's nothing to worry about," the man explained. He saw Wellesley standing in the lobby and froze. His body was so angular he might have been one of the museum exhibits.

Wellesley dropped Charlotte's hand. "What aren't we worrying about, Sid?"

"Oh. Hello, Welly," he said and paled to the color of his suit.

Jacob cleared his throat. "Word got out on social media that Wellesley Kincaid is visiting her new painting at Quarry." The lawyer shook his head. "The art world is very excited. There's reason to believe people are on their way."

"On their way, here?" Wellesley asked.

"Yes, to the museum," Jacob confirmed. "Some are already at the gate."

There was a moment of silence and then Wellesley took off the sunglasses. "Is this true?" She glared up at Sid who hovered over her repentantly.

The museum director looked at his feet. It was a long way down but he seemed to be contemplating the jump. "An intern tweeted it. The girl thought she was doing me a favor."

"She, Sid?" Wellesley spat, causing Stefano to gasp.

"It's nothing like that," Sid wailed but Daniel cut him off.

"You said there was a back entrance?"

"Yes," he said and looked plaintively at Wellesley who turned dramatically away. "There's a dirt access road behind the utility building. It's not easy to find. But I can show you."

"Great." Daniel put a hand on his hip. In full troubleshooting mode he was gunning toward the door. "You can show Lily where to go."

"Lily?" Charlotte asked. "How does Lily fit into this?"

"I'm happy to help," Lily interjected while Daniel exhaled a patience-mustering breath.

"You and Lily will take Wellesley out the back road in the Jaguar," he told Charlotte as if explaining something to a small child. "Sid will show you where it is. I'll drive the Saab out the front entrance with Jacob and Stefano. With any luck we'll fool the paparazzi. Questions?"

"How do the paparazzi know Wellesley's car?" Charlotte asked. She didn't disagree that a quick departure was a good idea, but she wanted to make sure Lily's involvement was necessary.

Daniel held up his phone. On the screen was a twitter account called @QuarryStory. The most recent tweet was a photo of Wellesley in the museum parking lot standing next to the Saab. The post had gone up twenty-three minutes ago. It already had three thousand likes and two hundred and fifty shares. It wouldn't be long before someone Google-mapped the property and found the back entrance. It might have happened already.

Wellesley took the phone from Daniel and studied the image for several seconds. When she looked up, her face was stricken and she swore under her breath. Charlotte's heart went out to her. She didn't know much about social media but the numbers did look frightening. Jacob said there were already people at the gate. There was likely to be a crush. Given her apparent anxiety, Wellesley was right to be concerned.

"When did I get so old?" she wailed instead. "Is it possible I have crone's disease? I look positively ancient."

"That's not what Crohn's disease is," Jacob scolded her.

"You're a goddess!" Stefano soothed.

But Daniel spoke over everyone. "I can't believe I'm saying this, but this is no time for vanity. We need to leave, pronto." He held up his phone. "This is not going away."

"Stop showing everyone that awful photograph!" Wellesley covered her face.

"This is not about the photo," Daniel told her. "It's about your safety." The tweet had now climbed past ten thousand likes. He looked at Charlotte. "We need to get out of here."

"I'm ready," Lily asserted and Charlotte wanted to kiss her.

"Yes, let's go," Sid said. He wrapped a long arm around Wellesley's shoulders. To Charlotte's surprise her aunt didn't shrug him off but leaned in instead for support.

"I'm so sorry," he spoke to the top of her head.

"Another story for my memoir," she replied and lowered the glasses.

They walked to the elevators and Charlotte took a chance to look around at the exposed rock wall of the old quarry. It was unfortunate she wouldn't get a chance to tour the acclaimed museum. *Valkyrie as Mother Nature* had been a revelation. She could only imagine the other amazing works on display. Perhaps she would come back on her own. Or maybe Lily would come with her. Charlotte didn't want to get her hopes up again, but Lily's constant blush made it difficult not to feel optimistic.

"You must come back and visit the museum under less chaotic circumstances," Sid said to Charlotte as they waited for the elevator. "I'll arrange a private tour."

Wellesley nodded her approval. It was imminently clear this was Sid's motivation in extending the invitation.

"I'd like that." Charlotte smiled at him. She wasn't above nepotism if it involved private museum access.

"And I assume you'll be here for the Human Left Gala." The museum director looked pointedly at Daniel. The man was going all out to make amends. "Daniel and I didn't have time to discuss the particulars. But I've put it on the calendar."

"That's great," Charlotte said, shooting a look at her twin.

"Fantastic," chimed Stefano.

"Thankyousomuch," Daniel stammered, uncharacteristically tongue-tied. It was as if he didn't trust himself to say anything else.

Sid waved his hand. "Then it's all settled." He fished a business card from the breast pocket of his suit and handed it Daniel. "Set up a meeting this week. I'll put you in touch with the caterer." He smiled benevolently. "And put me down for a table. I think your organization is terrific."

"I agree." Daniel took the card.

There was an awkward pause and Charlotte wondered if Sid even knew the Human Left's stated mission. Did he even care? Everything he did seemed tailored to impress Wellesley. He hadn't asked for the cost of a table because presumably no price was too high if it meant getting back into her good graces. Right now, it appeared he might be talked into signing over his life savings.

"Let me know if there is anything else you need," he said as the elevator arrived.

"We're still looking for someone to underwrite the invitations, pay for the swag bags and the liquor. Oh, and do you know Bono?" Daniel quipped, ticking off all the items left on his to-do list.

Sid looked stricken. "I don't. But I'm happy to make some calls."

Wellesley shushed him. "He's only kidding, but thank you."

Charlotte stood against the back wall of the lift with Lily in front of her and Wellesley to her left. Next to Lily, stood Sid, his long body poised mantis-like to spring at any intruders. Charlotte took the opportunity to study Lily from behind. It wasn't as if there was anywhere else for her eyes to go. She took in Lily's silhouette. God, the woman was fit. Swallowing hard, Charlotte raised her eyes to caress the curve of her ass and drape of blond hair against her shoulders. Her perfume was the same she'd worn at Birdie's and again after the softball game. The scent was sophisticated and feminine. It made Charlotte want to bury her face in Lily's hair, to kiss her neck. Hopefully there would be time for that later. Lily had indicated an interest in resuming their relationship. But right now, she had to drive the getaway car.

The elevators opened at ground level to reveal a small cadre of museum security guards in dark blue uniforms. "Surely, this isn't necessary," Wellesley said, but Daniel nodded his approval. Handing Lily's keys to a guard to retrieve the Jaguar, he outlined the plan. He would drive the Saab with Jacob riding shotgun and Stefano in back posing as Wellesley. The tinted windows would provide ample cover but Stefano demanded the Chanel sunglasses to get into character. The security guards would lend further authenticity. Leading the Saab down the driveway, motorcade style, they would create a spectacle. With any luck, the decoy would fool the crowd, allowing the Jaguar to escape the compound on the back road. It was all very exciting. Charlotte couldn't help but be a little thrilled. Growing up with Daniel she'd participated in many outlandish capers. This one beat them all.

The guard arrived with the Jaguar and Lily's team left first. A mile from the access road, a shortcut to the highway provided the anonymity of hundreds of cars and a quick trip back to the city. If they made it out undiscovered, they'd be home free.

"I don't think we should go to Georgetown," Wellesley announced. "I'd hate to be followed."

"I agree," Sid said. "How about my house?"

"I thought of that. But they might look for us there too," Wellesley said.

"Let's go to my place," Lily suggested, surprising Charlotte. "You enter the building through a private garage, so it's safe. It's not very big but it's clean, and I have scotch."

"Single malt?" Wellesley asked, brightening.

"At least half a bottle of Glenfiddich." Lily smiled.

"Wonderful. You can show us your art installation. I'm sure Sid would love to see it too."

"Oh, no! I didn't mean to suggest that," Lily said. She shot Charlotte a look but Wellesley was already inviting the museum director.

"Lily is an illustrator. She's created a private installation in her apartment."

"How intriguing," Sid said. Sitting next to Wellesley in the backseat, his long limbs were now folded around her like a protective harness. "A drink and a distraction, it's precisely what we need. Thank you."

"It's more of a work in progress, really," Lily hedged, sounding slightly panicked.

Charlotte covered Lily's hand with her own and immediately felt the connection throughout her entire body. The blush creeping up Lily's neck suggested she was having the same reaction. Wellesley and Sid were murmuring softly in the backseat and Lily began tracing light circles on Charlotte's hand. Arousal surged and Charlotte crossed her legs to fight the building need. But it was of no use. By the time the Jaguar hit the main road she was a hot mess. She knew she should be worried about marauding paparazzi but all she could think about was pinning Lily against the seat and kissing her senseless.

"Has anyone heard from the boys?" Wellesley wanted to know. The Jaguar entered the highway and she cracked the window.

"I'll check my phone," Charlotte said, and she reluctantly let go of Lily's hand. Encompassed in a cloud of lust, she'd completely forgotten that her brother was driving the decoy car. But there were no messages. Charlotte wondered if they'd made it out of the compound.

Sid's phone rang and Wellesley let out a small shriek. "It must be them!"

But the call was from the Quarry's chief security officer. The Saab had only made it as far as the front gate. Scores of fans had shown up hoping to catch a sighting of the famous artist. Satellite vans from three television stations blocked the entrance. The news feed had been slow all day. The networks were serving Wellesley up for supper.

Sid gave the chief officer the all-clear and Charlotte texted Daniel. His plan had worked. Wellesley had escaped with her anonymity mostly intact. The Jaguar exited the highway onto a two-lane minor road leading back into the city. Charlotte glanced in the rearview mirror and saw that Sid was holding Wellesley's hand. Was this the reason she'd braved an outing to Quarry? It certainly all fit. *Valkyrie as Mother Nature* was Wellesley's first major painting in more than a decade. According to Jacob, the piece had been commissioned by the man in the backseat. A former lover who was now holding Wellesley's hand like it was the most precious thing on earth.

CHAPTER ELEVEN

Pictures of Lily

They watched the media coverage on a wide-screen television in Lily's bedroom. Squashed together on Lily's queen bed like teenage girls at a slumber party, Charlotte, Lily, Wellesley, and Sid were riveted to the screen. All that was missing were popcorn and M&Ms.

An earnest young reporter stood in front of the museum's main gate addressing the camera. Clearly visible on the other side of the fence was Wellesley's Saab. Not visible, though presumably still inside the car, were Daniel, Jacob, and Stefano.

"The now-deleted tweet went out this afternoon at five p.m. from the Twitter account of museum intern, Tracey Braun," the newscaster began. "The account is called @QuarryStory and is designed to promote attendance." She paused for dramatic effect and the camera zoomed out to reveal a sea of humanity. "Tracey…has more…than done…her job…today."

It looked like iconic photos of Woodstock except everyone had cell phones. Charlotte glanced at her aunt. Snuggled next to Sid on the bed, she watched the coverage with complete fascination. It was as if she didn't know who might emerge from the Saab.

"Reclusive artist Wellesley Kincaid is believed to be inside the car seen here in the circular driveway beyond the gate. The tweet, sent out approximately ninety minutes ago, included this photo of Ms. Kincaid standing in front of what is thought to be the same car."

"Jezebel!" Wellesley swore as the newscaster's image was replaced by the photo of her taken earlier in the Quarry parking lot. She leaned back against Sid and closed her eyes. "I can't unsee it."

"I'm sorry, darling," Sid soothed and wrapped his impossibly long arms around her body. Charlotte chanced a look at Lily and found wide green eyes seeking her own. They shared a smile and Charlotte shook her head. She'd thought about Lily's bedroom, fantasized about it even. But never, in her wildest dreams, had Great-aunt Wellesley and her insect lover factored into the scenario.

The camera returned to the Saab, which was now moving back around the circle in the direction of the museum. The newscaster carried on.

"It looks like Wellesley Kincaid is returning to Quarry. After nearly an hour's hesitation…about greeting her public… the artist…has made up…her mind."

The Saab stopped. It was as if Daniel had heard the comment and decided to respond. The crowd grew excited and began to cheer. Charlotte wondered what her brother was up to. Why mess around when he'd been given the all clear? The back window lowered a couple of inches and a pair of Chanel sunglasses was visible. The crowd cheered more loudly and Charlotte smiled. *Okay, not bad.* This was why they'd come, after all. An image of Wellesley Kincaid to take home with them, proof that they were there. The car began to roll away and the front passenger window lowered too. Clear in the frame was a man's naked ass.

"Well done!" Wellesley slapped the bed, sending pillows to the floor as the Saab screeched off down the driveway.

"Incredible." Sid looked stunned.

"It was," Charlotte agreed. Lily had a hand over her mouth laughing.

The newscaster was acting as if it hadn't happened. Perhaps she hadn't seen it. She started talking again and the parking lot image of Wellesley reappeared on the screen. The artist grabbed for the remote. "Turn it off!" she screamed and mashed at the buttons.

"Aunt Wellesley, let me..." Charlotte started, but it was too late. Wellesley's assault on the remote had successfully obliterated the offensive image of the tweet. The screen was now purple-colored static with large Chinese characters across the middle.

"Thank God," Wellesley said. Leaning back against Sid, she closed her eyes. Charlotte retrieved the remote and wondered about which button to press. She turned to Lily and found her watching with amusement.

"I think my aunt shanghaied your TV," she whispered and Lily let out a laugh.

"Just turn it off," she said, and she ran a finger down Charlotte's back. "I'll unplug it later and reboot the whole thing."

"Ya sure?" Charlotte choked. The feel of Lily's hand on her body made it difficult to form a proper sentence.

"Yes," Lily said. She took the remote from Charlotte and clicked off the television. The sudden silence was deafening and Charlotte was more aware than ever that she was sitting with Lily on her bed. The thing that had been clawing at the back of her mind for weeks sensed imminent release. Wellesley and Sid were all that stopped her from pushing Lily back against the pillows. She fought for control.

Sid must have felt the shift in the room. Extracting himself from Wellesley's embrace, he rose from the bed and offered her his hand. "Shall we view the installation, Welly? Then I'll call my car and we can let Charlotte get on with her evening."

"Charlotte's evening?" Wellesley asked, and she swiveled her head to examine her niece. Hot and bothered from weeks of longing, Charlotte made no effort to hide her condition.

Wellesley's blue eyes sparkled with understanding. "Oh, forgive me."

Sid cleared his throat. "Let's give the girls a minute," he suggested. Offering Wellesley his hand he addressed Lily. "We'll be in the living room, when you're ready," he told her, one boat-sized shoe already out the door. Pulling Wellesley along, he closed it behind them.

Lily rose to follow but Charlotte took her hand. "Are you sure you're okay with this?"

"With what?"

"Showing them your art," she replied. Lily had never once invited anyone to see it. Wellesley had just made an assumption. If Lily wasn't comfortable about the impromptu exhibition, Charlotte had no problem shutting it down.

Lily gave her a hesitant smile and exhaled. The trademark blush was in place. "That's really nice. Thank you for asking," she said. "But honestly? I'm fine." She twisted Charlotte's fingers, ratcheting up the awareness of her body. Charlotte tried to focus on what Lily said next but was only about fifty percent successful.

"I'm proud of my art. It's not that," Lily explained, and her eyes were shyly confident. "This work is just very personal. The installation is like my journal, only illustrated. Does that make sense?"

Charlotte nodded. She'd never kept a journal for fear that Daniel would steal it and start a blog. "You don't have to show it to anyone."

"But it's Wellesley Kincaid." Lily let out an incredulous laugh. "The woman partied with Warhol. I've seen her work in the Tate Modern. And that's Sid Weimar. He discovered Judy Chicago. Did you know that?"

Charlotte shook her head. Not only was she unaware Sid had discovered Judy Chicago, Charlotte was unaware of Judy Chicago. What hadn't escaped her attention was the intensity in Lily's eyes when something excited her. Charlotte vowed to make it her personal mission to see this look as often as possible.

"Part of me wants to know what they think? Is that egotistical?"

Charlotte squeezed her hand. "Absolutely not, I totally get it." And she did. Aunt Wellesley was a force of nature, about as easy to resist as a summer breeze. "Let's go find out."

"Okay." Lily bit her lip. "But I need to do one thing first." Leaning in, she kissed Charlotte hard and fast. When Charlotte whimpered, Lily kissed her again, this time slipping her tongue into Charlotte's mouth. Charlotte wrapped an arm around Lily's waist and might have forgotten about her aunt entirely had Wellesley not cackled in the hallway.

"Your walls leave a lot to be desired," she said, pulling away. She pecked Lily's mouth. "But your lips do not."

Lily smiled at her. "Tell me more about my lips?"

"Later," Charlotte promised. She couldn't wait to say more about her lips and other places she hoped to discover. Right now, it was time to see the art.

They left the bedroom and Lily led Charlotte down a short hallway to the main living area where Wellesley and Sid stood looking out a picture window.

"I won't ask what you pay in rent," Wellesley said to Lily, clearly dying to know. "But I assure you it's worth it." She swept her hand across the storybook skyline in front of her. "I'd sketch it every day."

"Thank you. I love it."

Located on the tenth floor of a prewar building, the window looked down on the turreted tops of nineteenth-century townhouses of Dupont Circle. If someone told Charlotte she was in Amsterdam or Prague she would not have argued with them. Gazing out, she felt transported to another time and place. Shadows bouncing off wrought-iron spires and ornate weathervanes added to the effect.

"I concur," Sid said and pointed a long finger at the window. "It reminds me of a garret I lived in after college. It was in Montmartre. I was going to be a great artist." He shook his head remembering. "I didn't produce a single painting of merit but I met some wonderful people." His eyes caressed the top of Wellesley's head.

Lily gave him a hesitant smile. "I don't know if my work has merit for anyone besides myself," she said. "When I started the project, I was going through a hard time. I needed to work some things out." She shot Charlotte a look she couldn't quite read.

"I quite understand. Kayne West says the essence of art is pain," Sid replied, his brown eyes conveying professional certainty.

"How original!" Wellesley scoffed. "Nietzsche said it was gratitude."

"How German," Sid retorted and everyone laughed. Charlotte said a silent thank-you to the museum director for putting Lily at ease.

"I think it's somewhere in-between," Lily said and led the group back in the direction of the bedrooms. "I'm certainly grateful for the experiences that have shaped my worldview. But it hasn't always been easy."

"Easy?" Wellesley scoffed. "Unless we're suddenly discussing Spanish waiters, then easy is boring."

Sid hooted but Lily shook her head. "Easy is safe," she replied and Charlotte was reminded of their conversation in the parking lot. She was beginning to understand what had happened to their fledgling relationship. When Charlotte had broken their date, Lily had given herself permission to stop texting. It didn't take a psychologist to understand this was an act of self-protection. Lily was worried Charlotte was going to hurt her so she launched a preemptive strike.

"True." Wellesley gave a little laugh. "And I've never had the courage to take my own advice," she confessed. "When my first marriage fell apart, I did too. I became very fearful of the world, of being rejected. It was easier to shut people out, so I did. I backed away from friends and family. That's when I started painting." She gave Charlotte a fond look. "Anxiety is a difficult cross to bear. I've learned to manage but it prevents me from having a more public life."

"Have you tried medication?" Charlotte blurted. "There are lots of treatment options."

Wellesley smiled at her. "Pharmaceuticals have never worked for me. I walked in the valley of the dolls for a while but they left my brain fuddled and they don't mix well with martinis.

But maybe this CBD will be the ticket. It helps Rhianna. Who knows?"

"That's true," Charlotte agreed.

"And maybe I don't want to get better." The blue eyes crinkled. "The dark periods have inspired some of my most relentless muses. It looks like Lily and I have this in common."

"No argument there," Lily said and they paused outside the door to the second bedroom. "Apart from work, and Sunday museum visits, I've barely left the house in two years," she joked and shot Charlotte another unreadable look. "Let me turn on the lights."

"Of course, take your time," Sid told her as she closed the door behind her.

"Isn't this exciting?" Wellesley said and squeezed Charlotte's arm for emphasis. There was rustling noise behind the door followed by a scrape and then a click. Moments later, Lily reappeared.

"Are you ready?"

"Yes!" Sid and Wellesley chorused like small children setting out for an Easter egg hunt. Charlotte gave Lily an encouraging smile. She had no idea what was inside but she couldn't wait to find out. Lily opened the door.

Charlotte's first impression was one of scale. The volume of work was simply staggering but the artistry was even more so. The walls were covered in wide strips of beautiful white paper that looked like pages from a graphic novel. In the same whimsical style of the party T-shirts and softball jerseys, Lily had inked a pictorial diary. Each vignette was contained in carefully lined three-inch frames showcasing scenes from Lily's life. The entries were dated. Some scenes were heavily captioned with commentary, others entirely blank. Some days vibrantly colored, others just black. One whole section was entirely gray and another covered by a blue tarp strung between two ladders. The only section not inked in panels was the ceiling. A free-form collage, it was a riot of color.

"Oh my," Wellesley said thoughtfully as the group took in the spectacle.

As if prearranged, they split up into separate quadrants of the room to examine the walls. The comics were charming. Illustrated Lily moved through the world with a self-deprecating wit that was both heartbreaking and hilarious. Charlotte smiled at cartoon Lily petting a stray cat, pondering a birthday gift for her mother. She scanned the gray section of the wall and found frames of Lily watching television or crying. Charlotte was glad to see this section was well in the past. Charlotte wondered what was beneath the tarp. Had Lily recorded her impressions of the piano bar? The softball game? Lost in thought, she was surprised when Sid let out a ponderous sigh.

"My dear." He did not take his eyes off the illustrations but continued to walk about the room. Craning his neck, he examined a portion of the ceiling where cartoon Lily was running naked through a rainforest. "I have no words."

"I have one," Wellesley said. The blue eyes blazed with conviction as she tapped the wall where Lily had inked herself arguing with the dry cleaner. "Ambitious."

"Yes, the scale is most impressive," Sid agreed. "Are these your dreams?" he asked, eyes still on the ceiling.

"Yes," Lily admitted and flashed an anxious look at Charlotte. "That's the idea anyway."

"Marvelous execution," Sid murmured and steepled his fingers together under his chin.

"Yes, it's beautifully realized," Wellesley agreed.

Charlotte scanned the ceiling with renewed interest. In addition to her nude image, Lily was flying within a flock of birds, sitting in a field of flowers and holding a baby to her breast. Charlotte was surprised at how happy the last image made her. It was ridiculously premature to discuss children but still good to know that Lily saw them in her future. Charlotte smiled at a fantasy image of Lily as a rock star and then stopped short. Just below, Lily had drawn herself kissing a broad-shouldered brunette on a park bench. Was that supposed to be Charlotte? The illustration was sexy as hell. Lily had made Charlotte look like Wonder Woman. She was flattered and more than a little turned on.

She scanned the ceiling but found no other likenesses of herself. Her gaze returned to the tarp and she wondered again what was beneath it. She smiled at Lily and was surprised to find her looking worried. What could possibly be wrong? Wellesley and Sid obviously loved the piece but Lily looked like she was going to cry. Charlotte was confused until she realized that she had yet to register a reaction. Showing one's art was a supreme act of courage. Lily was waiting for her response. In two strides, Charlotte was across the room. She took Lily's hand and squeezed her fingers gently. "I love it."

"You do?"

"Yes, and I can't wait to see what's under the tarp." Charlotte let her eyes drop to Lily's dress.

"I can't wait to show you."

CHAPTER TWELVE

WTF Buddies

A rhythmic tapping on Lily's apartment door announced the presence of Precious LaRue, Quarry's head of security. The sound reminded Charlotte of the secret knock her college sorority had required to get inside the meeting room. But Precious LaRue was not here to discuss a homecoming float or a new item on the breakfast bar. A former detective with the DC police department, she was there to make sure Wellesley made it safely to her next destination. The level of attention generated by the tweet was still a cause for concern. A documented Wellesley-Kincaid sighting was the art world equivalent of catching a glimpse of the Loch Ness monster. According to the Montgomery County police, who were now monitoring the situation, fans were still trying to get onto the museum grounds.

The knock sounded again, and Charlotte followed Lily out of the art room into the entrance hall. She wanted to tell her again how much she liked her art, how flattered she was to figure in the dream ceiling. She wanted to kiss her. But there wasn't time. Certainly not for the type of kiss Charlotte was imagining. That type of kiss might take days.

Lily opened the door to find a small trim woman standing in the hallway. "Good evening, Ms. Chapman, my name is Precious LaRue." She offered Lily her hand. "I believe you're expecting me?"

"We are." Lily gave the woman's hand a quick shake. "Please come inside."

Dressed in the ubiquitous black pantsuit of a corporate professional, Precious might have been a colleague of Lily's at the law firm, or an upscale mortician.

"Hi, Ms. LaRue. I'm Charlotte. I'm..."

"Ms. Kincaid's niece," Precious finished the sentence. She gave Charlotte an appraising look that did not invite familiarity. After an awkward moment, where Charlotte had to remind herself that she hadn't committed any crime, Precious shifted her gaze down the hallway. "Is Sid here?"

"Yes," Charlotte said, struck by the contemptuous note in her voice. Had she just called her boss Sid? She pointed a hesitant finger toward Lily's art room where he was just emerging.

"There you are," Precious said, her tone now bordering on impolite. Sid either didn't notice or didn't care.

"Precious," he said simply and gave her a tired salute. Stretching his long arms into the air he rolled his neck, calling to mind a stork. Precious looked on with obvious disdain. Charlotte wondered if this was their normal working relationship or if Sid had done something to earn her wrath.

"Is Ms. Kincaid ready to go?" she asked. Her gaze, now trained on the doorway to the art room, was as flat as her voice.

"Is that Precious?" Wellesley walked out of the art room. Opening her arms, she gestured Precious forward. "Thank you for coming, darling. Have you met Charlotte and Lily?"

"I have," Precious replied and then shocked Charlotte by flinging herself into Wellesley's embrace. She clung to her for several moments before pulling away. "I'm so glad you're safe, Ms. Kincaid. I only wish I'd been on site to personally escort you off the premises."

"Me too," Wellesley said and patted her shoulder.

"My car is downstairs in the building's private garage. I'm ready when you are."

"How did you manage that?" Sid asked but was met with a withering stare.

Precious turned back to Wellesley. "I'm taking you to a board member's house on the Chesapeake Bay," she explained. "He has a private guest cottage. You won't be bothered."

"Great idea." Sid clapped his hands. "Have you spoken to Jared?"

"I have." Precious did not look at her boss but remained focused on Wellesley. It occurred to Charlotte that she was starstruck. Initially she'd thought this level of deference was a quirk of Daniel's but she'd now seen it in Lily, Precious, and about three hundred people on the news.

"I told him to leave a key under the mat and a bottle of Chenin blanc in the refrigerator," Precious said.

"Good thinking!" Wellesley clapped her hands.

"I also stopped and picked up Thai food in case you're hungry. I remembered you liked the pad thai," Precious explained and Charlotte knew her fangirl hunch had been correct.

"Thank you!" Wellesley leaned forward and kissed her on the cheek.

It seemed to soften her. Turning to Sid, she spoke in an even tone. "Please consult me the next time you decide to spirit a national treasure off the premises. As head of your security team, I might have an opinion."

"You weren't on site," Sid started to protest but the hostile energy coming from Precious made him reconsider. Tenting his fingers together, it looked as if he might be offering a prayer instead. "It won't happen again."

"Thank you," Precious said and gave him a little nod that seemed to indicate the matter was closed. Opening the door to Lily's apartment, she ushered the couple through. "Have a nice evening, ladies."

"Thank you, Ms. LaRue," they said in unison.

The front door closed and they were alone. It was the moment Charlotte had been waiting for all evening, dreaming of all month. But something wasn't right. Lily seemed stunned, tongue-tied. The green eyes were brimming with questions but none formed on her lips. Charlotte was suddenly very concerned. Perhaps Lily regretted allowing them inside her studio. Yes, she'd given consent, but the decision had been made hastily. And she'd been overwhelmed. What was Lily supposed to say when Wellesley Kincaid was inside her house? She opened her mouth to apologize but Lily cut her off.

"What the fuck just happened?" she asked.

"I'm really sorry," Charlotte responded but Lily didn't seem to hear her.

"I mean, what the actual fuck? Right?" she repeated. Her voice was louder this time and Charlotte braced herself for a lecture. Whatever Lily threw at her she deserved. They'd had no business barging into her personal headspace. Lily had told Charlotte the art installation was her journal, and still, she'd allowed the group to intrude. Charlotte had to accept both the blame and the consequences.

"I'm really sorry."

Lily surprised Charlotte by bursting into laughter. She shook her head. "I mean, am I crazy? Or, did all that really just happen?"

"You're not crazy," Charlotte answered immediately. She wasn't sure what specific events Lily was referencing. A lot had happened, after all. But it didn't matter. Charlotte wanted to do, or say, anything necessary to keep that smile on Lily's face.

Her eyes grew brighter. "I mean, Wellesley Kincaid came to my apartment. She saw my art! What the fuck?" Lily chewed her lip, thinking. It was adorable and Charlotte wanted to kiss her. "Right?"

"Right." Charlotte agreed. "What the fuck."

"I mean, my art is crazy personal, but I just let her see it." She threw up her hands. "Oh! And not just Wellesley Kincaid, I also showed it to Sid Weimar." Lily shook her head with wonder.

"You did that. That was you."

She gave Charlotte a shy look. "I also showed it to this hot woman who I can't stop thinking about."

Charlotte laughed. "Now *that* was bold."

"I know," Lily replied. "What the fuck has gotten in to me?"

"I'm not sure." Charlotte smiled. Lily didn't seem to blame her for the intrusion but she still needed to be sure. "I hope our studio visit was okay."

Lily nodded. Her smile still bright. "Yes, strangely, it's fine. But I'm still like, what the fuck? You know?"

"I do," Charlotte said. She took her hand.

"And I drove the getaway car," Lily went on, her green eyes flashing at the memory. "We took a secret backroad to avoid paparazzi. That qualifies as a WTF moment too. Don't you think?"

"Yes," Charlotte agreed. "It totally ranks."

"And I could go on," Lily said, her voice rising. "That sweet older gentleman mooned the camera!" She laughed again. "What the fuck?"

"Absolutely," Charlotte replied, thinking how cute Lily looked when excited. It had been crazy seeing Jacob flash his bare ass. Charlotte couldn't wait to get the debrief on the debriefing from Daniel. It was definitely a WTF moment.

"Oh! And how about us running into each other in the parking lot?" Lily blurted. She broke out in the familiar blush but didn't break eye contact. "That's three times the universe has put us together." She moved closer to Charlotte. "I couldn't believe it when I saw you there today. What the fuck is up with that?"

"That's a very good question," Charlotte agreed. If she hadn't seen Lily at Quarry they wouldn't be in Lily's apartment right now. "Maybe the universe is giving you another chance."

"I think that's why I kissed you in my bedroom," Lily said softly. "I knew your aunt was standing in the hallway but I didn't care. I had to let you know." Her eyes went a shade darker. "What the fuck has gotten in to me?"

"I have some ideas," Charlotte said and closed the distance between them.

The kiss was not gentle. The make-out session in Lily's bedroom had them both more than ready to take things to the next level and they came together in a grasping embrace. Charlotte wasn't usually the aggressor but something about Lily made her bold. And she didn't hold back. Pushing her tongue into her mouth, she stepped them against the wall.

"Oh, my God," Lily gasped and tried to take control but Charlotte wouldn't allow it. Cradling Lily's head in her hand, she wrapped the other one around her waist.

"Just let go, *please?*" Charlotte whispered and pushed a thigh between Lily's legs. It was the magic word. Lily ceased struggling and melted against her.

"Thank you," Charlotte said and kissed her again. She was more than willing to allow Lily to take charge. She was looking forward to it, actually. But later. Charlotte wanted her turn first.

Moving her hand from Lily's hair she slid it down her body and cupped a breast. It fit perfectly into her hand as if custom-made. The thought was completely ridiculous but Charlotte clung to it. She wanted to believe there was more at play here than an undeniable physical attraction that had them both blushing like teenagers. Squeezing Lily's breast, she moved a thumb across her nipple. Lily whimpered and Charlotte did it again. This time harder. Lily cried out and Charlotte started to pull back only to feel Lily's hand close over hers.

"Don't stop," she said and pushed herself against Charlotte's leg.

"Okay," Charlotte murmured, her lips now against Lily's ear. She bit down on a lobe and then licked a hot stripe down the exposed column of her neck. Somehow, they made it back to the bedroom where Lily guided Charlotte to stand in front of a full-length mirror. Charlotte didn't remember seeing the mirror earlier but now she couldn't take her eyes off it.

"Is this okay?" Lily asked. Lips swollen from Charlotte's kisses, eyes dark with desire, she watched her reaction from the glass.

"Yeah," Charlotte managed, and she felt a feverish wave of desire. Never before had she considered fucking in front of a mirror, but she was certainly considering it now.

"I'm glad," Lily said. "It helps me visually." She leaned in and nipped Charlotte's neck. "You know? In case I want to draw you later."

"Great," Charlotte said again, and she meant it. The illustration of herself on Lily's dream ceiling had been a wonderful surprise. Lily had hinted there was more under the tarp. She was a talented artist. Who was Charlotte to stymie her expression?

"Take this off," someone said. Charlotte wasn't sure who. But it didn't matter as they were both suddenly stripping. Charlotte kicked off her ankle boots then shimmied out of her jeans as Lily lifted the sundress over her head. Once naked, they held hands in front of the mirror. Charlotte's mouth went dry. The supple curves of Lily's body were magnificent. How had she missed the fact that Lily looked like a Bernini sculpture? Long glorious legs attached to wide hips and a narrow waist capped with small round breasts, Lily's body was perfect.

"You're gorgeous," Charlotte breathed but Lily was preoccupied. Charlotte could almost feel her bold appraisal of her breasts but had no thought of hiding. The sensation of being desired was splendid, intoxicating. She arched forward to hasten contact.

"I want..." Lily started and the need in her voice made Charlotte's heart clench. "Can I? Just? Please?" she asked. Charlotte nodded and Lily lay her face between Charlotte's breasts.

"Oh wow, yeah." Charlotte's hands rose automatically to grasp her waist and Lily pulled a nipple into her mouth. "Lily," Charlotte gasped at the sensation. It was electric, exquisite. She wrapped an arm around Lily to steady herself. Pulling her close she caught their reflection in the mirror and almost came undone. They looked like the cover to a romance novel. A very erotic romance novel.

The pulse between her legs quickened and Charlotte knew she was dangerously close to orgasm. Even without direct pressure against her center she was capable of coming apart. Madison had called her a lightweight but Charlotte wasn't concerned. Just because she came early the first time didn't mean the evening was over. She liked to think of sex like ordering from a fancy menu. The first orgasm was just an appetizer to be followed later by an entrée and dessert. She shut her eyes to slow the ascent while Lily continued to ravish her breasts, switching her mouth from one to the other. It wouldn't take much more. Every nerve in Charlotte's body was standing to attention though she was struggling to keep her feet. She pushed her thigh between Lily's legs for leverage. Their centers aligned and Lily cried out.

"That's so good," she breathed and began a slow grind against Charlotte's leg. Charlotte watched in the mirror for a few blissful moments and then exploded into orgasm. Watching Lily's perfect ass in the mirror was more than she could take. A surge of heat tore through her body radiating waves of pleasure that seemed to go on forever. She bucked hard against Lily's thigh and tried in vain not to fall. Fortunately, the bed was only inches away. Collapsing on the edge of the mattress she pulled Lily on top of her. Her pussy was still contracting from the orgasm and if the noises Lily was making were any indication, she wasn't far behind. Reaching down with one hand Charlotte grabbed Lily's knee and hiked it high against her thigh. Using the other she slid two fingers inside her from behind.

"Oh my God!" Lily said and Charlotte watched in the mirror as Lily spread her legs inviting Charlotte to take her completely. The image stunned her. Nothing Charlotte had ever seen rivaled the eroticism of watching her fingers penetrate Lily's pussy. It was incredible. The beautiful body bore down boldly on her hand sliding up and then back searching for release. Charlotte felt another orgasm begin to build but Lily got there first. Exploding beautifully, she cried out. Gazing in the mirror Charlotte vowed never to get angry when Daniel called her monkey arms again.

It was moments before anyone spoke. And then it wasn't much. Lily simply said, "What the fuck?" and then slid down Charlotte's body and buried her face between her thighs. There was nothing for Charlotte to do but enjoy the show. Propped against a pillow she laid a hand on Lily's head and gave in. What the fuck, indeed?

CHAPTER THIRTEEN

Maybe Charlotte

Hazy light from a streetlamp leaked through the sheer curtains in Lily's bedroom. Charlotte had no idea what time it was. It was bright enough to see the beautiful woman lying next to her but too dim to find her cell phone. It was most likely in the pile of clothes scattered in front of the mirror. *God, the mirror.* Charlotte squirmed pleasantly on the mattress. Recalling the erotic images in the reflection made her want to wake Lily and ravish her all over again. It would be so easy.

Lying just inches away, Lily was exposed from the waist up with a thin sheet wrapped around her hips and twisting down her legs like a mermaid's tail. Charlotte could see the swell of her breasts pressed into the mattress, the outline of a nipple. A lock of blond hair obscured her eyes but a happy smile played on her lips. Charlotte wondered if Lily was dreaming of her. Or maybe the expression was still in place from her last orgasm. Charlotte had only succeeded in making her come twice before they'd fallen asleep. She had given her the appetizer and the entree but not the dessert. Maybe she could remedy that soon. What time was it anyway?

She moved down to the bottom of the bed and fished around on the floor until she found her cell phone. There were two texts from Daniel, both demanding her whereabouts. Neither was urgent because it was only eleven thirty. Eleven thirty? The early hour surprised her. It seemed so much later. It seemed like days had passed, eons. Probably because the evening had been significant. Lily was only Charlotte's second sexual partner. Ever. Charlotte had had lots of sex. She'd had sex in a car, in a tent, on the beach, in a treehouse, in a regular house. One horny Thanksgiving, she'd had sex in her grandfather's toolshed. But it had all been with Madison, who'd been her first and only lover. Lily was number two.

From an intellectual point of view Charlotte knew this had the potential to magnify her perception of the event. But how much? She didn't doubt her attraction to Lily. But she barely knew her. And how did Lily truly feel about her? She said she'd been hurt badly. So badly she'd closed in on herself, kept away from friends and family. Charlotte had seen it in Lily's art installation. An entire year of Lily's life was in black and white. Maybe she wasn't ready for another relationship. She'd ghosted Charlotte once. Would she do it again? Charlotte needed to be careful. She needed to talk to Daniel.

Wrapping the bedspread around her body she slipped out of the bedroom and padded down the hallway into the living room. There was too much to text so she sat down on the couch and called her twin. He answered on the first ring.

"What the fuck is going on?"

Charlotte laughed out loud.

"What? What did I say?" he demanded.

"Nothing. It's nothing." She put him off then filled him in on their getaway and viewing the live news coverage on Lily's bed. They giggled about Jacob mooning the camera—naturally it had been Daniel's idea—and marveled at how many people had shown up to gawk at Wellesley. Charlotte described the arrival of Precious LaRue. She told Daniel about Lily's art.

"She drew a picture of you on the ceiling?" Daniel went right to the heart of the matter.

"It was her dream ceiling." Charlotte described the likeness of herself holding Lily on the bench. At least she thought it was supposed to be her. Lily's blush had been a confirmation of sorts and she'd not denied it. "The walls are more like a daily journal. The entries are dated."

Charlotte explained the basic setup of the installation. She told Daniel about the sad wall of black and white and Lily's astute observations of her everyday life.

"A journal? What are the recent entries like? Do you make an appearance? More importantly, do I?" Daniel asked her. Charlotte heard a beeping noise in the background followed by loud crackling.

"What's that noise?"

"Microwave popcorn. Tell me about the recent stuff."

"I didn't see it. But there was a tarp over a section of it. I assume that was it." Charlotte pulled the bedspread up to her chin. "We don't have a microwave. Where are you?"

Daniel ignored the question. Or perhaps he was squealing too loudly to hear her. "You have to see what's underneath the tarp! Go look right now! Where are you?"

"In her living room."

"Where is she?"

Charlotte considered lying. If she told him the truth, that Lily was sleeping in the other room, he'd demand Charlotte sneak a look behind the tarp. The notion of invading Lily's privacy would not faze him in the least. Not only would he insist Charlotte look, he'd insist she take pictures so he could see too. He'd also know that Charlotte and Lily had been intimate. He'd make Charlotte talk about it when she'd yet to talk to Lily, yet to look Lily in the eyes. What if things were weird? What if this was a one-off? Just because Lily had acknowledged the physical chemistry between them didn't, mean she was ready to pursue anything further.

"She's in the bathroom," Charlotte lied and then lowered her voice. "We're going to have some tea. I'll Uber home later. Don't wait up."

"You need to look," Daniel repeated. "If you want to know how she feels about you, the writing is on the wall." He laughed at his own joke.

"I'll try," she whispered and ended the call. Daniel wasn't wrong. Whatever Lily was feeling was inked on the wall in the other room. It would be easy for Charlotte to walk in there and see it for herself. She didn't need Daniel to tell her this. It was tempting enough all on its own. She pulled the bedspread around her shoulders and rose from the couch. The light coming through the picture window allowed for an easy walk to the refrigerator and a pitcher of cold water. Charlotte opened three incorrect cabinets, finding plates, spices, and assorted cookware, before locating a glass. The action made her feel like a thief and she laughed at herself. How could she even contemplate looking under the tarp when she was nervous looking for a glass?

Yes, she was curious. Who wouldn't be? But looking without Lily's permission was dishonest, a direct violation of her trust. Either she would show Charlotte when she was ready, or she wouldn't. Charlotte took a healthy sip of water and walked back toward the bedroom. Her cell phone beeped in her hand. She glanced down at an incoming text from Daniel and nearly spilled her drink.

Congratulations on getting laid btw
Long time coming, lol

Charlotte rolled her eyes. It wasn't an outlandish conclusion, but she'd hoped to keep it to herself for a little longer, at least until she knew how Lily felt about her. Yes, she had the option of sneaking into the installation room right now and seeing for herself. But she'd decided not to do that, hadn't she? Not two minutes ago a very grown-up decision had been made. The phone buzzed in her hand. More texts from Daniel. It was as if he was inside her head.

You need to see that art
Just a sneaky peek

Charlotte squinted at the door to the installation room. It didn't help her resolve that it was two feet away and stood slightly ajar. She might get away with it. She tested the door with her toe and it swung open without making a sound. Damn. It was almost too easy. Charlotte wondered if she was being tested. Another text came in from Daniel.

Go in there

You know you want to

And there it was. She did want to go in there. She did want to see. In the end, her body made the decision. She didn't recognize herself. It was as if she was watching the event on television, as if she had no control. But she had to know. If Lily had recorded a visit to the dry cleaner, buying fruit in the farmers market, what might she have expressed about the kiss on the bench? What were her thoughts on their failure to make contact after that? Were those panels drawn in black and white? Were they drawn in blue?

Charlotte peered into the darkened room but couldn't see much beyond the shadowy shapes of the ladders supporting the tarp. To view the wall behind it, to know what Lily was feeling, she would have to commit fully to the transgression. There was no doing it halfway. There was also no point wasting time. Charlotte needed to get in and out without being discovered. Closing the door, she pressed her hand against the knob hoping to muffle the sound. She'd seen a woman do this on a detective show once and had no idea if it worked. It certainly wouldn't hurt. Charlotte was completely out of her league and would take all the help she could get.

Swiping on her cell phone flashlight, she surveyed the room and knew she needed more light. The uncovered art was barely visible. To see what was beneath the tarp would require greater illumination than her iPhone could provide. A floodlight positioned conveniently near the wall would help considerably. Charlotte shone the flashlight to find the switch and the phone buzzed again.

Take pictures!

I want to see too

Daniel was not helping her concentration. She flicked the button on the side of the phone turning off her notifications. She would talk to her brother when she got home. Now it was time to see what was in Lily's heart. Setting the phone down on one of the ladders, she switched on a floodlight and recoiled against the glare. It was so bright she was surprised Lily couldn't see it through the wall. That astronauts couldn't see it from space. She clicked it off again immediately, then listened to hear if Lily was stirring in the other room. But the only sound was her own breathing. She hesitated and then turned the light back on. It didn't seem as bright this time and she allowed her eyes a moment to adjust.

Taking in the panels inked on the beautiful white paper, Charlotte was filled with a renewed sense of awe. She looked at the ceiling where Lily's dreams swirled together in a subconscious milkshake. The image of her holding Lily on the bench stirred her blood. Lily was truly talented, her voice clearly defined. It was poignant yet whimsical and the illustrations looked so professional Charlotte could also understand if Lily dreamed of pursuing a career as an illustrator. Her talent was prodigious.

The tarp was easily adjusted to allow Charlotte to see beneath it. Pulling one side back she held the other carefully as she took in the images on the wall. The first thing that struck her was the sight of her own name. Preceded by the word *maybe*, it appeared many times over in panel captions. What did it mean? *Maybe Charlotte. Maybe Charlotte. Maybe Charlotte.* So definite in its uncertainty. It told her everything—and nothing at all.

Looking more closely, Charlotte examined the panels by date. Her heart warmed at Lily's interpretation of the night they'd met. Lily had inked lovebirds swirling around them on the dance floor. Charlotte recognized Birdie's logo and smiled. The art was clever. Another panel had Charlotte hovering powerfully in the air over a softball diamond, the Washington monument in the background. Charlotte looked like a superhero, strong and impossibly sexy. She wasn't unhappy Lily saw her this way but wondered if the attraction was purely physical. Perhaps that's where the *maybe* came in. *Maybe Charlotte.* The two words appeared in the panels over and over again. Whatever it meant, Charlotte would take it. *Maybe Charlotte* was better than *not Charlotte* or *never*.

Carefully replacing the tarp, she retrieved her water and clicked off the flood lamp. She'd seen enough to know that Lily was more than intrigued. But she'd said as much in the parking lot. They had a spark. The night's activities had only confirmed this observation. Charlotte suddenly felt silly for spying. She couldn't discern Lily's true feelings looking at a wall. The art was her journal. Just like their relationship it was a work in progress. Only time would tell if things would turn out for them.

Careful to leave the door slightly open, Charlotte left the art room. Entering the bedroom, she sipped the water and gazed down at Lily sleeping. Curled in the fetal position she was hugging a bed pillow to her chest. Charlotte eyed the cushion jealously and contemplated a sneak attack. How would Lily respond to being woken with a warm tongue on her back, a soft kiss on her neck? She didn't have the chance to find out. Lightning crackled somewhere near as the forecasted storm finally broke. The accompanying thunder sent vibrations through the old building causing Lily to stir. Her eyes blinked open and she smiled at Charlotte.

"Hey," she said and rubbed adorably at her nose. "What are you doing up there?"

"Getting water," Charlotte answered. She sat down on the edge of the bed and offered Lily the glass. "Want some?"

"Thank you." Lily took a deep sip and then another. Charlotte watched her swallow. She saw Lily's neck constrict and then relax as the liquid traveled down her throat. Thunder crashed and they smiled at each other. The moment was decidedly intimate. Charlotte still had the bedspread pulled up around her shoulders but Lily was naked. Her breasts were so close. Charlotte couldn't decide whether to taste them or touch them first. She only had to reach out her hand.

"Do you want more?"

"It depends on what you are offering," Charlotte said and then smiled at her own bad joke. "Sorry, that was crass."

"I don't mind," Lily said, her voice low. She put the glass on the bedside table. Leaning back on her forearms she looked up at Charlotte. "What is it that you want?"

Lightning flashed again and Charlotte licked her lips. Hard rain began to fall and there was the distant sound of sirens. But Charlotte was focused on the world in front of her, the world of Lily's body. She longed to kiss her, touch her, lick her until she came hard against her tongue. Yes, that was it.

"I want to lick you," she said and pulled the bedspread over her shoulders like a cape. "Is that okay?"

Lily's eyelids fluttered. "Yes."

"Okay, good." Charlotte climbed onto the bed and straddled Lily's body. Pulling at the sheet bunched around Lily's waist, she freed it entirely and tossed it on the floor. "Because I can't think of anything else right now." She pressed herself into Lily and began to rock her hips.

Lily gasped. Holding Charlotte's waist, she pulled her down harder increasing the pressure against her center. "This feels so good," she whispered, moving to match her rhythm.

"I'm just getting started," Charlotte growled. The gauntlet had been thrown. *Maybe Charlotte*? By the end of the evening she wanted Lily to be screaming "Yes."

Charlotte kissed her way down Lily's body. Stopping to part Lily's legs she allowed her breath to tickle her inner thighs. She tested Lily's clit with the tip of her tongue and was met with a tiny whimper. Lily pushed her hips off the bed seeking more contact, but Charlotte continued to tease her. She wanted to make the act last as long as possible, draw it out.

"I've got you," she said and spread Lily's legs apart. Stroking her clit softly with her thumb she slid her tongue deep inside her, pulled out, then did it again. Lily moaned and began to thrash but Charlotte held her in place. Tracing lines up and down Lily's center, she continued to build her up.

Lily rolled her hips. "Oh, wow," she said and pulled a pillow over her face.

"I thought you liked to watch," Charlotte teased but Lily only moaned in response.

She was gloriously wet and Charlotte pushed her tongue inside her again and again. Lily just moaned louder. When she began to tremble, Charlotte slid two fingers inside her and moved up to lick her clit. Pushing her against the bed she took her, showing no mercy.

When Lily began to pedal her feet against the sheet, Charlotte knew she was close. Instead of easing off she worked her harder, pushing her to the brink and then over the edge with a ferocity that both surprised and thrilled her. Lily screamed as lightning flashed concurrently with her orgasm. The dual energy filled Charlotte's body with pure light. She felt powerful, radiant. Lily was moaning quietly above her, her beautiful body trembling.

She ran her fingers through Charlotte's hair but didn't speak. "You okay?" Charlotte planted soft kisses on the inside of Lily's thighs.

"I'm perfect," Lily said. "That was amazing." For a quiet moment they lay there wrapped in mutual bliss. The rain came down harder. Lightning flared again, and Lily pulled Charlotte close against her body. "I'm glad you're here."

"Me too." And it was true. There was no other place Charlotte wanted to be. Making love to this beautiful woman, in this beautiful city, during this beautiful storm was thrilling. It felt like her life was finally starting to happen. An alarm went off on the bedside table pulling her from her thoughts. It blared again and Lily slapped her hand on it.

"What's that?" Charlotte asked. She looked over Lily's shoulder at the cell phone.

"DC weather alert. There's been some flash floods near here. They're very good about alerting the public."

"Oh," Charlotte said and had a sudden sinking feeling in her stomach. She looked around for her phone but didn't see it. Had she left it in the installation room? Fuck. Her stomach dropped further. "My notifications are off," she stammered, hopefully.

"It doesn't matter." Lily put her phone back on the table and snuggled into Charlotte's side. She nibbled her ear. "If it's a weather emergency they'll blast through your notifications. They'll be desperate to find you." She bit down on Charlotte's lobe. "A feeling I can definitely relate to."

Charlotte's phone picked that moment to sound the alert. The shrill alarm coming from the room next door was unmistakable. A flash of triumph crossed Lily's face followed by a look of confusion. She detached herself from Charlotte and propped her head on an elbow.

Charlotte closed her eyes against the hurt blooming in Lily's.

"When did you leave your phone in the art room? Did you leave it there when I took you in with Wellesley and Sid? Or later, when you sneaked in by yourself?" Her voice was soft but her tone was not.

"It was later," Charlotte admitted. There was no getting out of this. She needed to tell Lily the truth and deal with the outcome. "I've got no excuse. The door was cracked open. I just went in."

"And turned on the light?" Lily sat up straighter.

"Yes."

"I can't believe this." She pushed back against the headboard and studied Charlotte for a long moment. Though the rain continued falling, the moment had altered decidedly. "Tell me. Was it worth it? Did you satisfy your curiosity?"

Charlotte felt sick. She struggled to find the right answer and came out with. "No."

"I'm sorry?"

"I only came away with more questions," she blurted. "The reason I went in there was because I wanted to know how you felt about me. I can't get a read on you. You ghosted me, Lily. And all over the wall you wrote the word maybe. Every time I see you, your eyes tell me yes. Tonight, everything told me yes. What's with all the maybes?"

Lily looked shocked and then gave a derisive laugh. "You're kidding, right?"

"No."

She shook her head. "Go get your phone."

"Now?"

"Yeah. Go get it. Then send me a text."

"What should I say?"

"I'll leave that up to you."

Charlotte wrapped the bedspread around her body and left the room. She retrieved the traitorous phone from the ladder where she'd left it, then stood in the hallway to compose a text. A few quick taps on the screen and she was done. The notification beeped on Lily's phone as Charlotte reentered the bedroom. Lily held it up for her to see. Above the message of apology, the identification read *maybe Charlotte*.

Again, with the maybe. "You put that in your phone?"

Lily gave her a sad smile. "No, you did."

"Why don't I remember that?"

"The first time you ever texted me, it was your name and phone number. Do you remember that?"

"Yes."

"Well, every time you texted me after that, my phone guessed it was you. Because you weren't recorded in my contacts it said *Maybe Charlotte*. It struck a chord with me. I kept saying it over and over in my head. *Maybe Charlotte*. I wrote it on the wall but it still didn't go away."

"Oh."

"Do you understand now?"

"Maybe," was all Charlotte could say.

Seven hours later she emerged from an Uber in a cloud of self-loathing in front of Wellesley's townhouse. Lily hadn't asked her to leave the night before—the city was flooding after all—but the mood had suffered a radical change. Charlotte had gone from feeling the warmest glow of intimacy to the coldest shudder of shame. The actual confrontation had been brief. After Lily explained what *Maybe Charlotte* meant, she'd told Charlotte her feelings were deeply hurt and had gone to sleep. Charlotte had lain awake feeling like a creep. She'd snuck out an hour ago when Lily was in the shower. It was cowardly, but Charlotte was exhausted, and honestly, what else was there to say?

"Ms. Kincaid?"

Lost in thought, it took her a moment to realize someone was calling her name. She looked around to see who it was. Almost half of the people she knew in DC lived inside the house, and although the voice was familiar, it didn't belong to one of them.

"Ms. Kincaid?"

"Yes?"

A woman was getting out of a white van. Charlotte hadn't noticed the vehicle, but it was parked directly in front of Wellesley's house. It wasn't until the woman was standing on the sidewalk that Charlotte realized it was Heather Carol, the perky newscaster from the Quarry debacle. Rage swept over her.

"My aunt's not here."

"Your aunt?" The reporter tried to frown, but her botoxed-brow refused to furrow and she only succeeded in looking pouty. "I don't know your aunt, do I? I'm looking for Charlotte Kincaid, the singing nurse from Children's Hospital who reached a million hits on YouTube last night. That's you, right?"

"I don't know what you're talking about," Charlotte stammered. What was this woman talking about? Wasn't she here to see Wellesley?

"You are Nurse Nightingale. I've seen the video. I've also talked to your supervisor. She says you're pretty special. I'm hoping to talk to you, too. Maybe do an interview and shoot some footage of you singing? But now, you've got me curious. Is Wellesley Kincaid your aunt?"

"I, um..." Charlotte tried to hide her reaction but was unsuccessful. The woman had taken her completely by surprise. She opened her mouth and then closed it again. The nonresponse confirmed the newscaster's suspicions.

She gave a radiant smile. "Okay, wow. That's really cool. I should have made the connection." She turned and called over her shoulder, "Jerry, get out here." She addressed Charlotte again, "Mind if we get this on camera?"

Charlotte struggled to catch up. The newscaster hadn't known of Charlotte's relationship to Wellesley Kincaid until Charlotte had exposed it. The perky woman had come to interview Nurse Nightingale, who somehow had a million views on YouTube. Had Laura's wife released the video? Had the head nurse talked on camera? Charlotte found it hard to believe.

A man emerged from the van holding a compact camera and reality began to sink in. Charlotte had just revealed Wellesley Kincaid's home address to the paparazzi.

"Jerry, no," Charlotte said as if talking to a wayward dog. The man stopped in his tracks. Heather looked surprised and started to speak but Charlotte held up a hand. There had to be a way to salvage the situation.

"Okay, I'll talk to you."

"Great!" The woman motioned to her cameraman. "Jerry?"

"Jerry, stop," Charlotte yelled and the man froze again. She rounded on the reporter. "My aunt had to leave the state because of the circus you people generated yesterday."

Heather looked chagrined. "I apologize. That certainly wasn't my intention. I go where the story is. And right now, the story is you." She pointed at Charlotte. "You've got a million hits for singing to babies at the hospital. That's news. Your connection to Wellesley Kincaid only makes you more interesting. I can't keep that to myself. It's my job."

"Can you keep her home address out of it?" Charlotte pleaded. "It's a safety issue. You saw what happened yesterday."

Heather looked thoughtful. Charlotte could almost see the wheels spinning in her head.

"You'll let me interview you at the hospital?"

"Yes," Charlotte said without hesitation. She wasn't excited about the prospect of exposing herself further but would do it if it meant protecting Wellesley.

"And you'll sing?"

"Sure," Charlotte replied.

"Great." The woman handed Charlotte a laminated business card. "Check your schedule and text me the best time."

"Really? That's it?" Charlotte was surprised.

"Yes." Heather nodded. "Yesterday freaked me out too. I've never seen anything like it." She smiled and suddenly looked much younger. "I want to do my job but there are limits."

"I agree."

She turned to leave. "I look forward to hearing from you, Charlotte." She pointed to the business card in Charlotte's hand and then told Jerry to get back in the van.

CHAPTER FOURTEEN

Subterfuge

Daniel tightened the laces on his neon-blue running shoes, then stood to address the Sunday brunch group. "Will someone please tell Charlotte to get off her ass and come to the gym with me?"

"Hey!" Charlotte protested, bringing Jacob immediately to her rescue.

In the dynamic of the Kincaid compound, as Charlotte had begun to think of it, Jacob played the role of patriarch and often peacekeeper. He cleared his throat. "It's not polite to reference your sister's ass in company," he told Daniel.

"But it's okay to show yours on live television?" Wellesley cracked and the group broke into raucous laughter. The story had yet to get old. In the week since the impromptu moon landing, they'd watched the news clip so many times Wellesley had memorized the newscaster's cadence. That Heather Carol had broken the Nurse Nightingale story a couple days later only made it more fun.

"An unexpected happening...on the Quarry campus," Wellesley announced now, in perfect imitation of Heather. "One...never knows...what one...might find...in the art world."

Stefano picked up the thread. "Wellesley Kincaid...cannot be...pinned down...to the public expectation. It's part...of her enduring brilliance."

"One can...only wonder...what the artist...will do next," Sid finished the mimicked soliloquy and filled Wellesley's glass from a stainless-steel cocktail shaker. Only recently out of the doghouse, he was careful not to spill on the tablecloth.

"She certainly gave them more than they bargained for," Jacob agreed. He was unexpectedly tickled by the stunt and enjoying his newfound notoriety immensely.

"Right now, the artist is going to have a martini," Wellesley said and plopped an olive into the glass.

"And I'm taking Charlotte to the gym," Daniel said. "We need to get her mind off Lily."

"What happened to Lily?" Wellesley set her martini down on the patio table in surprise. "You two were simpatico last week. What happened? Was the sex bad?"

"Welly!" Jacob protested but she waved him off. Like the French cigarettes she sometimes smoked, Wellesley had no filter.

"The sex was wonderful, actually," Charlotte replied. She'd learned that answering Wellesley's questions directly just saved everyone time. There was certainly no putting them off. The upside was that her aunt wouldn't judge her and might have good advice. It had to be better than Daniel's.

"So, what happened?"

"Charlotte got caught looking at the art Lily had behind the curtain," Daniel informed them.

"Bad girl," Wellesley tsked.

Charlotte gave Daniel a "thank-you" look and he stuck his tongue out at her. "Well, it's true."

"You told me to do it," she shot back.

"I held a gun to your head?" he asked, but looked guilty.

"No, you didn't," she said, letting him off the hook. She knew Daniel felt horrible about goading her to see the art. He'd apologized numerous times and offered to call Lily himself. He had a connection through Shoshana who knew a friend of Lily's from the law firm, or something. But Charlotte had declined. Daniel was right. No one had held a gun to her head. She'd been the one to lift the tarp and look. Charlotte took full responsibility for her actions. She'd told Lily as much the night of the thunderstorm.

"Ah." Sid steepled together his long fingers in a now-familiar gesture. The bridge of his nose was slightly burned from his time with Wellesley on the Chesapeake. "You dared peek behind the veil."

"Yes, and now I'm paying the price."

"Did you send her flowers?" he asked and picked up a scone. Charlotte imagined there was a note of smugness in his voice. "I, myself, sent her lilies."

"Oh course, she sent flowers," Daniel replied, bristling with indignation. Though he'd been the one to place the actual order. "Charlotte sent her an orchid."

"Oh." Sid's face deflated and Charlotte felt horrible. Why was Daniel attacking Sid? It wasn't Sid's fault Charlotte had violated Lily's trust.

"I sent her a bottle of single malt scotch and a jar of Marcona almonds," Wellesley said as if this was the most obvious thing on earth. She turned back to Charlotte. "Tell us. What was behind the tarp?"

"A lot of maybes," Daniel said.

"Maybe's that have now turned to no's." Charlotte sighed.

"Are you sure?" Jacob asked.

"Has she seen you on the news?" Wellesley demanded. "Surely that will change her mind. I've never been so proud of anyone in my life. I was thrilled when they said you were my niece."

"That was my fault too." Charlotte hung her head. "When that reporter ambushed me on the sidewalk, I thought she was stalking you. I didn't know about the Nurse Nightingale video yet. I didn't know the reporter was there for me. I gave away our connection."

"That woman is no dummy," Jacob said. "She would have put it together eventually."

"She isn't that smart if she hasn't figured out who mooned her yet," Wellesley said and they all laughed.

"I let her interview me in exchange for promising not to disclose your address," Charlotte explained. "I wouldn't have gone on camera otherwise."

"Or raised a hundred grand for the oncology ward," Daniel reminded her.

"That's incredible." Stefano clapped his hands.

"The numbers keep climbing," Daniel bragged. "But Nurse Nightingale wants nothing to do with the notoriety. A producer from *The Voice* called yesterday and Charlotte pretended to be the nanny."

"Not everyone wants to broadcast their art." Wellesley pointed a finger at him. "I understand it was you who put the original video of Charlotte on social mediocrity. That was wrong."

"I think you mean social media, Welly," Sid corrected her, and she turned on him.

"Do I?" She glanced back at Daniel and seemed to soften. "No matter how beautiful a work of art may be, it's the artist's prerogative when and *if* to share it. Haven't we just learned that with Lily? These things are very private."

"I know," he said, petulantly, "but Charlotte is so talented and I'm so proud of her."

"Nevertheless," Wellesley said and nodded at Charlotte. "I hope Lily forgives you. Has she seen the news story? You never said."

Charlotte bit her lip. "I've no idea. I've only heard from her once since I sent the orchid. She texted back to say she'd given it to her cleaning lady."

"Oof." Stefano mimed taking a gut punch.

"No, not a good sign," Wellesley concurred.

"That's why Charlotte needs to come to the gym," Daniel explained as if the issue were a riddle they were trying to solve together.

"Or she could come to the gin," Wellesley said and raised the martini shaker. They all laughed.

Charlotte considered the option. Normally, day-drinking held no appeal for her. It gave the world a surreal quality and often led to an evening headache. But she was really sad right now, and Wellesley was already pouring.

Daniel leapt from his chair. "No!" he said and flung his body between Charlotte and the glass. "I didn't raise you up from a pup to see you debauched by this shameless hussy."

"Hussy!" Wellesley clapped her hands together. The blue eyes were gleeful. "Am I a hussy, Jacob?"

"Without a doubt," he replied. "And for what it's worth," he leveled a look at Charlotte, "if you're choosing between these two options, I believe Daniel's to be more prudent."

"Thank you!" Daniel pumped a fist in the air.

"Brutus!" Wellesley shouted.

"Maybe I'll just take a nap," Charlotte said as her phone rang in her pocket. She checked the screen. "It's Mom."

"Tell her we're going to the gym," Daniel ordered and popped an apple slice in his mouth.

Charlotte promised him nothing. Rising from the table, she answered the call.

"Hi, Mom?"

Sarah Kincaid's words came out in a rush. "Honey, you were on the news!"

Charlotte smiled into the phone. She'd sent her mother the link to Heather Carol's report three days ago. "Yes, I know."

"The videos of you singing lullabies to children are incredible. I haven't heard you sing since high school." Her voice caught. Sarah rarely got emotional. Charlotte was at a loss.

"That's okay," she said honestly. "But this isn't about the singing for me, Mom. The lullabies soothe the children. It helps them sleep."

"You sounded amazing. No wonder it's had so much attention. They called you Nurse Nightingale!"

"I care more about being a nurse than a nightingale."

There was a long pause and Sarah blew out a breath. "I know that. And I'm sorry I gave you a hard time about changing careers. I just knew you had the potential to help people. I see now that you are. I'm so proud of you."

"Thanks, that means a lot," Charlotte said. It wasn't an easy topic for either of them so she changed the subject. "How's Rhianna?"

"Fickle," Sarah said immediately.

"What happened?"

"She's fallen for Sven. Wedges her long body between us in bed every night."

"Mom!" Charlotte did not appreciate the visual.

"It's true," Sarah said, laughing. Daniel motioned to Charlotte to give him the phone and she gladly let it go.

"Bye, Mom."

"Call me next week."

Daniel did not linger in conversation. "Hi, Mommy. I can't talk. I'm taking Charlie to the gym. What? One teaspoon of cayenne, not three. You just got that man. Don't kill him, yet. I'll talk to you tomorrow." Hanging up, he handed the phone back to Charlotte. "Come to the gym, please?" he said.

"Why is it so important?"

"It just *is*."

They bid the brunch group farewell and started back to the carriage house. Once out of earshot, Charlotte stopped him on the path.

"You're acting strange. Is everything okay?"

"I just don't want to go alone," he admitted, and Charlotte felt a stab of concern. Daniel had been acting funny all week. It was more than just guilt over the art. She'd been too caught up in her own drama to question him properly but there was something he wasn't telling her.

"Tell me what's going on."

"Does there have to be something going on? Can't you just come to the gym?" he challenged and she gave in. She knew he was lying but she didn't have the energy to fight him. Daniel was always there for her. He'd come with Charlotte on her first trip to the gynecologist because their mother had been too busy teaching. A trip to the gym, whatever the motivation, wouldn't kill her.

"How long are you planning to stay?"

"Two hours at the most. There's a spin class at noon. It's called Same Sex Cycle. I reserved bikes."

"A queer-themed spin class?" Charlotte was intrigued. She'd taken a few spin classes in Maine, but had never been a regular. Hopeless at the choreography, she'd always felt a little silly. But there was no denying the efficacy of the workout.

"Yes! The playlist is all LGBTQ performers," Daniel said, dialing up the huckster charm that always reminded Charlotte of the time he played Harold Hill in the *Music Man*. "Melissa Etheridge, George Michael, Sir Elton, Brandi Carlisle, Lesley Gore," he ticked them off.

"Lesley Gore was gay?" Charlotte was sure she'd never heard this before.

"Why do you think she was crying?" Daniel herded Charlotte into the carriage house.

"Because Johnny left her party with Judy?" Charlotte asked. She went back to her bedroom to change clothes.

"Exactly! But it was all about Judy!" Daniel yelled from the living room. "Nineteen-sixties America just assumed it was about Johnny. Leslie cried all the way to number one."

"How did you hear about this class?" Charlotte asked, emerging from her room in workout clothes.

Locking the door, they took the path through Wellesley's yard to the street.

"Someone at work," Daniel said. The answer was uncharacteristically vague, putting Charlotte on immediate alert. She pressed him.

"Who?"

"I can't remember," he said and his neck turned red. It was his biggest tell. He had to wear a turtleneck when he played poker.

Charlotte let the subject drop. Daniel's attraction to the spin class would be revealed soon enough. She found it easy to distract herself by looking at the historic townhouses. According to Jacob, Georgetown's ornate Victorian-style residences were built mostly after 1870. The period aesthetic remained intact due to the efforts of the historic preservation society that ruled the neighborhood with a wrought-iron fist. Homeowners didn't change as much as a bird bath without board approval. Wellesley had run afoul of them once in the 1970s over a porch railing and been threatened with civic action. But the vigilance paid off. The neighborhood was charming without being quaint or precious. Georgetown houses seemed to take themselves seriously. There was a confidence about them. It was as if they believed not only in the sustainability of their market value but of their own personal appeal.

The twins turned onto M Street and small shops appeared. Located in rezoned townhouses renovated for commercial use, the storefronts along the main thoroughfare housed mostly boutiques. On the left was a specialty coffee shop that roasted its own beans. You could smell the place a block away. Next door was a stationery store that sold handmade paper. Charlotte looked in the window of a silk-suit shop Stefano swore was a front for Colombian drug money. She'd never seen anyone inside and wondered if the rumor was true. Georgetown had been an unexpected bonus of moving to DC. She'd never considered living in an urban neighborhood but found she liked it very much.

"Rhi-Treats!" Daniel shouted suddenly. Charlotte looked around for a snake or Republican senator but saw only a pet store. Then she saw the poster. The Madonna picture of Rhianna was front and center. Half-bald, with Daniel's headscarf wrapped around her head, it was the campaign photo for Madsnax CBD dog treats. Madison had officially infiltrated Georgetown. Charlotte stepped closer. Rhianna looked bedraggled and half-starved.

"I can't believe this." Charlotte slapped her palm against the glass rattling both the window and her brother.

"Down girl," Daniel squealed. Slipping his body between Charlotte and the display, he narrowly missed getting smacked when she raised her hand a second time.

"Sorry," Charlotte muttered and dropped her arm.

Assured of his safety, Daniel examined the poster. "Madness in the house," he hissed then turned on Charlotte. "When will you tell that balloon-atic to cease and desist exploiting your baby?"

Charlotte rubbed her eyes. "I never seem to find the time." It *was* maddening. She knew she needed to contact Madison, tell her to back off once and for all, but it never seemed like a good time. It took a lot of emotional energy to pin down someone so slippery. The fact that Madison was in Maine made avoiding the job even easier. Out of sight out of mind. Until now, the tactic had worked remarkably well.

"Well, I think it's because you're a big fat chicken." Daniel snapped a picture of the poster with his phone. He then pulled Charlotte away from the window and back in the direction of the gym.

"You're right," Charlotte admitted. "Jacob even offered to help. But I told him not to worry about it. I don't want to engage."

"Well, I think that's stupid."

"Thanks for your opinion." Charlotte picked up the pace. She was suddenly very eager to get to the gym. It would feel good to work out her frustration in a spin class. Everything felt upside down. She couldn't get rid of Madison, and Lily wanted nothing to do with her.

"You should definitely talk to Jacob." Daniel was now jogging to keep up with her, his legs needing two steps to every one of hers. "I don't know what type of law he practices but it won't matter. A Washington, DC letterhead will be enough to scare Madison well…probably not straight." He laughed at his own joke. "But she'll stop the ad campaign for sure."

"Maybe," Charlotte said and immediately thought of another DC lawyer. Even if they were on speaking terms Charlotte wouldn't have asked Lily to get involved. She didn't want Lily anywhere near Madison. It was mortifying. Her ex-girlfriend was a vacuum of entitlement and treated Charlotte like a well-cared-for pet. Bring Madison and Lily together and you'd scripted Charlotte's worst nightmare.

"I'm happy to call her," Daniel said and opened the door to the gym. The name stenciled on the window read Keep It Up, DC!

"Thanks, but I don't want you to mess up the gala sponsorship."

"She wouldn't dare."

"Wouldn't she?"

They entered the gym, and Charlotte took a moment to look around. It appeared to be a climbing facility. A two-story rock wall dominated the back of the room, climbers hung at various levels. She turned to her brother. "Are we in the right place?"

"Yeah, spin class is in the back. It's a recent add-on."

"And how do you know this?"

"Geoff is friends with the owner's wife, they're big-time donors," he said casually. They walked into the lobby and approached the front desk where the attendant was helping other clients.

"When did the Geoffrey Problem become Geoff?" Charlotte asked and he stopped short.

"Lower the volume, please," he hissed glancing around. But no one was in earshot, so he filled her in. "Geoff and I met for a drink the night of your debauchery."

"I thought you hated him." Charlotte ignored the reference to her night with Lily and began to interrogate him. "Why have a drink?"

"Three reasons," Daniel said. "Number one, I wanted to brag that I'd scored Quarry for the benefit."

"That couldn't wait until Monday, because...?" Charlotte asked.

Daniel held up his phone. "Reason number two."

Charlotte gave an appreciative whistle. The image on the screen was hurt-your-eyes beautiful. "Oh, he's so pretty," she said and reached out a finger to stroke his face. Daniel yanked the phone back.

"He's just as beautiful on the inside as he is on the out."

"You sound like you're in love with him," Charlotte joked but when Daniel didn't respond she realized she'd hit a nerve. "Wait a second. Is that the Geoffrey Problem? You're in love?"

"Keep your voice down, please," Daniel hissed. "My feelings are only part of it. The problem was that Geoffrey was dating Paul. But that's no longer a problem." Daniel looked abashed and Charlotte started to catch on.

"Oh, so the Geoffrey Problem was that you couldn't have Geoffrey."

Daniel nodded and then looked over his shoulder. "Can we please talk about it later?"

"If you answer one question. Were you the catalyst?"

"Catalyst on a hot tin roof," he giggled and then looked guilty. "It's complicated, Charlie."

"I'm sure."

Charlotte wondered who this new man was that had her brother so on edge. Usually Daniel was in complete control of his relationships. Directing men in his life like actors on a stage, he dated them until he tired of the script and canceled the show.

"Will he be here today? Is that why we came?" Charlotte asked and was surprised when her brother sounded nervous.

"Yes."

"Will I meet him?" she teased. "Will we go get lattes after?"

"Maybe," he said. Signing them in, he retrieved their spin shoes. Handing Charlotte hers, he didn't make a joke about the size. It was another red flag. They walked down a short hallway toward a glass door.

"That's the studio." Daniel pointed his finger straight ahead. On either side of the door were men's and women's locker rooms. "Get changed in there," he pointed to the women's room, "then meet me on the bikes. We're in back." He started to open the door to the left but she grabbed his arm.

"What aren't you telling me?"

"Nothing," he said and tried to back away. But it was too late. Charlotte watched with satisfaction and concern as a bloom of red flushed up the back of his neck.

CHAPTER FIFTEEN

Spinning

When she exited the locker room, Daniel pounced on her like a worried mother by the deep end of the pool. Grabbing her arm, he hurried them back to the farthest corner of the brightly lit studio.

"What's going on?" Charlotte demanded but he shushed her. Only when safely positioned on the very last bikes, in the very last row, did he speak.

"Don't be mad," he said. His hazel eyes were wide, and her pulse quickened. All too often when Daniel prefaced a conversation with these words, calamity followed. Like the time he'd signed Charlotte up for the Miss Maine pageant— she'd won the talent portion—or the Maine Marathon—she'd finished in under four hours.

"What did you do?" she said and steeled herself for the worst. Daniel's behavior on the way to gym had made it apparent he was up to something. Charlotte was pretty sure it concerned his new conquest. But why would that make her angry?

Class time drew nearer and the studio filled as a steady trickle of people moved out of the locker rooms onto the bikes. A hairy man in a tank top took the bike in front of them and a pretty woman in pink claimed the one to Daniel's left. So far, Geoff was nowhere in evidence. Charlotte had only seen his picture on a cell phone but expected to recognize him immediately.

"Is Geoff back here with us?" she ventured. "Is that it? I'm okay being the third wheel."

"No!" Daniel yelped, surprising Charlotte. Each time the door opened he looked up like an underage kid holding a beer. "He's coming with a friend from law school."

"Geoffrey is a lawyer?"

"Nonprofits have lawyers too."

"So, what's going to make me mad?"

"I'll start by saying this seemed like a good idea yesterday." Daniel put a hand on Charlotte's knee and squeezed. If possible, he was looking even more worried than before.

"You see, Geoffrey went to NYU Law School."

It was then that Charlotte realized Daniel's anxiety wasn't about seeing Geoffrey. It had something to do with Lily. Dread flooded her body.

"What did you do?"

"DC is a very small town," he said, meekly.

"*Daniel.*"

"We thought Portland was small."

"Tell me."

"Okay." He took a deep breath. "Geoff knows Lily from law school. Lily works with Camille who is married to Hannah who is co-owner of Gowear."

Charlotte looked down at the faded sportswear logo on her Bates College T-shirt. "The outfitter company? What does Gowear have to do with spin class?"

"Geoff got Gowear to sponsor the gala's entertainment budget. Hannah and Camille are Richie Rich." He gave a little shimmy. "They also made a big personal donation."

Charlotte struggled to catch on. "That's wonderful. But what does it have to do with today?"

"Oh, Hannah also owns the gym," Daniel said and the connection slid into place. "I told you, they're Richie Rich. She owns a gym in Virginia too. They're donating membership packages to the silent auction."

"I met Camille at the softball game," Charlotte mused, remembering the woman who'd told her Lily's name was Lillian.

"Great!" Daniel said enthusiastically, as if this made a difference to Charlotte's current predicament. "Geoff suggested we all come here today so I signed us up. We thought if you and Lily ran into each other…" He held up his hands giving a what-are-you-going-to-do shrug.

"*We* thought? Who is *we*? You hatched this plan with Geoffrey?"

"We've gotten very close."

"And Lily's coming too? Does she know about your scheme?"

"I'm not sure." Daniel was mournful. "Do you want to sneak out?" He looked over his shoulder in the direction of the locker rooms. But it wasn't an option. At two minutes before the hour, people were now streaming in through the doors. The studio was filling quickly. There was no sign of Lily or Geoff but they could appear at any moment. The instructor had already dimmed the lights. Class was about to begin.

"Maybe they blew it off," he offered.

"Or maybe they just got here." Charlotte ducked her head. Lily had indeed entered the room. She was chatting with Camille and a man Charlotte supposed was the infamous Geoffrey. They each took a bike in the front row, Geoff and Camille flanking Lily on either side. At the sight of Lily's delicious body, the body that had been so recently pressed against hers, Charlotte's heart began to race. She gripped the handlebars and tried not to think of the way Lily had tasted or the sexy noises she'd made when Charlotte had touched her. She tried to focus on the fact that Lily was angry. That she may become angrier if she saw Charlotte lurking in the back shadows of her spin class.

"You've put me in a bad spot," she whispered and clipped her shoes onto the pedals. "She's going to think I'm stalking her." Charlotte kept her head low and her voice lower. She'd hoped that in time Lily might give her another chance, but it was way too soon to force the issue. Lily had made her feelings clear when she'd given Charlotte's orchid to the cleaning lady.

"Some people think stalking is sexy," Daniel tried, but Charlotte glared at him.

"Or creepy, or illegal," she said.

"I'm so sorry," he said again. "I'm a complete idiot."

Charlotte didn't argue.

The lights dimmed further and warm-up music began. Though Lily was only about twenty feet away, the night club ambience coupled with their relative positions in the studio made Charlotte feel safe from discovery. After class would be another matter. Charlotte supposed the best way to avoid detection would be to stay low and wait for Lily to leave. Surprising her in this brightly lit, freezing cold room didn't seem the best tactic if she had any hope of reconciliation.

"Why is it like the arctic in here?" She shivered in her simple Bates College T-shirt.

"Because the place is legit," Daniel said. He seemed relieved to be discussing something other than his colossal fuck-up and grew animated. "In about twenty minutes this place is going to be bumping. The temperature is the litmus test. Geoff says the colder the studio the harder the workout."

"Geoff says..." Charlotte mimicked and Daniel made a face at her. A moment later Geoff turned and gave Daniel a thumbs-up and the middle school tableau was complete.

"Subtle," Charlotte muttered and ducked her head. She was mortified. As long as Daniel's co-worker hadn't acknowledged them, Charlotte had been able to pretend it wasn't happening. But the cheesy thumbs-up made it real. She was beginning to feel like she was in a romantic comedy. The type of film that Madison had adored but put Charlotte to sleep. It didn't help that Geoffrey looked like Zac Efron.

The music lowered and the instructor, an impossibly fit woman wearing a rainbow-patterned cycling unitard, began an introductory spiel.

"Hey, DC! My name is Dharma and I'm so glad you came out to ride with me today! This is Same Sex Spin!" She paused to let the class cheer. "Before we start, I want to make sure that everyone has water." She held up bottles in both hands. "It's important to stay hydrated during the class. It's only sixty minutes but it's an ass-kicker, people!" She tapped the bottles against her butt and the class cheered again. "We have extra bottles up here if you forgot yours." Her eyes scanned the room letting the group know she was serious.

Daniel shot Charlotte a worried look but she shook her head. She didn't doubt the wisdom of Dharma. But a walk to the cooler was too great a risk. It was in the very front of the studio. Lily would certainly notice.

"Let's start by doing some stretches," Dharma chirped and began to lead them through a series of arm exercises. Charlotte tried her best to focus on the warm-up. Pretending this was a normal workout class and not a ticking time bomb was the only way to make it to the end. She would ignore Lily and spin.

"I'm thirsty," Daniel whispered, breaking her concentration. She refused to look at him. He could dry up and blow away before she'd let him anywhere near that water cooler.

The first song seemed to knock fears of dehydration from his mind. "I'm the Only One" by Melissa Etheridge. He let out a happy squeak and held up his hand for a high-five but Charlotte left him hanging. She was too angry. Yes, it was one of her favorite songs. Yes, she liked to sing it loudly while driving down old country roads, belting out the lyrics like a lost and broken soul. But she wouldn't give him the satisfaction. Fortunately, Dharma had enough positive energy for everyone in the room.

"Everyone up on your bikes," she said, sounding like a combination cheerleader drill-sergeant. "Who's ready to spin?"

The class cheered an assent. Charlotte pushed herself to a standing position on the bike and began to pedal. Eyes locked on Lily's back, she found it difficult to pay attention to the choreography when Melissa was crooning about drowning in desire. It did feel like Charlotte was drowning. She was drowning in desire, despair, in delirious hope.

Watching Lily move to the music Charlotte lost her place again. God, she was sexy. Charlotte was mesmerized as repeated motion on the bike caused the fabric of Lily's hoodie to slide up just a fraction revealing a thin crescent of skin above her shorts. Damn. She wanted to lick it, taste the salt. The thought made her instantly wet. How was she going to endure a sixty-minute class when she couldn't get through the first song? Cheeks burning, she glanced at Daniel to see if he'd noticed her discomfort. But her brother was lost in his own fantasy. Eyes locked on Geoff's ass he was pedaling the stationary bike so hard it looked like he was trying to catch up. No help there.

Melissa sang about fear and Charlotte looked at Lily again. Fear was the true obstacle. Lily had been hurt. She'd told Charlotte as much herself. What she hadn't said out loud she'd expressed on the wall. Some horrible ex-girlfriend had made Lily distrustful of love. And now Charlotte had done it again. How was she to undo it? Was it even possible? The song segued into Queen's "Somebody to Love." Fortunately, the entire class was as excited by the selection as Daniel. The collective noise of affirmation was just enough to cover his squeal. Charlotte punched her brother in the arm and he crossed his eyes at her.

"It's my jam," he said and started belting the lyrics.

"Calm down," Charlotte hissed and hit him again. Possibly too hard this time as he almost fell off the bike. Glaring at her, he righted himself but continued to sing, albeit more softly. In the front of the studio Dharma was ducking and bobbing like a middleweight boxer. Charlotte was still struggling with the choreography but Lily was having no trouble at all. Perfectly in sync with the instructor, she looked like she could be in a promotional video for the gym. Charlotte tried hard not to stare but failed miserably. Perhaps this was her problem. Dragging her eyes away, she forced herself to watch the hairy man in front of them instead.

It worked until the song changed and Charlotte made the mistake of checking on Lily who was now removing her hoodie. Beneath the garment she wore a T-shirt that left her midriff entirely exposed. The tiny morsel of her back Charlotte had been eyeing suddenly expanded to a full buffet of naked skin. *Good lord.* Charlotte sucked in a breath. God, she was in trouble. The simple act of taking off a sweatshirt seemed like a deliberate striptease. Charlotte was ready to take off her own clothes and pull Lily in the locker room. How was she going to make it out of the studio without detection if she spontaneously combusted in the back row? It didn't help her anxiety that Geoff continued to sneak looks at Daniel. Each time he glanced over his shoulder her brother puffed-up like a prized rooster.

"Stop it," Charlotte whispered.

"He's the one checking me out!"

"Because you're acting like Mick Jagger," Charlotte scolded and then hated herself. But Daniel didn't seem to take offense. If anything, he inflated and sat up higher on the bike.

Elton John's "Tiny Dancer" started and Charlotte forced herself to look back at the man in front of them. Oily hair coiled around the edges of his pink tank top like tiny wet spiders and sweat stained the garment red. Dharma was delivering the promised ass-kicking. The formerly frigid studio was starting to cook. Charlotte was three steps behind the choreography but it didn't matter. She was feeling the workout everywhere. Focusing on spinning helped dull the throbbing between her legs. It was the simple equation of mind over matter. If she pushed herself to be fully present in the class, she didn't think so much about Lily.

"I'm really thirsty," Daniel whined but she ignored him. The class was more than half over. He could make it until the end of the session or he could lick the back of the man in front of them. It was his choice. Going to the water cooler in the front of the classroom was not an option.

"Please," he begged and she turned her head mouthing the word "no" for extra emphasis.

"Can I at least go to the locker room?" Daniel nodded toward the door at the back of the studio. "I'm dying."

Charlotte wavered. The locker room was out of Lily's line of vision. The departure would likely go unnoticed. Sensing her hesitation, Daniel pressed his suit.

"I'll bring you some back," he promised hopefully.

"Don't you dare," she said. "I'll meet you at home."

"You sure?" he asked and she nodded.

"Go."

She didn't have to tell him twice. His smile was so bright he looked like a child let out early from church. As Dharma cued up Joan Jett and the Black Hearts, he unclipped his shoes from the bike and danced out of the studio to the throbbing bass of "I Love Rock and Roll." Charlotte was not surprised to see Geoff follow a few moments later. She watched the door to the locker room close behind them and breathed a sigh of relief. It would be much easier to dodge Lily without Jumpin' Jack Flash gassing around the studio.

The choreography hopelessly lost, Charlotte allowed her eyes to drift back to Lily. The song had begun to really rock and Dharma was shouting something about sliding her body to the side in a hip-hop move. Lily executed the move like a boss. Charlotte pedaled furiously trying to mimic her motions. This was a spin class, she reminded herself, not advanced ballet. To her surprise she soon began to recognize a pattern to the movements. Maybe it was her body yearning to be in sync with Lily's but Charlotte found she could suddenly follow the motions of the class. For several glorious minutes, she felt like a part of a flash mob in a YouTube video. Everybody moving as one, loving rock 'n' roll, dancing with Joan Jett.

The song began to wind down and Lily peeled off her T-shirt and used it to mop her face. Charlotte gasped out loud and then clamped a hand over her mouth. Clad only in a sports bra and bike shorts, Lily's attire was perfectly appropriate for a spin class but almost too much for Charlotte. It was as if Lily knew how much she was torturing her. Charlotte looked down at her knees. It couldn't be much longer.

"Don't let up yet," Dharma said, sensing that she was starting to lose the class. "Stay with me for the ride home."

The cool-down started and Charlotte grew nervous. Once the class was over, the lights would come on and the chance of being discovered much greater. If Charlotte was going to be found out, it would be soon. Dharma walked them through some breathing exercises as George Michael crooned "Careless Whisper" at a much lower decibel. This was the time for class members to ask questions. Several took the opportunity to suck up to Dharma while others began chatting and gathering their belongings. Charlotte was careful not to draw attention to herself. A pretty woman in pink tried to make eye contact but she pretended not to notice. This was Same Sex Spin. There was an implied pick-up vibe in the title. Charlotte didn't want to give the woman the wrong impression. There was only one woman in the room she wanted to talk to, and she was unclipping her shoes from the bike in the front row.

"I'm here every Sunday," Dharma said as more people began to unclip from their bikes. "Make sure you register online if you want a reserved spot."

But Charlotte was only half listening. Lily was off her bike and moving toward the locker room. Her gorgeous body was slick with sweat and Charlotte was torn between dragging her to a remote corner of the studio or sticking with the original plan of hiding from her completely. Lily walked toward the locker room and it looked as if Charlotte would get her second wish. But then something unexpected happened. The locker room door closed but Lily didn't go inside. Instead, she turned around and looked directly at Charlotte.

CHAPTER SIXTEEN

The Loophole

Charlotte couldn't move. She felt like she was underwater, lassoed to a stone. This was a happy coincidence as she found she had no desire to go anywhere. Lily was walking directly toward her and she was smiling. The lights were back on in the studio fully illuminating what appeared to be a sassy sparkle in the bright green eyes. It wasn't the reaction Charlotte was expecting, but she was glad to see it. After the agony of the week apart, she was happy to see any expression at all. Just looking at Lily made Charlotte feel better. And sassy? Sassy, Charlotte could handle. Madison's default reactions to disagreeable situations were anger and petulance. Compared to this, sassy was cake.

Lily propped her foot against the wheel of Daniel's vacated bike. "Hey," she said softly, "did you enjoy the class?" Her voice was low but the challenge came out loud and clear. Charlotte was puzzled. Lily didn't seem angry. It was something else, not aggressive but not entirely tender either.

"It was fun," Charlotte replied, carefully. She tried her best not to gawk at Lily's curves still glistening with sweat from the workout. She looked incredible. In another era her attire would be considered scandalous, illegal, actionable. Charlotte was glad she lived in the now.

"You really found your groove there at the end," Lily said, breaking Charlotte's train of thought.

"I did?" Charlotte replied. It sounded as if Lily was dissecting her performance. How was that possible? As far as she'd noticed, Lily hadn't turned around once during the workout.

"You seemed distracted during the first part of the class. Was that Daniel? You got better once he and Geoff took off." Lily smoothed her hair back. She seemed to be enjoying herself. Her manner was confident, bordering on cocky. It reminded Charlotte of the Lily she'd first met at Birdie's. It was sexy as hell.

Charlotte thought hard. It was clear Lily had been able to see her during the workout. She wasn't sure how, but did it matter? If Lily had seen Charlotte well enough to judge her spin performance then she'd also seen Charlotte drooling all over herself. Honesty was the only option. "It wasn't Daniel who was distracting me."

"I caught that." Lily smirked but didn't look unhappy.

"I didn't know you'd be here," Charlotte said quickly. If Lily was weighing the facts, she needed to have them all. "I wouldn't have come otherwise."

"Oh." The light in Lily's eyes dimmed.

"Not because I didn't want to see you," Charlotte clarified and just managed to stop herself from taking Lily's hand. "But because I didn't want to invade your privacy any more than I already had. I'm really sorry about spying on your art."

Lily's face softened. "Thank you for saying that."

"I don't know what got into me. It was a shitty thing to do."

"I've actually been thinking about that a lot," Lily said, and Charlotte was delighted to see a smile tugging at her lips.

"You have?" Charlotte willed the smile to grow, colonize Lily's eyes, take over her entire face.

"Yes, and as shitty as it was," Lily shook her head, "I don't think you're getting enough credit for what you did next."

"Next?" Charlotte searched her mind for what Lily might be referencing. "You mean the orchid?"

"I mean the *orgasm*."

"Oh." Charlotte flashed back to the urgency of the moment. After seeing her name on the wall of maybes, she'd felt an overpowering need to hear the word "yes." So, she'd made Lily scream it.

"The orgasm should be factored in," Lily explained. "My friend Camille, who is very smart, pointed this out." Taking her foot off the bike she stepped an inch closer to Charlotte. The distance between them was now minimal, and Charlotte struggled not to reach out. The animal pull she felt toward Lily wanted off its leash. There was something else at play too. Something even more primal if this were possible. Charlotte felt a claim on Lily. She felt connected in a way that she wanted everyone to know *this woman belonged to her*. The thought was wildly inappropriate but there it was. She struggled to push it from her mind and focus instead on what Lily was saying.

"The first thing you did, after looking behind the tarp, was to come into my bedroom and ravish me." Lily lowered her voice as if sharing a secret. "This was your response to my art. To give me one of the best orgasms of my life." She moved forward another fraction of an inch. Charlotte kept her hands on the bike.

"Yeah, I did do that," she breathed. She'd caught the scent of Lily's light floral perfume. God, what was it? Coupled with the very feminine smell of Lily's perspiration it was making Charlotte swoon. She gripped the bike harder as Lily studied her lips.

"I would have shown you if you'd asked me."

"I'm sorry."

"I forgive you." Leaning in, she brushed their lips together. Charlotte felt something pass between them. She wanted to weep with relief, to pull Lily against her body and revel in her nearness. But the man in the pink tank top was eavesdropping on their conversation, she was sure of it, so she took Lily's hand instead.

"Thank you."

Lily brushed her lips again and then broke out into the familiar blush. "I lured you here today because I couldn't stop thinking about you. I kept drawing your picture. It was getting to be a lot."

Charlotte's eyebrows shot skyward. "Wait, what?" You lured me here?" The notion was preposterous. "And where did you draw my picture?"

"Where do you think?"

"Oh." Charlotte thought of Lily's art room. "The wall or ceiling?"

"Both," Lily said. "I couldn't get you out of my head. I can't."

"So, you lured me to spin class?" Charlotte found this impossible to believe but Lily smiled.

"It honestly wasn't that hard." She shrugged her shoulders. "I knew Geoff was friends with your brother. So, I made a call."

"What are you? The Godfather of spin class?" Charlotte teased. "Bada-boom, bada-bing, it's done?"

"Does that scare you?" Lily's eyes sparkled.

"A little." Charlotte laughed. They were flirting again and it felt wonderful. "It's actually pretty hot."

"I'm glad you think so."

"Why didn't you just text me back?"

"Because..." Lily said and then looked away. "I don't know. Maybe I was punishing you a little bit."

Charlotte thought of the deliberate way Lily had moved on the bike, the provocative striptease. Knowing Lily had done this for her benefit was the hottest thing that had ever happened in her personal universe. "Mission accomplished."

The man in the tank top laughed, confirming Charlotte's suspicions. She lowered her voice. "Do you want to go for a walk or something?"

"Or something?"

"Anything you want."

A few minutes later they were standing outside on a busy Georgetown sidewalk. Lily had changed from spin clothes into a short-sleeved white T-shirt and pair of painter's overalls. She looked adorable and Charlotte wondered if she planned to go home later and work on her art. How would she interpret today, this moment? Did Lily know what happened next in the narrative?

Charlotte caught a glimpse of herself in the gym's plate-glass window. Still in her sodden Bates T-shirt and shorts, she looked like a drowned rat. When Lily asked Charlotte where they should go next the answer flew out of her mouth.

"My house. I want to take these clothes off."

The green eyes darkened a shade. "Who's punishing who now?"

"I didn't mean it that way."

"Too bad," Lily replied and they set off down the street.

Charlotte didn't take the most direct route back to the carriage house. Walking past the poster of Rhianna in the pet store window again would make her angry and she didn't want to spoil the moment. She'd begun to consider Daniel's advice to request a sit-down with Madison, but there was nothing she could do right now, so she put it out of her mind.

It was a glorious fall day. The sidewalks of Georgetown were filled with the unique combination of locals and tourists. Charlotte loved living in a place other people visited. It gave her an odd sense of pride. It was silly, she knew. She'd lived in DC only a few months. She had nothing to do with the stately monuments or world-class museums but she'd begun to claim the city as her own. And it was hers, in a way. If she moved back to Maine tomorrow, she'd always be able to reference that time she'd lived in Georgetown like her grandfather had with his time in the army or Daniel his summer on the Cape. The city had made an impression on Charlotte. She glanced at Lily. Sometimes she felt like a different person.

"You live in your aunt's carriage house?" Lily was asking now. "I had no idea she lived in Georgetown."

"I'm not sure anyone does," Charlotte replied. Heather had promised not to broadcast Wellesley's address if Charlotte did the interview. She'd kept her end of the bargain and could only hope the reporter did the same. "Daniel and I live there together."

She explained to Lily her brother's relentless campaign to win over their reclusive great-aunt.

"In the end, Aunt Wellesley gave us her carriage house, rent free."

"Did she give you a reason?"

Charlotte smiled. "She claims it was easier than recycling his letters. But I get the feeling she was interested in reestablishing some family ties. She hasn't had an easy time."

Lily sighed. "So, I gather. But her art is brilliant."

Charlotte nodded. "I agree. When Daniel got her letter, he became so excited, Mom made me check his pulse."

Lily shook her head. "It was surreal meeting her. I can't believe she's your aunt. I studied her work at NYU."

"Did you go there for both law school and undergrad?" Charlotte asked. There were so many basic things she didn't know about Lily. She had intimate physical knowledge of her but not much else. It was funny. A year ago, she would have found this shocking. Now, she just found it exciting, thrilling, hot.

"Yes." Lily gave her a wistful smile. "I never wanted to leave the city. But I got a job in DC so I had to move."

"Do you like it here?"

"I didn't always, but lately things have been looking up."

"You don't say?" Charlotte smiled.

"I do, actually," Lily countered.

"I've never actually been to New York City," Charlotte admitted and Lily froze comically on the sidewalk. Charlotte started to explain but then screamed when they were nearly mowed down by a boy on a motorized scooter. Pulling Lily out of the way, Charlotte dragged her beneath the awning of a hair salon. Despite the sweaty spin clothes, it felt wonderful to press her body against her. Lily seemed as comfortable in Charlotte's arms as Charlotte was holding her. When she pushed back it was only to look Charlotte in the eye.

"Tell me you're kidding about New York," she said and Charlotte laughed.

"I'm kidding about New York," she said.

"Thank God."

"Except that I'm not. I've really never been."

"But you sing show tunes!" Lily said as if this was some kind of guarantee.

"I know, it's weird," Charlotte agreed. She released her hold on Lily's body but didn't let go of her hand. Lily squeezed her fingers and they continued down the sidewalk. They walked a few paces before Charlotte felt the need to explain herself. "I've had lots of chances to go to New York City. It just never seemed like a priority."

"Oh?" Lily brightened. "Well, what if I invited you to come with me on a romantic weekend?"

"Well, then my priorities would change."

Lily grinned. "Okay, then it's settled. Me. You. New York City."

"Great." Charlotte didn't try to hide her happiness. The day was turning out differently than she'd anticipated. When she'd gotten out of bed that morning all she'd had to look forward to was day-drinking with septuagenarians. Now she was making plans to go to New York City with the most attractive woman she'd ever met. Charlotte was still trying to process the fact that Lily had lured her to the spin studio, that Lily had wanted to see her again. Charlotte was being given another chance. She vowed not to mess it up.

"Tell me more about your art," she said. "Have you ever had a show? Your work is so good."

Lily ducked her head. "Thank you. It's a question I've heard before. Why work as a boring old lawyer when I could possibly pursue a career as an illustrator?"

"Well...*yes*," Charlotte said.

"Insurance, mostly. Law firms have excellent insurance. They have medical, dental, vision." She ticked them off with her fingers. "Oh! And there's a retirement plan too."

"So, it's just about money?"

"Primarily," Lily admitted. "I made a choice to pursue a law career because it's a safer financial proposition. I do art on my own time. Changing career paths now wouldn't be simple.

Competition is tough, and the term *starving artist* doesn't appeal to me."

"Is that why you went to law school?" Charlotte asked.

Lily nodded her head. "Do you think I'm a coward?"

"Not at all. It's just a shame more people don't get to see your work," Charlotte said honestly.

"I could say the same thing about you," Lily challenged. "Why haven't you pursued a singing career? It seems to be an option right now. I saw you on YouTube." She shook her head. "Nurse Nightingale. You sounded so beautiful. I almost cried."

"You saw that?" Charlotte didn't know why she was so surprised. The Nurse Nightingale video was the feel-good story of the week and had had almost two million views. Daniel's video had been lifted from Facebook and gone viral. There was no way to trace the responsible party but it was hard to complain when the video had generated nothing but positive attention for Children's Hospital. The story had been picked up by almost every news service in the country. Donations had come pouring in, all mentioning Nurse Nightingale by name. Charlotte's status had been elevated from saintly to saint. She'd received calls from booking agents and television producers. Some people wanted her to sing to sick children, others wanted to write stories about her. She'd done exactly one interview with Heather Carol to protect Wellesley's privacy and didn't plan to do anymore. Nurse Nightingale was the flavor of the week, she didn't care to make her a new cuisine.

"Yes, I saw it. Geoff emailed me the link and you were amazing. I can't believe it was the same reporter from Quarry. How did that happen?"

"She ambushed me." Charlotte told Lily about the newscaster approaching her in front of the house, about trading her anonymity to protect Wellesley's.

Lily frowned. "That sucks."

"Yeah."

She brushed her thumb across the back of Charlotte's hand. "If it makes any difference, I loved it. I must have watched it a hundred times."

"You're kidding."

"No," Lily said. "And that estimate might be low. I even sent it to my parents."

"Really?"

"I know I told you this before, but you've made a big impression on me."

"You impress me too," Charlotte said. "Your art is amazing. I love your sense of whimsy. Wellesley has mentioned it more than once."

Lily slipped her hand from Charlotte's to cover her eyes. "I still can't believe Wellesley Kincaid was in my apartment. That whole night feels like a dream. If I wasn't able to Google the news coverage, I'd swear someone made it up."

"It happened."

They turned the corner leaving commercial Georgetown. Nineteenth-century townhouses now flowed, one into the next, like a receiving line at a society wedding. Charlotte felt transported by her surroundings and leaned into Lily's arm.

"Not everything that happened that night was on the news," she reminded her.

"The parts not on the news were my favorite," Lily said.

"Mine too." Charlotte hesitated and then asked Lily a question that had been bothering her all week. "Are you worried we let things move too fast?"

Lily tightened her grip on Charlotte's hand. "I don't think we had a choice. At least I didn't have a choice." She corrected herself. "Being with you makes me feel very…" She paused seeming to search for the perfect word. "Physical."

"Is that a bad thing?" Charlotte asked, suddenly very concerned. Maybe Lily didn't like feeling out of control. Maybe that's why she hadn't returned Charlotte's texts and had given her orchid to the cleaning lady. Just because her body was responding to Charlotte didn't mean she had to like it.

"I don't think so." Lily stopped on the sidewalk and turned to face her. "We have a spark. Like Wellesley said, it's rare. How can that be a bad thing?"

"I don't think it is," Charlotte said, relieved. Lily was making a case for the relationship. This was definitely not a bad thing. There were other questions Charlotte wanted to ask Lily. Did she regret their night of passion? Was she interested in moving forward? And, God in heaven, what was the name of her perfume? But the scientist inside Charlotte craved data, so she dug deeper. "Have you ever felt like this before?"

"Twice," Lily admitted. "In high school I had a crazy connection with a girl on my softball team. Her name was Katie. For three years we buzzed around each other like manic bees. Everyone teased us about it and I finally kissed her on prom night. We made out for two hours in the back of my parents' van." Lily fanned herself with her free hand. "I thought I'd died and gone to heaven."

Charlotte grinned. Her first year with Madison had been similar. The energy surrounding their most basic interactions had been electric, all-consuming. "Sounds hot."

"*It was.* Until later that night when she completely freaked out. We didn't speak again until after college."

"She freaked out that same night?"

"Yes."

"Ouch."

"Right?"

"Her loss."

Lily smiled. "I like to think so."

"Was the second time your recent ex?"

"Yes." Lily blew out a breath. "Her name was Mia and I was completely in love with her. She was a partner at Walker and Jenkins, my supervisor actually, so we had to keep everything secret. Somehow that made it all more intense."

"What happened?"

"Mia had serious commitment issues." Lily shuddered. "The hardest part was I thought she'd moved past them. She really had me fooled. When we finally went public, she decided we should both leave Walker and Jenkins. It was important to her we both make a fresh start."

"Did you think about becoming an illustrator?" Charlotte asked.

"No, that was never a consideration. Mia found me a job at another firm and she went in-house at Gowear." Lily smiled

ruefully. "It was great for a while. We moved in together. She bought me a ring. I even met her family."

"That sounds pretty serious," Charlotte said wondering what went wrong.

"I thought so too," Lily said. "Then two months before the wedding I caught her in our bed with an old girlfriend." She swallowed hard. "I packed a bag and she didn't try to talk me out of it."

"That was it?"

"Pretty much. Of course, there was lots of emotional texting and a few sessions of awkward breakup sex. You know how that goes."

Charlotte flashed to Madison storming the pillow wall in Aunt Wellesley's guesthouse. "I do."

"It took me a long time to get over it," Lily went on. "I was so depressed I had to take a leave of absence from my new firm and wound up getting fired."

"No."

"Yep. I was lucky Walker and Jenkins rehired me. It was Camille who kept the door open. She actually dated Mia before I did, so she had a unique perspective on my breakdown."

Charlotte was stunned. "Not the same Camille who is married to Hannah."

"Yes. DC is a small town."

"Daniel just said the exact same thing."

"Your brother's a quick study."

"Has anyone ever told you that Camille kind of looks like you? I mean you're much prettier, but she could be your sister."

Lily grimaced. "Believe me. Our resemblance is lost on no one. Turned out Mia has a type. The woman I found her in bed with could have been our third sister."

"Ouch."

"It was a blow. The art room saved me to a degree. But I completely lost myself for a while. For the last two years I've given it most of my free time. Mia really messed me up."

"Mia sounds like an idiot."

"Except that she isn't," Lily said, emphasizing the last word. "Mia's actually quite brilliant. She's one of the top patent attorneys in the country."

"If there was a brain in her head, she'd be the one holding your hand right now." Charlotte raised Lily's hand to her mouth and kissed it.

"Thank you," Lily said softly. "How about you?" She held Charlotte's eyes. "How many times have you felt like...this?"

Charlotte wagged a finger between them. "You mean *the bliss* of this?"

Lily blushed. "Yes, the bliss of this. Has it ever happened to you?"

"This is the second time," Charlotte admitted but didn't elaborate. Lily wasn't to be put off.

"Did you love her?"

"I thought so at the time. But it was college, and she was my first girlfriend. Maybe it was more about sex."

"What was her name?"

"Madison." Charlotte exhaled. Eventually she'd have to tell Lily about the lingering complications involving the bakery, but now didn't seem like a good time. Was there ever a good time to tell a new girlfriend that your ex had named a dessert after your vagina and sold it to a national distributor? They'd just gotten past the snooping incident. Charlotte didn't want to drive another wedge between them. She didn't want anything between them at all.

Fortunately, Lily didn't push the subject. "Do you think we're more than just a physical connection?"

"Maybe." Charlotte couldn't resist teasing her.

"Maybe?" Lily sounded worried.

"I'd like to do some proper research." Charlotte squeezed her hand.

Lily frowned. "Would that require taking a break from sex?"

"No," Charlotte said quickly. "What would be the point of that? It's not like I can forget the way you look naked."

"No way in heaven." Lily drew the last word out and Charlotte grinned. It seemed Lily didn't want to stop having sex either.

They'd arrived at Wellesley's house. The cottage was only yards away. Charlotte's bed a few feet further. "What do you think we should do?" She smiled down at Lily.

"Didn't you just say something about research?" Lily said and pulled her inside.

CHAPTER SEVENTEEN

Cover Up

Sunlight streamed through Charlotte's bedroom window, warming her naked skin. Lily, also naked, was sitting next to her on the bed. There was a sketchbook in her lap and a thoughtful look on her face. Pen poised, she considered Charlotte.

"I want you propped against the pillows with your arms above your head," she said and Charlotte smiled. In the last two months Lily had sketched her many times. In the beginning she'd been shy about suggesting poses. This was no longer an issue. Now she asked Charlotte to sit for her anywhere, anytime. Daniel called it Green-Eggs-and-Ham posing. In the car. At the bar. With a guitar.

"Like this?" Charlotte leaned back onto the bed and positioned her arms as Lily had requested. She felt her breasts lift and separate and knew they were being displayed to their best advantage. The thought made her nipples harden and a dull throb began in her clit. Art as foreplay. It was a totally new concept for Charlotte. But the eroticism of lying exposed before Lily was undeniable.

"Perfect," Lily said and began to draw. Her eyes flashed with arousal making Charlotte's clit pulse even harder. She wondered how long Lily would last this time. She rarely made it past a rudimentary outline of Charlotte's naked form before she dropped the pen and pounced. And Charlotte was always ready for her. *Like now.* She allowed her legs to fall slightly apart and was rewarded with a hitch in Lily's breath.

"You're going to pay for that," she said so quietly it was as if she was talking to herself.

But Charlotte heard every word. "I'll look forward to it," she said and opened her legs wider.

There would be time for sketching later. *Oodles of time.* Charlotte wanted Lily now. She wanted her on the bed, fully spread. She wanted her legs apart, ditch the art. To Charlotte's disappointment, Lily kept drawing. She heard the scratches against the paper and imagined they were being made on her skin. Her center was now throbbing wildly. She was desperate for Lily to touch her. Arching her back, she pushed her aching nipples forward and imagined Lily pulling one into her mouth.

"Stop that," Lily hissed. Her hand continued to move across the paper at a furious pace. Charlotte closed her eyes but it was of no use. Her need was simply too great.

"Lily," she said softly and that was all it took. Lily tossed the sketchpad to the floor, and climbed up next to Charlotte on the bed. Pressing the hard muscle of her thigh against her pussy, she whispered into her ear.

"Tell me what you want."

"Fuck me," Charlotte begged her. "Please. Be inside me." The pressure of Lily's leg was exquisite. But it wasn't enough. Impatient with need Charlotte cupped Lily's ass and begin to move against her.

"I've got you, baby," Lily cooed. The endearment warmed Charlotte almost as much as the tip of Lily's tongue now circling her ear. She bucked against her leg.

"God, you're so close," Lily said. Hours of research had given her unique insight into Charlotte's personal rhythms. Sliding a hand between them, she parted Charlotte's slit and slipped two fingers inside. A few firm thrusts were enough. Charlotte's muscles tensed and she exploded, spasms of pleasure rocking her body like a seismic shift. Lily didn't stop but continued to move inside her, the heel of her hand tapping Charlotte's clit like a punctuation mark at the end of each thrust. It was perfect, this woman, this moment. Intensifying everything was Charlotte's awareness of it all. Another orgasm began to build and Charlotte spread her legs wider, boldly asking for more. Lily obliged, fucking Charlotte even harder.

"Oh, Lily, yes!" Charlotte cried as a second orgasm ripped through her. She knew she was being loud, but didn't worry. Daniel was in Portland with Geoffrey, and the occupants of the main house all needed hearing aids but were too vain to wear them.

"Stop, you've got to stop," Charlotte said when she was finally able to catch her breath.

Lily pressed her palm down on Charlotte's clit. "Are you sure?"

Charlotte grabbed Lily's wrist as residual spasms rocked her body. "Give me five minutes?"

"How about four?"

"Okay, four." Charlotte pulled Lily into a deep kiss. Tears pricked the back of her eyes. She didn't know exactly when it had happened, but she'd fallen in love. There was no other way to explain the feelings she was having. Charlotte thought of Lily constantly. When they were apart, which was seldom as they spent every free moment together, she craved her presence like an addictive substance. It helped to understand the science behind physical attraction but you could only intellectualize things so far. Lily made Charlotte feel vital, special. There was something in the way she looked at her that stirred her blood. Charlotte hadn't said the words out loud yet because she didn't want to scare anyone, herself included, but it was always on the tip of her tongue. So, she kissed Lily. A lot.

"So good," Lily murmured against her mouth, and Charlotte flipped their positions so she was on top. She wasn't ready for the morning to be over. It didn't matter how many times she made love to Lily, Charlotte always wanted more. On the floor. Against the door. At the store.

They languished in bed for another hour before getting up to dress for brunch. Lily had become a fixture at Wellesley's Sunday morning get-togethers. Charlotte was proud of the way she'd seamlessly blended into her aunt's sophisticated-friend group. Conversant in art, law, and politics, Lily could always be counted on to have an informed opinion on the topic *du jour*. Charlotte often had no idea what they were talking about and had to Google the subject later.

Last month, seasonal temperatures had forced the brunch inside. No one had complained as Wellesley hosted the gathering in her library, a magnificent room with floor-to-ceiling bookshelves and eclectic *objet d'art* from all over the world. Undeniably the heart of the house, just being in the space made Charlotte feel smart.

This morning Stefano had prepared salmon and avocado tartines. He and Jacob had already eaten and were upstairs packing for their return to Miami. Charlotte would have a hard time saying goodbye to the older gentlemen but hoped to visit them with Lily after Christmas. Holidays were tricky at the hospital, but you never knew. Laura Minor had allowed her nursing staff to select a guaranteed day off of either Thanksgiving or Christmas, but you had to pick one. Charlotte had chosen to go home for Christmas.

It was a good thing, as Thanksgiving was three weeks away and two days ago Madison had suddenly started texting Charlotte again. It was bizarre. Charlotte had read the first ten messages, mostly stuff about the bakery, and then blocked the number. She couldn't have Madison blowing up her phone. It was annoying, not to mention risky, as Lily still knew next to nothing about the Madness. Charlotte hoped to ask Daniel about it later in the day when he returned. He and Geoffrey had gone home to collect his winter wardrobe and meet Sven, whom Sarah had invited to move in with her. It was difficult to imagine their mother dating someone, much less cohabiting.

But stranger things had happened, and recently. Daniel's romance with Geoffrey had taken off like a house on fire. Her brother was a changed man. Charlotte had never seen him so deferential. Wellesley joked that Geoffrey was orange juice to Daniel's vodka. And it was true. Wholesome and sweet, Geoffrey tempered Daniel's spirit.

Yesterday the duo was supposed to have had lunch with Madison's parents at their yacht club in Portland. Daniel knew the Hagens quite well. The last year of college, he'd lived with Charlotte and Madison, and struck up a friendship with Felix, Madison's father. The two were often the only men in the room and had bonded over a love of Cuban cigars. Daniel hadn't known he loved Cuban cigars until Felix had offered him one from the Tiffany case he kept in his breast pocket, but that was part of the appeal. The Hagens were fabulously wealthy. Sponsorship of the Human Left dinner, less than two weeks away, would be only a tiny line item in their annual philanthropy, a blip. Charlotte was no longer concerned that they would fail to honor their donation, just what Madison might do to make them earn it. Perhaps Daniel had heard something at lunch that explained her recent behavior.

Lily had shared with Charlotte the brutal details of her broken engagement to Mia and the lingering depression. So far, the only thing Lily knew about Madison was that she was Charlotte's college girlfriend. Charlotte hadn't even told her about the dog biscuits, much less the odious Charlie Pies. Every time Charlotte tried to frame the story her tongue twisted into knots. It was a huge problem. The more time that passed the bigger the secret felt. Daniel likened the information to the Yellowstone volcano. When it finally blew, it was likely to be catastrophic.

Charlotte put two tartines on her plate and considered the rest of the spread. This morning there were more food options than guests. She and Lily had joined Wellesley and Sid to form an intimate group of four. It was unclear if Sid had spent the night in Wellesley's bedroom or arrived earlier in his car. Immaculate in wool slacks and a crisp button-down shirt, his clothing did nothing to give him away. Thankfully, this was not information Charlotte required.

She claimed a small bunch of grapes and eyed a sausage link. Sex was hungry work and she hoped to get in more after brunch. Later in the day she was taking Lily to the hospital for the first time. She'd reconciled the public demand for Nurse Nightingale by agreeing to perform a weekly concert in the first-floor atrium. Charlotte still visited individual rooms—Laura Minor was not shy about calling her in for hard cases—but the YouTube video had added a fundraising potential that forced her to allow a greater audience. The atrium provided this opportunity. Every Sunday afternoon at four, patients and parents, doctors and staff gathered to hear Charlotte sing. She didn't relish the personal exposure, but the donations provided housing for qualified families who'd come to DC to receive treatment for their children. If Nurse Nightingale stopped, so did the cash.

"Hungry this morning, *Harlot*?"

She was surprised to hear Daniel's voice from the entrance hall. Dressed in a vintage Ralph Lauren blazer with leather patches on the sleeves, he looked like a model for a cologne ad. Charlotte was willing to bet that he smelled good too. Scratch and sniff, her brother was groomed down to his chiseled bone structure. Next to him, Geoffrey was equally splendid wearing an equally marvelous jacket. Wellesley rose to welcome the newcomers while Charlotte added several slices of kiwi fruit and a piece of prosciutto to her plate.

"This is unexpected. When did you get back from Maine?" Wellesley air-kissed Daniel's cheeks and then Geoffrey's.

"We flew in two hours ago," Daniel said. There was an edge to his voice that put Charlotte on immediate alert. Something was bothering him. His next sentence was going to be cutting. Gauging from the way he was looking at Charlotte, it would be at her expense.

"We stopped by the carriage house first. But Charlotte and Lily were watching horror movies so we went to Geoffrey's instead."

Charlotte searched her brain for the reference. What the hell was he talking about? They hadn't been watching movies. There wasn't even a television in the house. And why was he mad at her? Geoffrey walked over to the sideboard that served as a makeshift buffet. Picking up a plate, he whispered in her ear, "Ignore him."

Wellesley was nodding at Lily. "Horror movies on Sunday morning? How beautifully sacrilegious."

"Horror or gore?" Sid wanted to know. He sat angled next to Lily on the couch, his long body like a question mark. If Wellesley showed any interest in a subject, he was all over it like a fitted sheet. Daniel had begun calling him the holla-back boyfriend. "Guillermo del Toro has really raised the bar. Did you know he started his career as a makeup artist?"

"I didn't," Lily said. She looked to Charlotte for help.

"We weren't watching horror movies," Charlotte said firmly.

Daniel feigned shock and put a hand to his hip. "Then why all the screaming? I'm sure I heard screaming."

Wellesley's eyes narrowed with understanding and she smiled knowingly at Charlotte. "I enjoy a dab of horror in the morning myself."

Lily blushed maroon while Sid prattled on oblivious. "*Pan's Labyrinth* was truly frightening. I closed my eyes during the violent bits. But even that wasn't enough. The noises were also terrifying. I had to cover my ears too." He bobbed his endless neck. "I don't know how you girls stomach it."

"I've never seen the film," Charlotte told him politely and sat down next to Lily on the couch.

Sid didn't hide his dismay. "But it won the Oscar *and* the Goya."

"We'll put it on the list," Lily said and took Charlotte's hand.

Wellesley was quizzing Daniel. "How was the home visit? Did Sarah fall in love with Geoffrey too?"

"She did, indeed," Daniel said. "I thought Sven was going to challenge him to a dual."

Geoffrey flashed his perfect teeth. "They were both very nice." Finished at the buffet, he sat down in a chair and crossed his feet at the ankles. The man was so beautiful he was almost too hard to look at. Charlotte and Lily had a joke that he was actually a hologram.

"How is Sarah?" Wellesley asked. "Will she be in town for the gala? I'd love to see her again."

"No." Daniel looked at Wellesley as if she'd just suggested he hunt and kill a baby seal. "Next year maybe. But I have too much on my plate right now to add another bite." Charlotte was marginally disappointed her mother wasn't coming but largely shared Daniel's perspective. Being responsible for Sarah and Sven at the gala would force her to focus on something other than Lily. Charlotte felt much closer to Sarah after their heart-to-heart and looked forward to seeing her at Christmas, but she wasn't ready for their worlds to collide. Not yet. Maine felt far away, and Charlotte was happy to keep it that way.

Geoff dipped his head adorably. "My parents are coming, Ms. Kincaid. They're huge fans of yours. When I told them I'd met you, they accused me of lying." He looked so earnest Charlotte wanted to hug him.

"Welly, please," she said her eyes resting easy on his face.

Geoffrey smiled but didn't commit.

"Tell us about your family, Geoff," Sid cut in. The old mantis appeared to be jealous of Wellesley's attention. "What does your father do? Does your mother work?" Daniel shot Charlotte an incredulous look but kept silent. Alienate the museum director and possibly jeopardize the gala. Fortunately, Geoffrey's parents could more than fend for themselves, even if it was in absentia.

"They met in school," Geoffrey offered. "Dad's an orthopedist and Mom's an obstetrician. They've both been to Quarry." Adroitly he pivoted the attention back to Sid. "Mom says it's her new favorite gallery. And that's saying something. I've been at the Human Left six years and this is the first time they've bought tickets to the gala."

Sid beamed. "How are sales going?"

"Ask the coordinator." Geoffrey nudged Daniel. "He's done an amazing job."

"Did you sell out?" Charlotte asked her brother. It had been a while since she'd checked in on the event but she assumed things were on schedule. Daniel was a master tactician, aware of every weapon at his command. The Human Left Gala already existed in his head as a completed picture. Right now, he was just putting things into place. If he needed Charlotte's help, he would ask for it.

"Almost," he said, and he gave her a look she couldn't read. "We filled another table last night."

"Congratulations."

"Should be interesting," he said, the look still unreadable.

"Tell them the latest, baby." Geoffrey raised an eyebrow.

"Bono canceled."

"What?"

"Oh, my God!"

"I thought it was a done deal."

The group reacted with appropriate shock. It was a huge blow. Bono was the main draw of the event. It had to be why Daniel was acting strangely.

"He has tissue buildup on his larynx," Geoffrey explained.

"Oh, nodes!" Charlotte clutched at her throat.

"Oh, yes."

"They're treatable but he can't perform. Thankfully he's got friends in high places."

"Who's higher than Bono?" Lily asked.

Daniel scratched his chin. "Okay, not higher, but definitely on the same plane. I think hers might be a Lear."

"Is it Celine?" Sid clapped his huge hands together. "I met her once at a dinner party. What a wonderful wit."

"Bigger."

"Beyoncé?" Lily guessed.

"Good guess, but no."

"Gaga?"

He pointed to the ceiling and Wellesley gasped. "Streisand?"

Daniel didn't deny it. There was a moment of stunned silence and then everyone started talking at once.

"When did this happen?"

"How many songs?"

"Who talked her into it?"

"It was all Bono," Daniel explained. "He orchestrated a rich-person favor swap. Barbra's singing at our benefit and he's playing her great-nephew's bar mitzvah in the spring." He shot Geoffrey a look. "I'm trying to score us an invite."

"La Barbra." Wellesley looked intent. "I'll look forward to meeting her. Well done, Bono."

Daniel put his plate down in shock. "You're coming?"

"I had no idea you were entertaining the idea," Sid said and Wellesley huffed out a breath.

"Well, I'm not missing Streisand." She shook her head. "I blew my chance to see her live with Judy Garland in nineteen sixty-three. I swore if I got the opportunity again, I wouldn't pass it up."

"How did you blow it?" Geoffrey asked politely while Daniel started pacing the floor.

"Not it, darling, *him.*" She blinked her big blue eyes. "My husband caught me with the gardener. We had a huge fight and missed the concert."

"I see how that might have been an issue." Geoffrey gulped while Lily stifled a giggle. Daniel was parsing logistics.

"Aren't you worried about being recognized?" He stopped pacing and stood in front of her.

"I'm not," she said. "The CBD tincture is miraculous. I find I care less and less."

He bit his lip. "Yes, but it may be a logistical nightmare *for me* if other people know you're there. Remember what happened last time?"

"What if I'm not recognized?" Wellesley said. She rose from the couch and walked over to an ornate trunk sitting beneath a map of ancient Arabia. Charlotte had never noticed it before but this was not surprising. It would take years to examine everything interesting in Wellesley's library. Lifting the lid, Wellesley reached in and pulled out an armful of wigs.

Daniel gasped. "What are those?"

"What do they look like?"

"You're coming to the gala incognito?"

"Incognita," Wellesley corrected him.

Lily squeezed Charlotte's fingers. "I love your family," she whispered in her ear.

Charlotte closed her eyes. *And I love you.*

Daniel leapt from the couch. Food forgotten, he pounced on the trunk. Charlotte knew from a lifetime of experience that he loved nothing more than dressing up a human doll. She was glad not to be his model today.

"Where did you get a trunk full of wigs?" He stroked an auburn-colored pageboy.

"Breast cancer," Wellesley said, matter-of-fact. She ran her fingers through the soft strands of the platinum-blond bob she'd taken from the pile. "I gained two material things from the Big C. A very expensive wig collection and a morose self-portrait. Are you familiar with *Lady in the Shadows*?"

"Is she still in Spain?" Sid wanted to know. His petulance made Charlotte wonder if he'd been outbid for the piece.

"Yes," Wellesley said. She put the wig on. "What do you think?"

"Too Carol Channing," Daniel said firmly. "Try this one." He handed Wellesley the auburn wig and gave the blond bob to Geoffrey. "I want to see Geoff in the platinum."

"I'm not wearing your aunt's wig," Geoffrey was definite about this.

But Wellesley let out such a delighted squeal that he had no choice. Soon they were all trying on wigs. Charlotte marveled at how much different hair changed one's appearance. Sid in a black shoulder-length number looked like a decrepit rock star while Lily in the same piece looked like Cleopatra. Geoffrey was full-on Doris Day in the blond bob. Charlotte felt her best look was the auburn pageboy. Once the wig was in place she refused to give it up, no matter how many times Sid asked to have a turn.

In the end it was decided that Wellesley would attend the gala in a glossy Jackie Kennedy wig. The bangs framed her face nicely and made her nearly unrecognizable. Add a pair of tinted Versace glasses and she was easily Sid's fictional sister Jeanette, a rich widow from Brooklyn. When Jacob and Stefano entered the library to say goodbye, the group was discussing Jeanette's personal design aesthetic. Everyone was wearing a wig.

"I see you let Daniel mix the martinis again," Jacob observed as Stefano bent to examine the trunk.

"Where did you find these?" he asked reverently. He picked up a silk turban with a fringe of blond bangs and pulled it onto his head.

"They've been right here the whole time," Wellesley said as if everyone kept a chest full of wigs in the library. "Allow me." She motioned for Stefano to move closer.

"I forgot you had them." Stefano let Wellesley make adjustments to the turban then turned to face Jacob. "Remember these?"

Jacob nodded. Behind his glasses, his eyes looked misty. "I do."

Wellesley put her hand on Stefano's shoulder. "The boys moved in here to look after me."

"I hadn't realized," Charlotte said, marveling at the sudden emotion in the room.

"Once I recovered, I insisted they stay."

"We were having so much fun," Stefano mused.

"So, the party just continued."

"How long ago was that?" Charlotte asked.

"Ten years," Jacob said without hesitation.

"Yes," Wellesley said fondly, looking at the two older men. "I told you two good things had come out of my cancer. I should have said four."

CHAPTER EIGHTEEN

Nurse Nightingale

What's going on?

Charlotte sent Daniel the text and then slid the phone into the pocket of her jeans. Lily was in the bathroom. Until Charlotte knew what was bothering her brother, it was better to keep her suspicions to herself. But she was worried. All through brunch he'd given her strange signals. It might be a hangnail, or it might be Barbra fucking Streisand. Something was bothering him. Until he texted Charlotte back, there was no way of knowing. Her phone buzzed and she checked the screen.

napping

Really? Daniel knew she was referencing his brunch behavior. The faces he'd made at her between bites of tartine had been comical. There was something he wasn't telling her, something important.

you were acting weird at brunch
wtf is going on?

His one-word response made her cringe.

Madness.

Fuck. Ignoring her texts had been a mistake.

what did she do?

Charlotte hoped the drama didn't involve the gala. But if Madness was indeed upon them, it could be anything. She slipped the phone into her pocket. Now was not the time to deal with it. Lily would be back from the bathroom any second. A voice tickled her ear.

"Nervous about performing?"

Like now.

"Not at all."

Lily's lips were covered in a fresh coat of gloss that smelled like honey. Charlotte wanted to taste it but kept herself in check.

"Do you ever get nervous?" Lily gave her a sweet smile.

"Not singing, no." What made Charlotte nervous were cryptic texts involving her ex-girlfriend. Until she knew what Madison was up to, she would exist in a state of mild panic. The phone buzzed again. Shit. The answer might be in her pocket right now.

"Never?"

"Middle school," Charlotte said and told Lily the story of shaking so badly during a performance of *Into the Woods* she'd knocked over a fake tree. She didn't tell Lily about the Madness. The story felt too big to spring on her in a hospital lounge. But she needed to tell Lily about her ex, and soon.

"Did it hit anybody?" Lily asked and Charlotte nodded, trying to stay in the conversation.

"It fell on Tommy Clohessy. Took him down too."

"Oh no!"

"Yeah, but he was playing the wolf so everyone cheered."

"That's lucky."

"It was." Charlotte nodded. She was still lucky, extremely lucky. There was still time to tell Lily the whole embarrassing truth about Madison. Waiting had been a huge mistake, one Charlotte wished she could correct. But she'd been loath to infect a single moment of precious Lily time discussing her nightmare ex-girlfriend. Floating above the Madness on a love balloon, Charlotte had allowed herself the indulgence of ignoring it. The phone buzzed again. Shit.

"Ten-minute warning, Charlotte." Ethan knocked lightly on the door. The concerts were arranged through the hospital programs person, but the lanky security guard had inserted himself into the setup. He also continued to distribute Madison's weekly goodies to the long-term care ward. Laura Minor called him Charlotte's groupie.

"It's a big crowd today. The kids are really excited," he said and gave his horsey laugh.

"I hope I don't disappoint them," Charlotte replied and he frowned as if the notion were preposterous.

"You won't!" His Adam's apple bobbed earnestly. When Charlotte had first suggested Ethan might have a crush on her she'd been joking. Now she wasn't so sure.

"This is my girlfriend, Lily," she told him carefully. If Charlotte couldn't be upfront about the Madness of her past, she'd take the present head-on. Ethan's face fell, but Lily inflated beside her.

"Nice to meet you, Ethan." She took the security guard's hand.

"You too," he said, recovering nicely. "Your um, Charlotte is a star around here."

Lily smiled. "She's a star with me too. I can't wait to hear her sing."

"You've never heard her sing?" he said and his eyes narrowed a fraction. "I try not to miss a performance."

Lily didn't let the challenge go unchecked. "Oh, I've seen her sing," she said and winked at him. "I've just never seen Nurse Nightingale perform."

"Oh. Well." Ethan coughed into his hand. "It's not just the singing that makes Nurse Nightingale special. Her donations make a huge impact."

"The money generated from the YouTube video has been incredible," Lily agreed.

"Yes, but she also donates candy, candles, cookies, popcorn, socks…" His eyes gleamed as he ticked off the list of Madison's gift subscriptions. "And lots of other cool stuff. Once a week it's like Christmas morning. And I get to play Santa."

"Really?" Lily gave Charlotte a confused look.

"It's not a big deal," Charlotte said. The phone buzzed in her pocket again. Shit.

"I can't wait to hear all about it," Lily replied.

Ethan seemed worried. He made an elaborate show of checking his watch. "See you in eight minutes?"

"Sure," Charlotte said, and he all but ran from the room.

Left alone with Lily, she took the opportunity to steal a kiss. Pressing her lips to Lily's she tried her best to convey what she was feeling. If Madness truly presented itself, Charlotte wanted Lily to know how she felt, where she stood. Lily seemed to get this, and gave back in equal measure. She slipped her tongue into Charlotte's mouth stoking the embers still burning from earlier in the day. Or perhaps the fire had never gone out. Charlotte couldn't be sure. Every time she tried to access the heat it was available. They kissed until the need for air made it necessary to pull away. Gasping, Lily rested her forehead against Charlotte's.

"We should stop."

"Yeah," Charlotte agreed but then kissed her again with more urgency.

Lily smiled against Charlotte's mouth. "I'm serious. We should stop. I'd hate for Ethan to walk back in. Pretty sure we just ruined his day."

"Oh, Ethan." Charlotte didn't want to think about the security guard right now. Nor did she want to think about Daniel's texts or her crazy ex-girlfriend in Maine. Charlotte only wanted to focus on what was right in front of her. The woman in her arms meant everything. But she needed to be honest.

"The poor guy is so into you."

"Yeah. He really is."

Lily laughed and Charlotte's heart swelled. The banter between them was so much fun. The relationship felt shiny and full of possibilities. She dreaded the conversation ahead.

"For the record, I think he's got great taste," Lily said.

"But you're the only one who gets to taste me," Charlotte teased and Lily's eyes lit with interest.

"Just how long is this concert going to take?"

Charlotte snorted. "I thought you couldn't wait to hear me sing!"

"I can't." Lily stole another kiss. "But I'm also looking forward to the encore."

Charlotte's phone buzzed again. Shit.

"Your phone is blowing up." Lily sat back.

"Daniel drama," Charlotte said. It wasn't the whole truth, but it wasn't a lie either. Letting go of Lily's fingers, she slid her hand into her pocket but made no move to remove the phone.

"Aren't you going to check it?" Lily asked.

"Do you think I should?"

"He was acting strange at brunch."

"Okay, yeah." Charlotte pulled out her phone and tapped the screen. She loved that Lily knew Daniel well enough to gauge his moods but hated to address this now. Holding her breath, she thumbed through the scroll. Shit. Shit. Shit.

Madness coming to gala with a date

RSVP'd on Felix's table

Please advise

"Everything okay?" Lily asked after a few moments. "Not problems with the gala, I hope." Her pretty face was furrowed in concern. Charlotte wanted to reach out and swipe the crease from her forehead. But she couldn't. The news she was about to deliver was only going to make things worse. She searched for the right words.

"There are no logistical problems with the gala," she said.

Lily picked up on the semantics immediately. "So, other types of problems?"

Charlotte played with the fabric at the corner of her jacket. "Can we sit down for a second? There's something I need to talk to you about."

"That sounds ominous." Lily gave a nervous laugh. When Charlotte didn't respond she looked worried. "You're scaring me."

"I'm sorry." Charlotte led Lily to a pair of chairs by the window. How much of the story should she share? Was it better to tell it all right now, or let it go in pieces? Eventually she'd have to cough up every sordid morsel of Charlie Pie but maybe it all didn't have to come out at the same time. Charlotte took a deep breath and decided to wing it. "Remember I told you that I had a girlfriend in college?"

Lily stiffened. "You mean Madison? Your first love? The relationship that was mostly about sex?"

"Yeah...That's right." They'd only spoken about Madison once or twice, but apparently Lily had been paying attention. "I never told you this, but her family owns the company sponsoring the gala."

"Madison's family owns Hagen's Shipping?"

"Yes, Daniel just got their RSVPs and Madison's name is on the list. She's coming with a date."

"Okay," Lily said slowly. She opened her mouth as if to continue her thought but then closed it again.

Charlotte rushed to fill the silence. "I didn't know about it until today. I would have said something. I promise."

Lily studied her. "I'm a little confused. Why do you care? If Madison is just someone you dated in college, why does it matter if she brings a date to the gala?" Her voice took on an edge. "Why would that bother you? Unless there's more to it." She gave Charlotte a look that almost stopped her heart.

"No!" Charlotte reacted with surprising ferocity. Grabbing Lily by the forearms, she stared into her eyes. There was no plan to make a formal declaration, here, in a vacant hospital lounge on a Sunday morning but out it came. "I'm in love with you, Lily. Don't you know that? Can't you feel it? I love you." She pressed Lily's hand to her chest. "I love you."

Lily looked surprised but then began to smile. "I do know it," she said and brushed her lips against Charlotte's. "I can feel it every time you look at me. And I love you, too." They kissed for a heated moment before she pulled away. "But loving me doesn't explain why you're worried about Madison coming to the gala. Can you explain that?"

Charlotte swallowed hard. Lily's honey-flavored lip gloss was smeared beneath her mouth. She wanted to kiss it away, stay in the moment, but it was time to come clean. "I told you we dated in college."

"Right."

"We also dated after college."

"Okay, when did you break up, *exactly?*"

Charlotte sighed. This was the part she'd been dreading. "The first time was two years ago."

"And the last?"

Charlotte tried to remember the date of the first softball game. "I'm not sure exactly. Four months?"

Lily bristled. "You're asking me?" The green eyes flashed and Charlotte stroked her arm.

"No, God no," she implored. She couldn't bear to see the hurt look on Lily's face, but it was important to tell the truth. "Madison had a hard time accepting our breakup. She was always looking for ways to bring us back together. When I still lived in Portland, she had a way of finding me out at clubs, seducing me. Sometimes she'd just come over to my house in the middle of the night and crawl into bed with me. I'd feel guilty afterward, we'd get back together for a week or so and then the cycle would start all over again. It was a problem and one of the reasons I moved. It was easier than avoiding her."

Lily was incredulous. "You moved to DC to get away from an ex-girlfriend?"

"It wasn't the only reason." Charlotte ran a hand nervously through her hair. "I also had a great job offer and a free place to stay, but yes, it was a major factor. I broke it off for good the night you kissed me after the softball game." She lowered her voice. "I haven't spoken with her since. That's how I know it was about four months ago."

"And now she's coming to the gala," Lily said this almost to herself but Charlotte nodded.

"Daniel can't exactly turn her away."

"No, he can't," Lily agreed and then smiled like she'd just heard something funny.

Charlotte was confused. "Why are you smiling?"

"Because you have a stalker," Lily said and then laughed out loud.

"Madison's not a stalker, she's..."

"An ex-girlfriend who's still obsessed with you? It's the same thing and frankly I'm relieved."

"Why would that make you happy?"

Lily threw her hands in the air. "Something had to be wrong with you. I've been trying to figure it out what it is. I mean you are kind and beautiful, smart and generous." She ticked off Charlotte's attributes. "You're a fantastic softball player, a dedicated sister, niece, and nurse. You give me earth-shattering orgasms. Every. Damn. Day. Oh! And you sing to sick children in your spare time. I thought you were perfect." She made a face. "It was starting to scare me."

Charlotte was stunned. "So, you're not mad?"

Lily took Charlotte's hand. "Do you still love her?"

"No way. I'm not sure I ever did. Not in the way I love you."

"Then there's nothing to worry about." Lily kissed Charlotte on the nose and then on each eyelid. The gesture was so sweet it made Charlotte want to cry.

"I'm not sure about that," she said and let her voice fall away. How much more of the Madness should she tell Lily? She still didn't know about Charlotte's cunni-lingering association with Madsnax Bakery and the Charlie Pie. She didn't know about Rhi-Treats either. Perhaps the revelations were better left for another time. Lily made the decision for her.

"We'll talk about it later," she said. "You can tell me everything, confess all your sins."

Charlotte searched her eyes and found only trust. "Are you sure?"

"Don't you have a concert in three minutes?"

They walked down a short hallway and turned a corner. Just off the elevator lobby was the performance room. Outside, an oversized dry-erase board advertised upcoming events. Today, written large were the words "Nurse Nightingale," followed by hearts and numerous exclamation points.

"Ethan's been busy."

Lily squeezed Charlotte's hand. Their conversation had been a big step forward. Charlotte had confessed her love for Lily and Lily had responded in kind. They loved each other. It was official. Anxiety concerning Madison faded behind the brilliance of the declaration. There were still things to talk about but they could do that later. Right now, it was time to sing.

CHAPTER NINETEEN

Madness

Precious LaRue opened the door of the black Cadillac SUV and stood back to allow Lily and Charlotte to exit. When the security director had learned Wellesley was attending the Human Left Gala, she'd insisted on acting as chauffeur. It might be possible to disguise the famous artist in a Jackie Kennedy wig and Versace glasses, but there was no dressing down a vintage Saab. Both had factored heavily in the viral tweet that had summoned the masses and necessitated a backroad getaway. Precious did not want a repeat performance. And if there were any mishaps, she would be the driver.

"Thank you, Precious." Wellesley stepped out of the SUV and kissed the security guard on both cheeks.

"No problem, Jeanette," Precious said. She didn't crack a smile but Wellesley beamed.

Daniel had scoured every closet in the Georgetown townhouse and found a mint-green wool dress with a matching cape from Reagan's first inaugural. Paired with patent leather pumps and a clutch of the same color, it was full-on masquerade.

Wellesley loved it. Tonight, she was not the reclusive artist Wellesley Kincaid. She was Sid's sister Jeanette, a retired accountant from Brooklyn.

"You look very sophisticated." She waved a hand at Lily's blue, floor-length column dress. "*Très* Erté. Did Daniel dress you both?"

Charlotte slid one hand into the pocket of her loose tuxedo pants and the other around Lily's waist. At one point in her life she may have taken offense at the suggestion that her twin brother picked out her clothing, now she was just grateful. Her silk tuxedo was perfect. Adroitly androgynous, the finely cut jacket accentuated her broad shoulders but tapered nicely at the waist showing off her slim hips. The trousers hugged her ass but then cascaded loosely over her legs. Charlotte had never felt more glamorous. Having Lily on her arm only accentuated the sensation.

"Yes, Daniel chose our clothes," she admitted. "But he gave us options." She smiled at her aunt then glanced suspiciously at two older couples exiting a vehicle. It was not Madison, not yet. But it was only a matter of time. Daniel had placed Charlotte and Lily as far from the Hagen Shipping table as possible but there were only one hundred and fifty people attending the event. If Madison showed up, Charlotte would see her.

If Lily was aware of Charlotte's discomfort or feeling any of her own, she didn't betray it. "Daniel has excellent taste," she was telling Wellesley. "It would be stupid to turn down his fashion advice."

"And futile," Charlotte reminded her.

"That too." Lily laughed.

"What time did he leave this morning?" Wellesley linked her arm through Precious's and the foursome walked toward the elevator lobby. Precious had parked in a spot designated for security vehicles, putting them only a few yards away from the two public elevators and fire stairs leading down to the museum floor. Sid had wanted to be on-site early and would meet Wellesley in his office.

"I'm not sure," Charlotte confessed and immediately felt guilty. This was the biggest night of Daniel's life and she only had him in the periphery. But the parts of her brain not absorbed with the spectacle of Lily in the beautiful blue dress were focused on the inevitable meeting with Madison.

"I heard him using the coffee grinder at six thirty," Lily offered as they made their way past a white hospitality tent adjacent to the elevator lobby. Inside, guests were sipping champagne and waiting to be called for a lift down. Charlotte did a quick scan of the tent and recognized Madison's parents. *Shit.* She'd been expecting to see them but wished she had more time to prepare. Charlotte had known Felix and Julie Hagen since she was eighteen years old. She'd stayed with them, traveled on their yacht, and they'd never been anything but nice to her. Julie had mothered Charlotte without stepping on Sarah's toes and Felix had provided fatherly advice whether she'd asked for it or not. One of the toughest things about breaking up with Madison was losing her relationship with them. And now they were sponsoring Daniel's event. Charlotte couldn't walk by without saying hello.

She touched Lily's elbow. "Honey?"

Her eyes flicked to the hospitality tent. "Is she in there?" Lily now knew almost everything about the Madness—Rhi-Treats, the hospital deliveries and the Madsnax jingle. Lily even knew about Charlie Pies. She didn't know their origin story, but it was the only piece of information Charlotte had held back. How did you tell your new girlfriend that your ex had mass-marketed your vagina as a blueberry pop tart? Even Daniel didn't know.

"Not Madison. But I see her parents. I need to say hello."

"Do you want me to go with you?" The tentative look in Lily's eye made Charlotte feel protective. Lily's ex-fiancé had kept Lily a secret—the woman's job had been more important to her than acknowledging a relationship with Lily. Charlotte felt just the opposite. She wanted everyone to know Lily was her girlfriend. She wanted to shout it from the rooftops, sing songs about her beauty. She'd even considered getting a tattoo. Lily needed to know this too.

Charlotte squeezed her hand. "Of course, come meet them." There was a good chance Madison was in the tent but Charlotte didn't care. Lily's feelings were more important than postponing the inevitable introduction.

Precious was tracking their conversation and of no mind to meet out-of-town guests. Even those paying for dinner. "We'll see you in the museum."

Wellesley's encounter with Madison the night she'd come to Washington made her feel close to the situation. Tipping down her glasses she peered into the tent. "Is she in there? Should I say hello?"

"You can tell everyone hello downstairs, Jeanette." Precious steered Wellesley toward the elevator. Jackie Kennedy wig or not, the security director didn't want Wellesley exposed to paparazzi who might be lurking hoping to get a picture of Barbra Streisand. It was much easier to protect Wellesley in the confines of the museum. Barbra had her own security but wouldn't arrive until after the dinner.

Wellesley looked disappointed but didn't argue. Clutching the security director's arm, she walked off dutifully.

"You ready?" Charlotte asked Lily. The Hagens were now talking to a woman wearing a shiny black beret. Felix was laughing and holding an unlit cigar.

"Sure." Lily pressed her lips to Charlotte's cheek. "Let's go." Hand in hand they walked into the tent.

When Julie Hagen saw Charlotte, she threw her hands in the air like she was signaling a touchdown. "Charlie!" A smile lit her intelligent face. Excusing herself from the woman in the beret, she came forward to say hello. Charlotte embraced Madison's mother and was instantly awash in the familiar scent of Chanel No. 5.

"Hi, Julie."

"Charlie!" A louder voice boomed and Felix Hagen's aftershave was added to the mix. Charlotte let go of Julie to hug Madison's father.

"Hey, Felix."

"You look beautiful Charlie, *très chic*." Felix assessed Charlotte's tuxedo with an approving eye and then looked expectantly at Lily.

Charlotte was quick to introduce them. "Felix, this is my girlfriend, Lily. Lily, this is Felix and Julie Hagen. They're friends of mine from Maine and one of tonight's major sponsors."

Lily offered her hand to Julie and then to Felix. If Madison's parents were surprised to be introduced to Charlotte's new girlfriend, they didn't show it. "Nice to meet you Lily. I love your dress."

"Thank you, Mrs. Hagen."

"Call me Julie, please."

"Julie."

"You two make a nifty couple." Felix gummed the unlit cigar. "How did you meet our Charlie Pie?"

Charlotte winced at the old nickname but Lily took it in her stride. Still clueless about the name's origin, she thought the pop tart was a sweet idea. "At a bar, actually."

Felix chortled. "An oldie but a goodie."

"Charlotte was singing," Lily explained. "I thought she had the most beautiful voice."

Julie pressed a heavily ringed hand to her heart. "Charlie sings like an angel!"

"We've been watching you on YouTube." Felix patted Charlotte's shoulder. "Nurse Nightingale. It's really special what you're doing."

"Thank you." Charlotte was touched.

"Daniel says you've raised quite a bit of money for Children's Hospital. We couldn't be prouder. Madison was lucky she got you to record the Madsnax jingle before you went viral. Though I guess you probably know she had something to do with that." Julie rolled her eyes as Felix launched into the jingle.

Charlotte kept a smile plastered on her face. What was Julie talking about? What did Madison have to do with the Nurse Nightingale video? Had she been the friend to take it from Daniel's Facebook page? When Felix finished the song, she was very direct.

"I'm confused. What does Madison have to do with Nurse Nightingale?"

"I think it was Melanie's idea actually," Julie backpedaled but Felix barreled on, oblivious.

"Mel is a social media whiz. She paid a YouTube influencer to promote Nurse Nightingale, and then linked the bakery jingle to it. The Madsnax site got thousands of hits. Brilliant marketing."

Charlotte was shocked. "That's how Nurse Nightingale went viral? Madison did it? I had no idea."

"Technically, it was Melanie," Julie dropped her voice. "She's here tonight with Madison." She looked over her shoulder. "They just left for the elevators. I'm surprised you missed them. They moved in together, you know."

"I hadn't heard." Charlotte tried to keep her face blank. Why the barrage of texts if Madison was happily involved with another woman?

"I like Mel just fine," Felix said. "She's a little aggressive but that just makes her a better businesswoman."

Julie put a warning hand on his arm. "We're still getting to know her."

"There's no denying she's done great things for Madsnax," Felix continued. "It was Mel's connection with the distributor who took Charlie Pies national. It was also her idea to add them to the swag bags tonight."

"They're serving Charlie Pies tonight?" Charlotte asked faintly.

Lily touched her elbow. "Does this mean I'll finally get to try one?" Charlotte had almost forgotten her standing there. She reached for her hand.

"You've never eaten a Charlie Pie?" Julie was shocked. "They sell them at Whole Foods."

"I've seen them!" Lily admitted. "But I've never actually eaten one. This one," she jostled Charlotte's arm, "is never in the mood."

"That deal put Madsnax in the black," Felix told her. "Any way you slice 'em, Charlie Pies are delicious."

"I can't wait."

Charlotte was mortified. She knew they were talking about a blueberry pop tart and not her vagina but it was hard to shake the memory of Madison gliding one up the side of her leg.

Felix pointed out a neat stack of boxes beneath the catering tables. "Everyone gets to take a box home tonight. Melanie and Madison will be taking pictures for their website. I'm sure they'd love one of Nurse Nightingale."

"Charlie Pie with a Charlie Pie," Julie joked.

Charlotte smiled through clenched teeth. "I'll look forward to that."

An attendant approached the Hagens to take them to the elevator. They bid Charlotte and Lily farewell promising to see them later downstairs.

Lily squeezed Charlotte's fingers. "You okay, baby?"

"I can't believe Madison was responsible for Nurse Nightingale going viral."

"You can't?" Lily raised an eyebrow. "From what you've told me, which isn't a lot I'll admit, this is exactly the type of thing she would do."

"You're right."

"Want some champagne?"

"Yes, please."

As Lily went to get drinks, Charlotte took the opportunity to look around the tent. She recognized no one. Precious had taken Wellesley down earlier in the service car to meet Sid in the administration office, and Daniel had been troubleshooting preparations on-site since noon. Everything had been meticulously planned but anything might happen in the final moments before an event. If a problem surfaced, Daniel would need to be fast on his feet. But he was a master. He'd once dealt with an eleventh-hour infestation of ladybugs by passing off the men in hazmat suits as part of the entertainment staff. Tonight, he was dealing with Madison, Barbra Streisand, and Aunt Wellesley in a wig. It would be surprising if something didn't go wrong.

Thankfully, Charlotte and Lily had no other obligations but to enjoy themselves, a task so much more easily accomplished if Madness weren't afoot and Charlie Pies not on the menu. But these things were out of Charlotte's control, so she accepted a glass of champagne from Lily and they stepped out of the tent to look at the stars.

"Are you upset she promoted the video?" Lily asked when they were away from the crowd.

Charlotte took a moment to consider the question. "Yes and no," she said finally. "I'm angry she interfered with my life again. But I'm not sorry how it worked out. Does that make sense?"

Lily pressed her fingers. "Absolutely."

"I mean, I like being Nurse Nightingale. We raise a lot of money for the hospital and that's a good thing. It just sucks Madison had anything to do with it. You know?"

Lily nodded.

"The worst thing is that Madison's likely to be smug about it. She'll expect me to thank her." Charlotte pinched her forehead, and Lily wrapped an arm around her waist allowing her to vent. "She already stepped way outside the bounds bringing Charlie Pies tonight. Daniel will freak if she stalks Barbra Streisand with those things." She burrowed her face into Lily's neck. "I can't believe this is happening."

"Don't let it get to you." Lily stroked her arm quietly. "And I've got a great idea of how to make you feel better." The tone made her intentions clear and Charlotte took a thoughtful sip of champagne. Sex would certainly let off some steam but where would they go? Other than the elevator lobby, there wasn't a structure for miles.

"What do you have in mind?" Charlotte rubbed her thumb up Lily's arm. Draining her glass, she set it on the grass.

"My car?" Lily smiled and it dawned on Charlotte that Daniel had driven Lily's car to Quarry.

Hello Laurel Jaguar.

"Do you know where it's parked?"

"Back left quadrant. Daniel sent me a picture."

"Did he hide a key?"

"Of course."

"Daniel is the best."

"He really is."

Ten minutes later, Charlotte's head was buried between Lily's thighs. The long slit up the side of her dress made her the best candidate for a wrinkle-free orgasm. Daniel would kill them if they messed up their clothes. Lily had offered an apology but Charlotte thought she got the better end of the bargain. Lily tasted like heaven. Gripping her thighs, she swirled her tongue around her clit before plunging inside her. Lily cried out, and Charlotte did it again, reveling in the intimacy. This was right where she wanted to be. The Madness was over. Lily was her everything.

"That's so good." Lily had her hand in Charlotte's hair. Her hips moved in a sensual motion that allowed Charlotte to gauge her progress while still losing herself in the combined bliss of taste, smell, and touch. When Lily pushed forward asking for more, Charlotte gave it to her. Licking her hard and fast, she pinned her to the seat.

"I love you so much," Lily breathed. Hitting her climax, she ground her pussy into Charlotte's face and rode out the orgasm with beautiful abandon.

They lay there for several moments collecting themselves and then Lily began to giggle.

"I don't know about you. But I certainly feel better."

"Me too." Careful not to mess her tux, Charlotte slid her body up and hovered over Lily in a plank. Their lips met. "I feel incredible. But we've been gone a long time. Maybe we should go in."

"Mmmmm," Lily murmured. "But you didn't get a turn."

"What are you talking about?" Charlotte smiled. "That was my turn."

The elevator ride down to the museum was not nearly as much fun as the time in the Jaguar. Crowded with well-dressed men and women, Charlotte and Lily were obliged to keep their hands to themselves. They stepped from the car and went directly to *Valkyrie as Mother Nature*. A couple was standing in front of the painting discussing Wellesley.

The man was very excited. "Bob just told me Kincaid is here tonight," he said. "Someone tweeted a photo." Charlotte shot Lily a look. She stepped closer to listen to the conversation but Lily opted for a more direct approach.

"Excuse me, did you just say Wellesley Kincaid is here?" The couple turned to look at them.

"Someone tweeted a picture," the man explained and took a phone from his pocket.

"Are you sure it's from tonight?" Lily asked and he looked affronted.

"I'm pretty sure I know Wellesley Kincaid when I see her," he said and tapped the screen.

"Henry is a nationally known expert on Kincaid," the woman informed them. "He teaches a class at Middlebury and has written the definitive book on her early work."

"How impressive. Have you ever met her?" Lily asked.

He shook his head. "No one knows her. I've heard she's quite mad." He stopped scrolling and pointed at an image on his screen. "Which explains this."

It was a picture of Wellesley wearing the Jackie Kennedy wig. Standing in the upstairs elevator lobby holding onto Precious, she was peering intently at the camera. The photo was arguably horrible but the responsible party was a gut punch. The tweet had been posted by Madsnax Bakery.

The man gestured to *Valkyrie as Mother Nature*. "Her mind might be gone but her work is still first rate."

"What a nice thing to say," Lily said and the man frowned at them.

He gave Charlotte an odd look. "Hey! Aren't you her niece, that singing nurse?"

"You tell us," Lily said and grabbed Charlotte's hand to pull her away. "You're the national expert, right?"

They found Daniel in Sid's office conferring with Precious. His expression was one of controlled panic. "Where have you been?" he asked and shook his phone at Charlotte. "I've been trying to call you."

Charlotte dodged the question. "It doesn't matter. We saw the tweet. Where's Wellesley?"

"Jeanette is having a wonderful time with Geoffrey and his parents," Precious informed them. "We have them seated away from the crowd in a private gallery."

"Oh, good." Charlotte was relieved.

"But there's a problem with Streisand." Daniel's voice was grim. "When the tweet went out the press blocked the gate again. Her driver saw the crush and turned around. They're on the way back to her estate. It's a logistical nightmare."

"It's Madness."

"I know. We had words."

"Can the police help?"

Precious shook her head. "They cleared the road but Ms. Streisand had already left. Now we're using a helicopter. I had one on standby in case we needed to get Ms. Kincaid out. Our pilot is plotting a course. Fortunately, Ms. Streisand's estate has a private landing pad."

"That's what I call an Airbnb." Daniel crossed his heart.

"The problem is that Ms. Streisand is still en route to the estate. Her car should arrive there in forty-five minutes. Our chopper will be waiting but the soonest I can have her on stage is ninety minutes. It may be two hours."

"When is the music program scheduled to start?" Lily asked.

"In an hour," Daniel eyed a small wrinkle on her dress. "Where have you two been? The silent auction is nearly over. You missed the bidding on the Kennedy Center tickets and they're about to serve dinner."

"What's your plan?" Charlotte sidestepped the question again.

"What makes you think I have a plan?"

"You always have a plan."

Daniel avoided her eyes. "I do have a plan. But you're not going to like it."

"You want me to sing."

"Just until Barbra gets here, Charlie," he said quickly. "These people have paid a lot of money to be here. So much, much money. I can't think of anything else that will appease them. You're the famous singing nurse. This is a benefit to help people. It's kind of perfect."

"Okay," she said simply.

"Really?" Daniel was clearly expecting more of a fight. "That's it? I thought I was going to have to offer my firstborn."

"Keep your baby." She smiled at him. "I want to help. Tell me what you need."

"Really?" he asked again.

"Yes. Give me the set list before I change my mind."

"Set list?"

"I know you have one."

He gave her an impish look. "We'll start with 'Edelweiss.'"

CHAPTER TWENTY

The Gala

The stage was round and spun slowly in the middle of the museum's central atrium like a lazy Susan. Patrons' tables framed the space making it a true performance in the round. Barbra's people had been clear—the stage moved so Barbra wouldn't have to.

"What if I throw up?" Charlotte asked Daniel. They were standing together in between tables reserved for the Human Left staff and sponsors from Gowear. Charlotte had chatted briefly with Little Orphan Olive and waved to Camille, who looked impossibly glamorous on the arm of Hannah, but found she had no stomach for small talk. She had no stomach at all.

Daniel thought for a moment. "Maybe bring your purse up there with you. You can use it as a barf bag."

"You know I don't have a purse."

"Then bring mine."

Geoffrey was in front of the crowd introducing Karen Kennerly, the Executive Director of the Human Left. After her remarks, there would be a keynote address from a famous human rights activist from Chile, and then Charlotte would perform three songs. Daniel wanted her to stick to lullabies. The world knew her as Nurse Nightingale. Why disappoint them? It certainly made things easier for Charlotte as she wouldn't need to brush up on lyrics. But she was nervous. She still hadn't seen Madison who was somewhere in the crowd. What if she found Lily and told her the truth about Charlie Pies? It was a hard-to-imagine scenario, but it was Madness, and anything was possible.

Lily had eaten dinner with Geoffrey's parents and Aunt Wellesley in a private room. Currently, a board member was giving the group an intimate tour of the gallery. They would join the rest of the party only when the lights went down and the music began. The sophisticated gala crowd had settled into excited awareness that a true celebrity was among them but Precious wasn't taking any chances. Charlotte wouldn't get to see Lily until after the performance and was trying to stay calm. Daniel had saved her a plate but she had no appetite. In fact, she felt slightly ill. She'd never had aspirations to be a singer. How was she opening for Barbra Streisand?

"Where's the bathroom?"

Daniel gave her a worried look. "Are you okay?"

"I need to go to the bathroom."

"The closest one is off the lobby but you can use the one in Sid's office. I'll come with you."

"I'm a big girl."

"Let me go with you."

Charlotte glared at him and he backed down. "Don't take too long."

"I won't."

She felt a wave of nausea. Was she truly going to be sick? She hurried toward the public bathrooms by the elevator. Privacy would be nice but she couldn't risk it. Thankfully, the space was empty. She splashed some water on her face and felt a little better. What was she so scared of?

Right on cue, the bathroom door opened. "Hey, Charlie," a familiar voice said brightly. It was Madison.

Charlotte turned off the faucet. "Hi." She eyed Madison in the mirror but didn't turn around.

"You're angry with me," Madison said looking guilty. "I can tell from the way you're standing."

"Why am I angry?"

"You're angry about the Madsnax tweet, and I'm sorry. Daniel already ripped me a new one, and I deserve it. I really do. I didn't mean to out Wellesley and mess up the gala. I was just trying to promote the bakery. I didn't think."

"You never do."

"That's not fair."

"Were you thinking when you paid someone to post the Nurse Nightingale video on YouTube and link it to the Madsnax jingle? Tell me what you were thinking then, Madison. I'm curious." Charlotte wiped her hands on a towel. "Because you turned my whole world upside down."

Madison paled. "That was actually Melanie's idea."

"Chivalrous."

"It wasn't me."

Charlotte turned to face her. "And Rhi-treats? You put that horrible picture of Rhianna on blast."

"Also, Melanie. I knew you'd be angry but Melanie is hard to say no to. You've no idea."

Charlotte snorted. "I think I can imagine."

Madison looked hurt. "What's that supposed to mean?"

"Really?" Charlotte took a calming breath. "Because of your tweet, I get to stand on a rotating platform and sing lullabies to a bunch of strangers. Strangers who only want to watch me sing because you paid someone to make me famous."

"But you're making money to benefit the hospital. Daniel told my dad," Madison argued.

"That's not the point. It wasn't my idea. I didn't give my consent."

"It wasn't my intent to hurt you." Madison was defiant.

"Then why did you bring Charlie Pies to the event? How do you think I feel knowing that at the end of the evening each guest will take home a blueberry pop tart named after my vagina? What if my new girlfriend finds out? How do you think Lily will feel? You're jeopardizing something I care about. Have you thought about that?"

"I'm..."

"You're trying to promote Madsnax, I know. Can't you just leave me out of it, for once?"

"Don't you want me to succeed?"

"I want you to leave me alone. Please? Can you just leave me alone?"

"Charlie, I'm sorry."

"Can you please just go?"

"But, Charlie..."

"You heard her, get out of here," a voice said and Charlotte watched horrified as a stall door opened and Lily stepped out into the bathroom.

"Lily," she said dumbly as her girlfriend walked calmly to an adjacent sink.

"Hey, baby." Lily smiled at her.

Madison narrowed her eyes. "Who are you?"

Lily lathered her hands with soap and turned on the water. "I'm Charlotte's lover. My name is Lily. She just asked you to leave and I'm seconding the motion."

"Her lover?"

"Yes." Lily shut off the tap and turned to face her. "I love Charlotte. Charlotte loves me. We're lovers. And you're her ex, Madison. That covers everyone, right?" She cocked her head to one side. "They call you Madness. It seems to fit."

"How dare you," Madison seethed but took a step back.

"How dare I?" Lily answered. "How dare you?" She pointed a finger in Madison's face. "How dare you compromise this gala with a self-serving tweet?"

"It was an accident." Madison looked to Charlotte for help. "Tell her! I said I was sorry."

Charlotte looked away while Lily pressed on. "It's grounds for a lawsuit and not the only lawsuit if the stories I've heard are true. I'd love to talk to you about the dog biscuits sometime. I'm an attorney, you know."

"I'm..." Madison gasped.

"Leaving? Great," Lily said and stared her down.

"Charlie?"

"Goodbye, Madison."

"Fine," she said and turned on her heel. The bathroom door closed and Lily let out a sigh.

"I thought she'd never leave."

"That was amazing." Charlotte moved toward her hesitantly. She took Lily's hand. "Thank you for standing up for me."

Lily gave her a sad smile. "You let her get away with too much."

"I know. I'm working on it," Charlotte said. "I guess you know about Charlie Pies then."

Lily nodded. "I had that pussy joke figured out a long time ago. I mean, it's kind of obvious, isn't it?" She squeezed Charlotte's fingers. "I just never said anything because it clearly makes you so uncomfortable."

"You knew?"

"I guessed."

"I hate them," Charlotte said and began to cry. Lily had already known. She shut her eyes to stem the tears but it was no use. "Thank you for being so nice."

"Nice?" Lily wiped a tear from Charlotte's cheek then leaned to kiss her. "I love you. Did you honestly think we were going to break up over a blueberry pop tart?"

"I didn't want to." Charlotte snorted and Lily pulled her into a hug.

"Well, we're not. This isn't some dumb television show. We know who the bad actor here is and it's not you. It's never you," she whispered in her ear. "I'm lucky to be with you. You're possibly the nicest person I've ever met. And you were way too nice to Madison just now."

"Can we not talk about her?" Charlotte pulled away.

"Great idea." Lily pecked her mouth. "I've got a better idea anyway."

"Yeah?" Charlotte thought she recognized the look.

"Dinner was really nice but I never got dessert." Lily traced a finger down the front of Charlotte's shirt.

"Please don't say you want a Charlie Pie."

Lily laughed. "Maybe." She let her finger drop a few inches.

"Maybe?"

"Yes. *Maybe*, Charlotte. Maybe, it's time to see what all the excitement is about." She zeroed in on her target. "But maybe I want the original."

Charlotte didn't try to hide her smile. "And I'd like for you to have it."

"Okay, great." Pushing Charlotte into a stall, Lily locked the door.

EPILOGUE

One Year Later

Lily carefully rolled the wide strips of mulberry paper off the wall and put them into protective tubes. One by one, the meticulous drawings, depicting the last four years of her life, disappeared out of sight. Sid was sponsoring an art opening in Georgetown. The show was going on the road.

"I can't wait to see the catalogue." Charlotte smiled at the image of Wellesley flying off in the helicopter with Barbra Streisand the night of the gala. The two had become instant friends and were currently vacationing with Stefano and Jacob somewhere in Greece. The CBD tincture had allowed Wellesley to reclaim her life fully. As Daniel said, it was a miracle substance. Rhianna was now getting dog treats that were CBD-free in weekly deliveries from Madsnax. Lily had brokered the arrangement to include fresh croissants for Sarah and Sven. Charlotte was truly the luckiest woman in the world. She let her eyes drift to the panel of Lily proposing to her on the dance floor at Birdie's. Lily's new work chronicled the best time of Charlotte's life. "When will the T-shirts be ready?"

"Hmmmm." Lily was lost in thought. "What did you say, baby?"

Charlotte sank into the warm green eyes. "The swag, when will it be done?"

"Stop calling it swag! We're just getting a few shirts made. Sid said they'll be ready next week. I still can't believe this is happening."

"Oh, it's happening."

"I feel a little exposed," Lily admitted. "But I'm also excited to hear what people think. Is that vain?"

"No! It's human." Charlotte reached for her hand. "You have a unique point of view. People are going to respond."

"At least I don't have to watch them respond," she said. "I still don't know how you sing in front of people."

"I don't perform in front of that many people."

"Excuse me?" Lily pointed to the panel of Charlotte standing front and center in Washington Nationals Park. "You sang the national anthem at a major league baseball game."

"I really wanted to throw the first pitch." Charlotte stuck out her lip.

The public had not grown tired of Nurse Nightingale. Charlotte had become a minor local celebrity and was occasionally asked to perform outside the hospital. She was choosy about the events and generally only accepted invitations that benefited the public. Daniel wanted her to release a Christmas album and buy a beach house.

He and Geoffrey were talking about moving in together. It was a big step, but as long as Daniel wasn't required to share a closet, Charlotte thought he was ready. His plan to move to Washington to become more sophisticated had yielded him a sophisticate in Geoffrey. She studied the panel of the two men dancing at Sarah and Sven's August wedding. Matching suits, matching smiles, they really were a perfect pair.

Sarah had surprised everyone by insisting on a traditional ceremony. She'd denied herself pageantry the first time around by eloping with the twins' father, so she'd given Daniel free rein. There'd been lots of fanfare, though thankfully Sven had talked him out of the doves. The result had been a picture-perfect barn wedding. Charlotte and Lily had spent a week in Portland attending pre-parties and even hosted one of their own. The bakery jingle was still on the radio, but they hadn't seen Madison. In fact, there hadn't been a peep from her since Lily had negotiated the free snacks. It was as if a curse had been lifted.

All in all, the Maine trip had been wonderful. Charlotte looked for the panel of them making lobster rolls and realized it had already been packed. Likewise, the panel of Rhianna in the oak tree. It was one of Charlotte's favorites. Lily had thought she was joking about the dog's abilities and sketched the scene over and over.

"Are you having trouble with this?" she asked Lily for the hundredth time. Gallery show aside, removing the art from the wall was a huge change. Lily had spent hours in this room working out her feelings through the panels. Seeing it taken down couldn't be easy.

"Nope." Lily studied the ceiling. "I never meant it to be permanent. I never meant it to be anything."

"Yes, but it turned into something really special."

Lily climbed down from the ladder and put her arms around Charlotte's neck. "You're something really special."

Charlotte kissed her tenderly. "Thank you. I feel the same way."

Lily laced their hands together and held up the engagement ring she'd given Charlotte, a diamond solitaire set in platinum that had been her grandmother's. "This is the only thing I need to be permanent. I get to spend the rest of my life with you." They shared another kiss. "Do you know what I mean?"

Charlotte gazed at the beautiful, complicated woman in front of her and many thoughts went through her mind but only two words formed on her lips.

"I do."

Bella Books, Inc.

Women. Books. Even Better Together.

P.O. Box 10543
Tallahassee, FL 32302

Phone: 800-729-4992
www.bellabooks.com